# Bewitching Her Monsters

## BEWITCHING MONSTERS BOOK ONE

## YVE VALE

# BEWITCHING HER MONSTERS

BEWITCHING MONSTERS
BOOK ONE

YVE VALE

Published by Entraverse Publishing

Sedona, AZ 86339, USA

YveVale.com

*To Mr. Vale,*
*thank you for being my Alpha… reader,*
*my sounding board, my cheerleader,*
*and my inspiration for many aspects*
*of my fictional guys.*

*For my fellow authors and the book community.*

# AUTHOR'S NOTE

$\mathscr{T}$he Bewitching Monsters Series is a dark yet often humorous paranormal monster why choose romance. The female main character will end up with more than one of the love interests. Group scenes are on the agenda.

This series also has male/male romance within the group that will occur with and without the female present.

But there's no cheating.

If you believe love is love, you enjoy having some laughs too, and of course, some spicy times, then please charge forward!

PLEASE NOTE: This series also contains several dark elements that some readers may be sensitive to. For more information, visit: ValeRomances.com

# 1

## AUTHOR INTERRUPTED

JADE

Attempt number three:

*G*oliath pulls me to his broad chest and growls, "You are coming with me, menace."

I twist and scramble to get away. But some part of me wants him—a very needy part between my legs.

"No, you... brute!" I kick to make him drop me.

Not a smart move since he's carrying me over treacherous and rocky terrain.

His clawed feet are the only things keeping us from slipping down the mountain and plummeting to our deaths.

"Stop, Nora," he orders, clasping my head to his shoulder and trying to comfort me. It's the first time he's called me by my name. This should settle me somewhat, knowing I'm not just some nameless sacrifice to him.

But the toxin in my system is making clear thoughts

impossible. I *can't* settle down. My actions might get us both killed. I don't want that.

After a few more minutes of scrambling over the mountainside to escape our enemies, Goliath sighs with relief when we see a narrow entrance to a cave ahead.

Once we are at the mouth of the cavern, Goliath sets me down. "Don't move," he warns in a whisper.

For the first time today, I listen to him. If there's an animal out here that is bigger and scarier than his beast, then we are fucked. His monstrous bearlike form is four feet taller than my height. I have to crane my neck backward to see his face. Holy crap, he's big.

I shiver with the thought of how big his other parts will be. I believe I'm about to find out.

After a quick investigation, he returns, apparently having deemed the cave safe for me to enter. He picks me up and carries me inside. Just enough light filters in to see it's previously been used as a shelter. A flat, smooth rock the size of a small bed is clear of debris at the far end. He sets me down.

Without an ounce of hesitation, he rips off my jacket and shirt, yanking them over my head and revealing my breasts. "I need to be inside you," he says roughly.

I try to cover my chest, but he won't let me.

"Mine." He circles his massive arm around my waist and pulls me closer. His claws dig into my flesh.

I can't control the whimper that leaves my throat, and it causes his enormous member to inflate. He presses it against my stomach.

He sweeps my legs from under me, and I fall backward. But his large hand catches me and sets me on my back gently. The rough stone beneath me scratches my sensitive skin, and I try not to squirm as Goliath rips my pants off and spreads me open for his viewing pleasure.

His long tongue sweeps out, taking his first taste of my slick center. He groans with approval and strokes his hardening length.

"You can't claim me," I protest.

"I have won you in combat. And you want me," he argues, flicking his tongue out to brush against me again. "Don't you?"

"But—"

"No. You are mine. And I am yours... finally." His eyes glint with mischief. "Do I need to make you ready for my cock? Is that it, my treasure?"

I can't say anything as I stare at the threat to my vagina's health and well-being. Even with proper and thorough preparation, that thing will destroy me.

I nod my consent. I might as well get a couple of orgasms out of this before it's death by dick.

He feasts on my center. His long, thick tongue slides through my folds and plunges into my channel.

It takes next to no time at all before my body quakes with an impending orgasm. He shoves two giant fingers into me, and I scream. When I stop trembling, he lines up the baseball bat sized appendage he calls a cock, and I...

*Wait, wait, wait...* This monster has a *baseball bat*-sized cock?

And doesn't he have claws???... *In* her vagina?

*Come on now...*

He really *is* going to kill her. Ugh. Author problems.

Nora is dead by dick, and I'm not even past writing chapter four.

Frustrated, I lean back in my chair and stare at my computer screen.

*Can I call him a monster if he can retract his claws while they're fucking?*

*How big of a monster cock is too big?*

Age-old questions.

Knowing I need some outside opinions, I open up a chat

with a couple of fellow authors and begin asking them what they think.

They are all for the biggest dick imaginable…

> Mere: A knot the size of a grapefruit and a wine bottle size dick.

All I can think is, ouch.

My FMC's poor cervix. But this is a fantasy land where all things are possible. Maybe women there have truly magical pussies, and they won't get their organs rearranged by a monster-sized cock with the girth and length of a wine bottle.

> Clara: You could be vague about how big is big.

> Bekka: There is no limit but our imagination.

They're right. I just need to lean into the fantasy.

Sighing, I rub my face and realize my muse is a bit broken. I don't really like Goliath or Nora. I won't get anywhere without an inspirational boost.

Oh, well. Time for my ritual to get the magic flowing again.

Off to my little kitchen, I steep my tea and glare at the herbal blend as I wonder if this is what's failing me. Maybe I need a change. Maybe I need a *lot* of changes.

However, I know the true culprit of my writer's *malaise* (Never call it a block. It gives it power). I haven't been the same since Rob. Perfect name, really, since he's the thief that robbed me of my muse.

For comfort, I head to my support group in the other room. They're my hostages, who I keep for their happiness as well as mine. My fur babies.

"I have a confession. I'm a romance writer who doesn't believe in love at the moment," I whisper to my guinea pig.

"Sorry. I shouldn't confess that to anyone. Not even you. If I don't get inspired here soon, your food is on the line."

As a paranormal romance author, I should believe in magic and love, if only in my imagination. And usually, I do. But right now, I don't believe in tiny magical moments in life.

Sure, I have my favorite crystals and know their metaphysical properties. I've researched all the mythical creatures. I tell myself it's all in the name of research. But deep down, I want magic to be real. Sometimes I wish my grandmother wasn't crazy, and I was a genuine witch, as she's claimed.

Maybe it wouldn't be *Hogwarts'* level of magic. But I *have* seen miracles and the power of positive thinking. I just haven't felt it in a while.

It seemed 'magical' when I first met my ex-boyfriend. But apparently, that kind of magic doesn't last. Maybe it was only magic lust.

The weird part was that I wasn't really attracted to Rob.

So if it was magic that I felt when I met him, it was a black magic spell.

# 2

## WALKS INTO A BAR

ADE

Slamming my teacup down a little too hard onto my banged-up writing desk, I curse my continued writer's *detour*.

I shuffle out of my writing cave and into my bedroom, flopping onto my disheveled queen bed with a grunt. I pull the tangled blanket over part of my body and give up on the effort it will take to completely cover myself up.

Maybe I should make my bed once in a while?

But what's the point in keeping it tidy when it's just me here now? Besides, I take about five to ten power naps a day, anyway. Sometimes I believe I must be a damn cat trapped in a human body.

Now I'm wondering about the various animal shifters and what combination of fancy peens I could use in my next book.

Speaking of animals, I need to feed my horde of rescues. Groaning, I lift myself off the bed to slip into the spare bedroom, where I have my odd collection of friends.

My guinea pig squeaks as soon as he sees me. He's one of

the extra fluffy breeds, reminding me of the 'Trouble With Tribbles' episode from the first Star Trek series—a mop of fur with feet.

I open up Trouble's cage and lift him out to give him plenty of affection, holding him to my chest and placing several kisses on his little head. "How are you doing today, buddy?"

Trouble makes his chirping sounds again, and I swear in my head I hear him tell me he's fine, but I get the mental image he wants food. Sometimes I wonder if it's just my imagination or if I'm really picking something up.

Animal whisperers are real... right?

I blow off this thought as nothing more than my overactive imagination. I've always had a crazy mind. It's why I'm an author.

However, when I was a kid my abuela told me stories that she was a powerful bruja—a witch. She passed away when I was little, so unfortunately, I never had the chance to know her as well as I would have liked. From what I remember, she was an intense character, beautiful and strange. My mother often said I inherited my grandmother's eccentric ways. Since she hated her mother, she wasn't happy about that.

But my mother isn't wrong that I'm an oddball. When I was little, I believed I could see all kinds of crazy stuff. I thought I saw auras, glowing strings connecting people, and swirling energy in the air.

I believed sometimes I could see what people were really like on the inside—glowing eyes, fur, and even monstrous faces. No wonder I used my imagination to make up stories for a living.

When I was around eleven years old, my mom screamed at me, trying to convince me I couldn't see what I was seeing. She cursed and ranted for an hour straight, telling me that she wasn't going to allow me be a crazy witch like her mother.

So, from that day on, I forced my wild imaginings to stop. Mostly.

But also I was just distracted by my hormones at that point in my development too.

I'm brought back to the present as my rabbit does zoomies around her cage, trying to get my attention. Without a voice, she usually rampages around to communicate her need for attention.

"Sorry, Sage."

I set Trouble down in his habitat with a last pet, and give him a healthy serving of food and an apple slice for a treat.

Sage stands on her hind legs and scrambles to take the raisin I pass over the wire fence. Her soft furry lips brush against my fingertips. She is always gentle, no matter how excited she is to get her goodies.

I open the door to her cage and give her the evening dose of attention, snuggling her and rubbing her soft ears.

I glance at the clock and realize I've wasted the entire day sitting at my desk and not writing much at all. However, I did get some edits completed on my other book due to be released next month.

And... I forgot to eat all day, and it's close to midnight.

After giving my fur babies their food and love, I wander into the kitchen and find I have nothing much for a human in the fridge.

I haven't exactly been taking care of myself since Rob left. And if I'm being honest, I wasn't great at it when I was with him. It's not like he kept me balanced. He wasn't the best guy to rely on for... well, anything.

Without someone to remind me to take a break, I get so deep in my tunnel-vision that I forget the world outside my stories exists. Hence, the hunger pangs right now.

I know my chronic self-neglect has got to be addressed—*mañana*.

Left with very few choices this late at night, I'll go to the bar down the street with a limited after-dinner hours menu. Then

I'll grab a few items at the 24-hour market on the way back for tomorrow's meals.

Wham, bam, thank you, ma'am, problem solved.

I look down at my outfit and realize I'll have to put something else on. A dirty and now fur-covered sweatshirt and pajama bottoms won't cut it, not even this late at night.

I change into yoga pants and a clean sweatshirt. Yeah, I know it's not a big step up, but I at least *appear* cleaner than I did a moment ago.

I grab my e-tablet for notes, hoping the odd characters who often frequent my neighborhood bar might inspire me.

Slipping into my well-loved and aged green '69 Mustang with my engine purring, I drive the short ride to the bar. Yes, I did buy it because it was a sixty-nine.

From the parking lot, I see that the dive bar is busier than normal. Despite that, I easily find a table with a good vantage point to watch the other patrons.

Jimmy, the old barkeeper, nods to me as I sit down. He's an odd duck but registers as relatively harmless on my douche-o-meter.

The long bar is filled with regulars. Most of them are guys in their mid-thirties and forties. They don't bother with me anymore since I've turned them all down at some point. They aren't a bad lot, but I have to have some spark for a potential date. And even though a couple of them are attractive and seem nice enough, I felt nothing for them.

The floor server, Lora, brings me a hot herbal tea set up without needing to ask if I want it. "The usual tonight, Jade?" she asks with a big grin. Lora doesn't mind me taking up space for hours since it isn't often busy this late at night, and I always leave a generous tip.

"Sure, thanks," I say, glancing around the dimly lit room as she walks away.

My attention instantly darts across the sea of tables to the entrance. It's as if gravity has become a vortex, and I'm falling into its well. I think I may have stopped breathing.

Four men—no, these are not *mere* men—file in the door and sit down, mostly facing me in the large, round corner booth. These guys seem to have walked right out of one of my novels. They're so good-looking that I have to turn away since it's like staring directly into the sun.

Their sheer hotness has burned my retinas.

My skin flushes. My mouth goes dry as something else gets wet. My clit perks up, begging for attention.

To distract my body from any more inappropriate reactions, I slurp my tea.

*Crap!* It's too hot, and I scald my tongue and choke.

I'm waving at my face to stop my freak out. If they look over at me now, I may just die. My obituary will read: "She died horny, survived only by her closest friend, her vibrator, Mr. O'Mygawd."

I take a deep breath, turning my gaze out my window and do my best to ignore the romance cover models, who are (weirdly) in some neighborhood dive bar in the middle of the night.

*Light bulb!*

This is perfect for my writer's *hump*.

An avalanche of questions hit me. But the first one is: *what* is the hot squad doing *here*? *Of all places?*

As I sip some water, I casually glance around the room, skimming my eyes over them again.

Damn. Their presence feels like an electric shock to my body every time I look in their direction. I thought that only happened in books. And yes, I confirm my earlier assessment… they are perfection incarnate.

I power up my tablet and take notes on their appearance.

On my third slow perusal, I go deeper with my assessment. It helps that I'm becoming accustomed to their stupidly ridiculous attractiveness.

I need to continue staring to desensitize myself, right?

The first guy sits on the edge of the circular booth, looking as if he's ready to bolt out the door. His strong jaw is clenched, and his knee is bouncing with frustration.

The word *alphahole* pops into my mind. Got to have one of them in the story.

He has short, dark brown hair sticking up as if he's been running his fingers through it in agitation. His golden-brown eyes seem to glow with passion and intensity. Roguish stubble covers his strong jawline. He's wearing a black t-shirt that strains against his muscular chest and biceps.

And *fuck me*... gray sweatpants. *Really?*

Of course, he has on the SoCal standard—flip-flops. He's lucky he's in temperate, near-coastal Southern California, where it seems to be the footwear of choice, even in winter. He must be close to six foot tall, maybe taller. With all that muscle, I assume he has a physical job, or he hits the gym as frequently as I take naps.

Although he wears sandals and exhibits anxiety, he still radiates total dominant alphahole energy.

I'd say he's in his early thirties, but I would also guess he has had a rough life. Something in his eyes suggests that he's had his share of grief. And grief recognizes grief. But right now, he looks downright upset.

I wonder why.

A breeze sweeps over me, and a shiver runs up my spine. Inspiration is here.

A scene filters into my mind.

These four have lost someone important recently... maybe a day or so ago. Mr. Alphahole was close to their fifth *missing* buddy. They're worried they will be targeted next. And they should be worried—

Someone barks out a laugh at the bar and I'm distracted, losing my train of thought. So I move on to the rest of the guys to see if they will inspire me, too.

The man (or should I say beast) next to him looks to be four inches taller and bulkier than Mr. Grumpy. Almost matching his skin tone, his hair is an unusual color that reminds me of light-colored sand. His eyes are fair too—maybe a pale gray?

I wish it wouldn't be weird for me to go up and see.

His features are bold, and everything about him appears massive. He's the human equivalent of a tank. But this one has stoic, somber vibes and appears to be made of beautifully sculpted stone compared to the alphahole next to him. I want to crack his calm persona and see what's underneath that cool exterior.

The third hunk is all that and a side of *oh-damn-me-to-hell-for-what-I'm-thinking*. He's the tallest of the four of them, but not much taller than Mr. Stoic. And if anyone was born with extra muscles, it's him. He has short black hair and a definitively masculine face. His obsidian eyes lock onto whoever is speaking with an intensity that could make lesser beings crumble. He's fuming too, but he's better at concealing it.

Finally, the guy on the other end is the smallest and sleekest of the oversized bunch. He scans the room every few minutes with a smoldering mien with ice-blue eyes. This one might be able to *literally* light my panties on fire.

I watch them as discreetly as I can while eating my grilled cheese sandwich and a side salad. Imagining them as some super elite spies isn't completely ridiculous, although they would have a hard time blending in with their disarmingly good looks, not to mention their immense size.

From my understanding, the best spies blend into a crowd with their mundane appearance.

I wouldn't be a horrible spy. Well, except for everything it entails—like coordination and finesse. I imagine running would be involved in that line of work, too—not my jam either. Now, if I could briskly walk away from a threat, then I'd be good with that. In addition to my aversion to real-life danger and running, I'm just this side of kooky and would attract unwanted attention. And I'd likely blow my cover since I'm not the best liar, even though I make up stories for a living. I've been told my face is far *too expressive.*

Okay, on second thought, I'd make a terrible spy. But I can write about being one, so I'm not going to cry about it.

Covertly as possible, I take a picture of the guys with my tablet's camera. Sure, maybe it's not ethical, but it's not like I plan on sharing it anywhere. It's for... *research.*

But when I look at the picture, it's fuzzy. Their figures are there, but blurred, and they have strange auras around them. I wipe the lens clean, because I'm sure I must have put my greasy hands on the lens.

I try again—blurry. Figuring it must be the tablet, I pull out my phone and snap a few shots. When I study them, the pics are still blurry and flared with colors. Well, damn. I guess I will just have to commit these guys to memory using my tired brain.

Frowning, I stare at them. I wonder if I'm blowing their attractiveness out of proportion. Am I just that much of a thirsty bitch? Maybe I only *want* them to be hotties since I've been alone the last few months.

And maybe not everyone would think they are damn fine.

Lora wanders around the tables and checks on them. Then she makes her way to me. "How are you doing tonight?"

"Mostly good." I shrug, being honest.

We've chatted quite a bit over the years. Enough to know we are both around the same age. I'm about to hit forty, and she had her fortieth birthday last month.

"Is it just my romance brain and hormones, or are those guys stupid-hot?" I ask.

"Yeah, they could change my oil anytime," she jokes.

"If only it were as easy as making an appointment for a lube job." I smirk.

"I'd tell you to go flirt with them, but they seem tense."

"I picked that up." I shake my head. "Nah, I'm good. My FMCs always have better luck than I do in the boyfriend department, so I'll focus on setting those guys up with my characters for now."

"Make sure I get a copy." Lora smiles. "Need anything else?"

"Not tonight, I suppose. Can't take those guys in a doggy bag."

Lora takes my card to run my tab. And I jot down some other observations about my new harem… for my next book.

When I glance up again, all their eyes are on me.

*Oh, shit.* They must have caught me staring.

Blushing as bright as Barbie's Corvette, I quickly drop my gaze, pack up my stuff, and rush to Lora at the register. I sign my receipt and bolt before I can further embarrass myself.

After stopping by the 24-hour corner market to grab some food for tomorrow, I head home.

I feel another wave of embarrassment over being caught staring by those guys.

They obviously had more important things to deal with than some middle-aged, horny author leering at them. My skin flushes pink again as I pull into my driveway and cut the engine.

When I get out of my car, I realize I've forgotten to check my mail the past few days. As I approach the curb to open my mailbox, I see a shadowy streak fly down the dark road. It appears to be a gigantic dog.

I hurry to my porch. Out of the corner of my eye, I see him hide across the street, tucked in the shadow of my neighbor's house.

His eyes lock onto me.

I go inside briefly to set my groceries down just inside the door, returning to the porch to see if he will come closer to my house, seeking safety.

Yeah, I know. I'm *that* person, the one who rescues every lost animal I see. But I can't leave him out there.

I bend lower to make myself seem less threatening. Not that I'm all that intimidating with my five-foot-five inches.

"Hey, gorgeous, are you lost?" I ask.

Yes… I *do* talk to animals as if they're humans. And maybe plants too.

The beautiful, giant dog raises his brows and turns his head to look behind him to see if I'm talking to someone else.

*Hilarious.* He's a smart one.

He dips his head downward and doesn't move forward.

I lean all the way over, trying to look smaller and less intimidating to the big lug. Whoops, my cleavage is on full display. At least I didn't subject those hotties at the bar to a desperate play like that.

"I have special treats for *good* boys," I say sweetly, trying to tempt him into the house.

He coughs, which sounds more like he choked. I hope he doesn't have some kind of lung infection. *Poor thing.*

"Come on. I have a warm place for you." I slowly walk backward toward my front door.

Some dogs don't like it when you seem too eager to snatch them up. Of course, he's too beautiful for me to let him live rough. Life on the streets is no good for any dog, but something draws me to this one. He's special.

So I'll have to play it cool to snag him.

# 3

## DOGGY RESCUE

### ARRAN

*T*he crazy witch leans over to lure me in with her luscious, hypnotizing breasts. Then she tempts my wolf-half with treats.

I have to stay strong.

"*You're* the one who was following me, remember?" She places her hands on her hips. "And now you're going to play me like this?"

I'm shocked that she's just calling me out. It's a damned challenge, is what it is.

But my wolf is intrigued and right now, he wants nothing more than to dive into her cleavage with his snout.

*Down, boy!*

Dammit, it's been far too long since we've had a nice rut. But this witch might kill me. My wolf's arguing it might be worth it.

"I guess you think you're pretty smart," the woman sasses me. "Well, we'll see… you know, you'll be more comfortable inside. Come on, I have something soft and warm for you to rest your head on."

I can't help it. My brows rise, wondering what's up with her. Is she really trying to seduce me? Is this a trap? Some part of me wonders if she is actually clueless about who she's dealing with. She must be. Otherwise, she's either crazy brave, crazy powerful, or just plain crazy.

The witch casually spins and saunters back toward her front door.

*And now she's playing hard to get?*

With a shake of her head, she peeks over her shoulder and says, "Poor skittish baby."

*Skittish baby!*

I slowly stand up and follow her. I have to know why she was watching us at the bar. Thankfully, she didn't live far away. I wasn't thinking it through when I shifted and chased after her car.

"You want something to eat? You want some of my meat?"

*What the actual fuck?* But my legs carry me after her.

She opens the front door and keeps it wide after she slips inside, waiting for me to decide to fall into her devious trap or not.

I am *not* a skittish baby, so to prove this, I trot inside confidently and glance around, sniffing the air.

Now that I'm within biting distance, I pause and stare up at her.

Slowly, she shuts the door, allowing me the chance to bolt instead of attacking her. But I cautiously watch her as she does. The witch won't intimidate me.

In the full light of the house, her eyes widen as she sees how massive my wolf really is.

I'm huge, even for a wolf shifter. I could give a mastiff a run for its money.

"You *are* a *big* boy, aren't you?" She chuckles, mostly to herself. "But I'm sure you get that all the time from the girls."

She waggles her eyebrows. "You can stay as long as you'd like, but don't cause any trouble," she warns me. "I have some other hostages here who I'd rather you be friends with if you're going to be my new friend."

I chuff with that. I cannot believe the set of crystal balls on this witch!

"Oh, sweetie! Would you like some water?" the witch asks with genuine concern. She hurries toward her kitchen with her groceries and tosses them in the fridge. She gets out a dog water bowl, fills it with filtered water, and sets it down in front of me.

*Huh?*

My wolf almost accepts this offering.

But I remind him she might have poisoned it.

He disagrees. Why the fuck is *he* on Team Witch? He usually hates witches—and for a good reason.

I don't drink. Instead, I give her my best approximation of an indignant look.

She frowns and glances at my neck. "I don't see a collar, but it could be lost in your thick fur."

Why she keeps joking about me being a dog, I do not know.

The witch places her hands on her hips again. "Are you going to tell me your name?"

I give her a quizzical look.

"Yeah, I know you can't talk. But fair warning, I'm going to touch you. Okay?" She cautiously reaches out for my neck, likely to curse me or put a magical chokehold on me.

I give her a low growl to back off.

"Fine." She pulls away. "I guess any touching will have to wait until we get to know each other better."

I blink at that comment. She *is* a strange one.

"Let's get something in you, since you look like you want to eat me." She shrugs and heads for the fridge. She bends over, rummaging through her stuff, and gives me a marvelous view of her full, juicy ass. "Do you like it raw?"

I cough again.

What is it with this woman and her sexual innuendos? Does this game ever work?

Shit. It probably does. If she were a supe and not a freaking witch, I'd be all over that plump ass. As it is, I want to take a bite out of it for several *conflicting* reasons.

She takes her sweet time bending over and pulling stuff out of her fridge.

What would she do to me if I were to shift and grab those wide hips from behind? Would she let me rip the seam of those tight leggings and slam home?

*Focus!*

I sniff the air for magic…

She must have activated some sort of lust charm for me to be thinking like this.

*Sneaky little witch.*

But oddly, I don't scent witch magic in the air. That makes little sense. Why would she allow her enemy into her home without protections in place?

And other than the random and *uncharged* crystals on shelves, there's nothing that screams this is a witch's house. Is this even her home?

I trot around the small but cozy place, sniffing the cushions and inspecting a few photographs. From the scents in the room, I can tell this *is* her home. She's been here for a while. Tucked behind a bunch of other framed pictures, there's one of her with a guy and some other friends.

My wolf snarls when he sees the male has an arm around her waist. Maybe he's a warlock who is truly evil, since my wolf can't be this possessive over a freaking witch.

I admonish him, *You can't like a witch.*

"Hey now, whatcha doin'?" From the kitchen island, she lifts onto her toes to see over the couch and what I'm up to. "Oh, don't get bothered by him. He's out of my life… mostly," she whispers the last word.

Hmm. Maybe *he* is the one who is making her spy on my

friends and me. I study the picture again to memorize his face. My wolf is agitated and aggressively bumps it with his nose. The frame falls to the ground, and the glass shatters.

"Oh, no." The witch quickly yet calmly approaches me. "Step back. I don't want you to get your feeties hurt."

*My feeties?*

Does she *really* think I'm a dog? She must. Either that, or she's incredibly condescending and has a death wish.

She looks at my front paws to make sure I don't have any glass on my fur. Picking up the bigger pieces of shards, she piles them on top of the broken frame to collect them. "I don't know why I kept this picture. Maybe because it reminds me of when I believed Rob wasn't such an alphahole."

I have a name for the man. Good.

But *alpha*hole? Was she dating a jerky wolf shifter? Maybe that's why she works for the Witch Council as a spy—for revenge.

I have so many questions.

Is that why she's so comfortable with me in my wolf form? Maybe she has already dated one?

Her eyes water, but she doesn't let the tears fall. Turning her face from me, she brushes away the moisture and stands.

"Why don't you come over here and eat?" She motions me over to the kitchen.

I don't follow. Rather, I continue my inspection of the living room, intent on figuring out what this witch is up to.

The witch doesn't force me to go to the kitchen. Instead, she sweeps up the glass with furtive glances my way. She's trying to figure me out, just as I am trying to understand her.

I suppose I should just shift and interrogate her.

"Do you have anyone who will miss you?" she asks, sounding sad.

*That's a fucking threat if I've ever heard one.*

And the sadness? I suppose she regrets that she needs to

eliminate me. Perhaps she is one of the few witches with a conscience.

Just as I'm about to snarl and show her I won't go down without a fight, she stops me cold.

"I'll call animal control in the morning to find your humans. I'm sure someone is worried sick about losing such a beautiful dog." She looks about ready to cry again.

Holy crap. She *really* does think I'm a regular dog.

She must be a magically weak witch and can't sense I'm the supe she was watching earlier.

She might know nothing about the four of us. And they sent her on a reconnaissance mission without many details about her targets. Maybe the council only picked her to watch us because of her proximity.

I sniff the air again and only get a faint hint of witch magic, but I don't know why it suddenly appeared now. So she doesn't practice her craft—much. Or she doesn't know how to use it. I almost didn't scent her muted magic at the bar either. But oddly, the magic was stronger there while she was watching us.

The witch pulls her computer tablet and phone out of her purse. But after she glances at me, she shoves it back inside and takes all her personal belongings with her as she heads toward the bedrooms. "There's food in the bowl if you get hungry. I hope you don't mind staying out here alone. Oh, and please don't eat my sofa. I'm going to bed. Don't worry, we'll get you sorted in the morning."

# 4

# HAUNTING DREAMS

## JADE

*T*his dog is the most intense animal I've ever encountered. And I've dealt with some animals I was sure had human souls. I have a couple of highly intelligent brats in my spare room right now.

I leave the huge canine to check on my little ones. When I open the door, they look at me like I've disturbed them. "We have a visitor, so don't get freaked out. Kay?"

They obviously don't reply, because, yeah, they're animals. I'm not that weird.

I suppose I talk to my furry friends because it's a bit of a lonely life, writing all day long and promoting stuff online. And I often go days without human contact—physical human contact. Sure, I network online and interact with my author friends there. I make comments on their posts and support them as much as I can. And that's rewarding, but it isn't the same as physically touching or talking with a living person in front of me. Sometimes I miss seeing a friend's smile and the crinkle of their eyes when we joke around or hug each other. Maybe that's why I go to the bar at least once a week—to experience humans.

I carry my purse into my bedroom and shut the door behind me. I don't think my new friend will chew up my stuff, but I don't want to risk having to go through the hassle of replacing my credit cards, ID, phone, and tablet.

I don't hear him whine or bark, so I relax and lock my bedroom door. It's an instinct now. I do it out of habit. Lessons learned and all that.

Using my ensuite bathroom, I brush my teeth and wash my face.

The bed invites me to a good time. And I pull back the covers, *real* slow. Okay, maybe those hot guys tonight worked me up a bit.

I pull my vibrator, Mr. O'Mygawd, from the side table drawer and imagine my new harem picks. I wonder which one of them I would choose first. The intense leader? The stony giant? The smoldering player? The broody bad boy?

A shiver runs up my back. The room feels like it dropped a couple of degrees. *Odd.*

There's no reason for the drafty breeze. I didn't hear the dog crash through the window or—I chuckle to myself—open the front door.

I'll need to make my noises quietly, since I don't want to upset the dog. He might think I'm being hurt in here when I come. I'd hold off, but the urge to rub one out is overwhelming. It's like I still feel their eyes on me. And I envision a world where they are interested—one where *all* of them are interested.

Ha! Fat chance, but it's my job to dream this shit up.

Got to fight the good fight. Research and all.

I feel my pussy wet with just the thought of them closing in on me. Each of their muscular bodies presses closer and closer until they tower over me.

Taking up all the oxygen in the room, they all reach out and caress me. A kiss on my neck. A hand on my breast. A firm cock against my ass. Another against my stomach. I feel dizzy with need and I sway.

"You are ours now," the dominant one claims me. "We are going to stretch you with our cocks, and then our cum will fill you so full you'll be leaking for days."

They tear the clothes off my body, and I cry out, "Yes, claim me."

Each of them tears off their own clothes and frees their cocks, stroking themselves with their massive hands. Not that they need the extra stimulation to get hard.

Strong hands push me down and I go willingly. On my knees in front of them, I open my mouth, understanding what they desire from me. What I desire from them.

One after another, their thick cocks face fuck me, rammed down my throat.

But it's only the last guy, Mr. Blue Eyes, who comes in my mouth. I swallow him down as he shouts, "Drink it all, my pet."

After he withdraws, I'm lifted into the dominant one's arms, and he spears me with his enormous cock, stretching and filling me beyond anything I have ever experienced.

Grumpy Alphahole comes up behind me, fists my hair, pulling my head back so he can plunder my mouth with his fingers, wetting them.

Then he slips his wet fingers down over my ass crack and slides two into my ass.

Bouncing me on his massive dick, Mr. Dom rams into me, keeping a brutal pace.

The quiet one squeezes my tit.

And the fantasy overwhelms me…

"Fuck!" I shout when the orgasm crashes into me.

I blush for some reason, even though I'm alone. It's not like the dog is going to judge me—probably. Although *he* might, since he seems way too smart.

Maybe I feel a bit smutty because I'm using real people to jerk off to?

Whatever. Another strange, cool breeze skims over my naked flesh, and I decide to throw on a long t-shirt before falling asleep. I have the unnerving sensation that I'm being watched. But that feeling just might be because I have a new presence in the house in the form of a highly intelligent dog.

But even with that feeling, I fall asleep, content with the knowledge I have found some inspiration. Now that I have my new characters, I just have to come up with the beginnings of a plot.

I can't wait to play with these guys some more...
***

I fall instantly into a strange dream...

"Hey!" A huge red demon runs directly at me, but I'm not afraid.

In this dream, I'm supposed to know him. His large horns curl above his head. Blood covers his hands and soaks into his shirt.

I realize he looks very much like one of the hot squad from the bar. Maybe this is actually one of my own dreams and not one that I've picked up from some stranger.

Yeah, I sort of believe that I *might* dream other people's dreams.

"Are you alright?" the demon asks while he studies my body for injury.

My avatar glances down, and I see from my build and bulging pants I'm a man. I'm also splattered with blood. "I think so. Let's leave before anyone else shows up."

"Let them come! I will rend them apart too." The demon flexes his muscles, and his eyes flare with a spark of fire.

I notice there are bodies and body parts strewn about in the dark alleyway. A distant streetlight makes the wet blood gleam.

My heart pounds, but not from fear.

I grab the demon's horns and pull him in for a possessive and passionate kiss.

Our hips grind against each other, and I can feel his hardened length, ready to be unleashed. We've been worked up from the adrenaline of violence. *Righteous justice.*

Pulling back, I curse. "We need to find the others. These bastards would have attacked them too."

The demon rests his forehead against mine. "When this is done, I'm fucking your ass so hard that even you won't recover."

"Promises, promises." I chuckle, but it's a sad thing. "If we survive this night, I'm going to fuck you all, even Blockhead."

The demon roars with a laugh. "I don't think he'll be pleased with that."

I chuckle too. "Maybe not, but it will be fun to watch him squirm when I tease him."

*Now, this is getting interesting…*

Then a voice whispers in my mind, *"Who are you?"*

Abruptly, I wake up and shiver. My skin is goose-bumped. And a wave of cold air washes over me. What the hell?

I believe in ghosts, not that I give it much mind… usually. I always assumed they were like energetic echoes of someone from the past. However, now I sense a presence, one that feels aware of me.

"Leave me alone!" I state firmly, and I feel the energy fade away.

I shiver. It's one thing writing about the paranormal and supernatural worlds and ideas. It's another thing to be living in them.

With how violent my dream was, I wonder if a spirit was influencing my dark nightmare. I'm not comfortable with that.

Well, I was okay with that panty-melting kiss. But everything else? No, thank you.

Maybe I'm losing my mind?

That's what Rob would tell me when I recounted my strange dreams.

## 5

## WITCH PLACE

ARRAN

*T*his witch must really think I'm only a dog. Why else would she allow me free rein over her home while she slept?

I hear her brushing her teeth and readying for bed, so I wander back to the room where she keeps her hostage-friends. They smell like small animals, but I wonder if she's somehow trapped shifters in there. That's concerning.

With my enhanced ability, I hear her slip into bed. I shift into my human form and open the door to her menagerie.

"Who the fuck are you?" an angry-looking guinea pig demands with a hiss, when I step naked into the room.

"No. What the fuck are *you*?" I growl, my voice low.

He scrambles backward into the corner of his cage, surprised I've heard him, I think. But that is a talent of mine— hearing the thoughts of magical creatures. Less than half of the shifter population can hear these unique animals' thoughts or the thoughts of other shifters.

The little thing glances at the other animals in the room, back at me, and toward her bedroom. "Don't hurt the witch," he says threateningly.

"Why shouldn't I?" I tower over his cage, wondering if he might shift into a human form. But I don't scent shifter magic on him. "Are you going to fight me?"

Instead of answering me, he pees. Fair enough. He probably expects that I'm going to eat him as an appetizer before the main course, the witch.

When my mind thinks of sneaking into her room and making her a meal, I imagine feasting on her pussy instead.

Goddess, I need to get laid soon. I've never been this distracted on a mission before.

"Tell me what you are doing here?" I demand.

"I'm a magical creature. I like to think of myself as her familiar, but—" he trails off and sighs.

"But what?"

"Jade doesn't know I can speak. She can't hear me like you do."

"She's really that stupid that she allows both of us into her home?" I rub my face, because now it seems unfair to kill her.

"Not stupid," the furry pig explains defensively. "I don't think she knows much about magic. But then, other times... it seems like she does. Like she might hear me, but not really."

This little twerp doesn't seem too bright either.

From down the hall, I hear a strange humming sound.

Is she casting a spell?

Giving up on her magical creature, I sneak down the hallway to investigate and press my ear to her bedroom door.

She's making little mewling sounds, and my dick twitches as a whiff of arousal leaks through the door's crack.

Is she trying to lure me in like a siren? Because the scent is intoxicating. It must be her witch magic.

Does she intend for me to shift, race in there, and fall into her trap? Maybe the whole ignorance angle is a guise of getting me to lower my guard.

She shouts out what sounds like an orgasm.

*Fuck.*

My cock is not immune to her dangerous seduction. I press my palm against my length, hoping to calm my raging boner.

Within moments, her breathing evens out, and she sounds to be asleep. Still, I wait another half hour before trying her door to sneak in.

Locked.

Interesting. The witch must have a clue as to what I am. Why else would she lock her bedroom door to keep out a regular dog?

I debate crashing through her locked door and torturing answers out of her. But that won't likely work out well for me, since her grip on my libido is overwhelming.

I imagine pinning her down, demanding the truth, and my hand wrapping around her fragile throat. However, I'd end up as the tortured one as my cock would throb with the sounds of her whimpers and pleas.

Instead, I decide to check out the other rooms down the hallway. There's a guest bath, but the other one is an office.

Traces of her magic are strongest in here. I wonder why. It doesn't appear to be a witch's casting space.

The walls are lined on three sides with bookshelves filled with books—not old creepy witchy books, but modern paperback novels. I pick one up and see it's some magical fantasy romance. After a quick perusal, I find most of them are, except for a few classic fantasy books like the *Lord of the Rings* trilogy. I'm not much of a reader anymore, but I recognize that title and a few others.

I don't see any family grimoires passed down through generations lying about, not that I'd expect witches to leave their spell books out in the open and unguarded.

But with how reckless this witch appears to be with her life,

I wouldn't have been surprised to find them next to these romance novels.

I glance at another title. Uh… *Monster Lovers' Manual*?

*What the actual fuck?*

Is this witch into screwing monsters? Or is it just research for her seduction magic?

Either way, the true beast inside me perks up.

The more I discover about this woman, the more confused I am. I rub my forehead to ward off the severe headache coming on.

Waking up her laptop with a touch of a key, I'm happy to find that she doesn't have a passcode to log on. I do my best to bind my magic so that I don't fuck up her electronic device. I have to see what information she has on us.

Most low-powered witches and warlocks are able to use computers with minimal issues. But almost all supes have some problems, if not actually blowing them up. Since my magic is more tied in with my shifting and not as active as other supes, I can usually use electronics sparingly. That ability fails if I get riled up or otherwise engage my limited magic.

I scan her desktop files and see a shared user folder labeled 'BAR GUYS' and today's date. I click on it and skim through her notes.

She has described all four of us in detail. Also, she was trying to figure out what we were talking about. And she isn't far off, but her language is a bit flowery for what I'd expect from a spy or assassin. I skim over most of it, because she goes on quite a lot about our bulging muscles and strong jawlines.

She describes Flint as *stony*, I'm an alphahole, Maxum is hot as hell, and Calder has *smoldering* eyes. I chuckle at that.

There's no way she's not on to us. But why she would take weird notes like *this* is beyond my comprehension.

I glance at the romance books on the shelves. But if *lust* is her magic, then maybe it does make sense. I've never run across a lust witch. However, my hardened cock very much wants to learn more—much, much more.

I shouldn't be having this lustful reaction right now. Yesterday, I lost the one person who meant the most to me in this world. My heart is broken—so my physical response to her *has* to be a manipulative spell she cast around us at the bar.

The smart thing to do is to take off now and warn the others. But I don't want to risk losing my position here, where I can spy on her without her knowledge.

Besides, I need to know if she's the one who killed Osen.

# 6

# INVITED

## JADE

*M*y sleep is restless and filled with strange dreams. I'm not sure if it was the late-night greasy cheese sandwich or the new animal energy in my home.

Still in bed, I stare at my ceiling, allowing my mind to wander and dream up some more details about my new characters. I find some of my best ideas come when I'm in the in-between headspace somewhere before falling asleep and just after waking up.

Half-awake, I groan when I hear a knock at my front door.

*This flipping early!*

Checking the clock, I see it's past noon. Oh… so no longer morning. I suppose I can't be this indignant about a midday visitor.

I can't believe I slept this late. Not that I usually get up at the crack of dawn. Being single and fueled by inspiration and manic writing episodes, I've become unreasonably flexible with my sleeping patterns.

I figure whoever is at the door is just here to save my naughty soul. So I close my eyes, hoping they will realize it's a hopeless cause, and move on when I don't answer their call to salvation.

I'm fairly certain that upon my death, I'm going to the Underworld and chatting up Tartarus about writing smut.

The knock comes again. Hmm. Maybe I ordered something that needs a signature? I didn't think 'Living The Smut Life' stickers would require that level of security. But what do I know?

I slide into my comfy sweatpants, since last night I've felt weirdly underdressed wearing only tight leggings around my new dog. I pull up my long, gray-streaked brown hair into a messy bun and check myself in the mirror. Not horrible for forty, but too many of my younger years had been wasted on Rob and other ex-jerks. It's time I wish I hadn't wasted.

Shrugging off the negative thoughts, I rush out to the living room. Realization dawning on me that I probably shouldn't be running since I have a new, skittish dog here now.

The dog is standing at attention, watching me closely, but doesn't seem overly spooked by my sudden appearance. He must have expected me with the door knock. Clever boy that he is.

I appreciate he didn't automatically and incessantly bark at someone on the porch. If no one claims him, I might keep him if he can play nice with my other fur babies. Oh, damn, I need to let him out to go to the bathroom if he didn't already use a rug in my house. Ugh. I'm not used to having dogs.

Hearing scuffling feet at the door, I remember I have someone waiting for me. I remind myself to let the dog go out to the fenced backyard after I deal with this intrusion.

I spy through the peephole and see the stupidly handsome dominant guy from the bar waiting for me.

I spin and slam my back to the door as if to brace it closed.

Or brace me from the panic I feel. I pant with nerves. My body heats.

Is this a hot flash? Nerves? Arousal? Check all the above?

"Fuck," I murmur to myself. "How did he find me? And what is he doing here?"

I suck in a breath to calm down and count to five to clear my head. My hand clasps the 'protection' pendant hanging around my neck that my abuela gave me.

The dog watches my whole chaotic display with interest.

Studying the canine, he seems like the type who would attack this visitor if this guy is a bad dude.

I swing open the door and plaster on a fake smile. "How can I help you?"

The man's eyes narrow on me, and he doesn't immediately respond. Finally, he tilts his head as if he's confused. "You look familiar."

My face burns with a blush. He knows *exactly* who I am. Stop bluffing, dude. "We might have both been at the bar down the road last night."

He grins, and his dark eyes trail down my body, taking me in—not in a creepy way, but *not not* in a creepy way either. "Ah, yes, of course."

He has a hint of an Irish brogue, but there's something else that I can't yet place.

His quiet attention is disarming. Hell, *he's* disarming. And he looks like he could literally remove my arms with no effort.

He must stand a foot taller than me, at least six-foot-five inches of sculpted muscle, highlighted by his form-fitting long-sleeve shirt and expensive-looking jeans that hug him in all the right places.

*Eyes up, Jade! On his face! Be a good girl... Ugh. Don't say good girl right now.*

"Did you need something?" I ask and sort of hope he'll growl and tell me it's me he needs. Then he'll throw me over his massive shoulder and carry me off to ravage me.

*Keep it together, naughty girl.*

He smirks as if he's read my mind.

Shit, my face probably gives me away. I don't think I can get away with casually checking my mouth for drool. Even if he can't read my face, I'm sure he just assumes that's what's going on in my mind. This man exudes barely bridled masculine power.

He's ruggedly handsome with a strong brow, perfect black hair, and the darkest brown eyes I've ever seen that look like volcanic obsidian.

I'm ready to fall into his gaze when he finally answers me.

"I'm looking for a lost… canine."

I'm suddenly protective of the mutt and close the door enough to block this man's view into my house. "Yeah? What does this dog look like?"

"Much like the one I just saw sitting in your living room."

Whoops. Too late. I'm not great at being covert.

"Is he yours?" a bit of loss seeps into my voice. I don't want to let the grumpy dog go. I was hoping we could go for a walk before I reported him to animal control. If no one claimed him, I wanted to adopt him. Make him feel safe.

The huge male pats his pant leg, and commands, "Heel."

The dog looks unimpressed.

"He's a friend's," McHottie confesses. "I was hoping he would come with me."

Reluctantly, I step back so the dog can feel free to join his owner's friend.

"Come with me, now," he says. His voice has a tinge of irritation.

"Does he run off a lot?" I ask, giving the dog time to warm up to the idea of going.

"Enough."

When the dog doesn't move, I ask, "Does the dog know you very well?"

"He should." McHottie studies me again. "But apparently, he prefers your company. And I can understand why."

I laugh heartily because this guy is so far out of my league, and I'd guess at least ten years younger than me. The thought is so absurd, and I think I snort at one point. "Uh, yeah. Okay. Well, I offered him free meat." I blush again because now it sounds naughty.

"Beautiful women don't usually tempt that beast. So it must be something about you."

I glance around this guy's massive body to see if someone is filming me for a prank video.

He turns to see what I'm looking for. "What's wrong?" His hand goes out as if to block someone, protecting me from an attack.

Odd. Maybe he's a cop or something? I could see him in a uniform—military or otherwise. Although, I doubt he would be low ranking with his dominating presence.

"I was looking for the prank camera," I admit.

When his dark eyes turn back on me, all I read is confusion. "Prank?"

"Umm… Well, it sort of sounded like you were hitting on me. Which is ridiculous."

"It is?" He frowns. "Why? Are you involved with someone?"

"No."

"Good." He smiles, and his whole face lights up, blinding me with his perfection. "Would you like to go out with me tonight?"

"That's funny." I shake my head.

I know I'm not ugly. But this guy? There's no flippin' way he's into me, especially how I look right now. No makeup, crazy messy bun, and dumpy oversized clothes—guys can't really like me like this. Currently, I don't even qualify as a hot mess. I'm just straight-up messy.

Rob didn't appreciate how I looked. He called me a sloppy pig. But whatever. I don't care.

"Oh, yeah. I suppose it *is* last minute." He nods like that's the reason I'm laughing and smiles again. "If you aren't busy now, I'm not doing anything since I've found my friend's beast."

"Beast?" I glance back at the dog, and he appears to be giving McHottie the stink eye. "Is that his name? It seems fitting. But he seems like a smart one."

"He's not *that* smart," McHottie says with a chuckle. Then he rubs the back of his neck nervously and shows off his humongous arms. I swear they are thicker than my thighs. And that's saying something since I'm not thin.

"So, how about that date?" he asks quietly, his voice a deep rumble that vibrates through me all the way to my clit.

I cross my arms defensively. Then I realize I've just pushed up my ample breasts with no bra on and in a thin t-shirt. "So, are you into older women or something?"

McHottie clears his throat. "Or something." Then he steps closer, and his shadow looms over me.

I'm equally turned on and a bit intimidated by his size. I think he might be an oxygen hound since I can't seem to get enough air.

"I'd like to get to know you. Is there something wrong with that?"

"Nope," I squeak. I'm tempted to take a step back... or maybe a step closer, and see what he does. But I'm starting to think he might actually be into me. "Uh. But I just rolled out of bed."

"Hungry?"

Oh, god, yes. I want to say for some sausage, but I don't. "Yeah. Can you give me a minute or several to get ready?"

"Sure." He retreats to the edge of my porch. "I'll be right here."

I shut the front door and quietly lock it, because, yeah. I

don't know this guy. And I want a quick shower. I can't trust the new weirdo dog to protect me if this guy has ill intent.

Not that I expect McHottie to be a dildo, but I've learned the hard way not to let down my guard even with—especially with —people I'm attracted to.

When I turn, the dog looks at me with raised eyebrows.

As I stroll by him, I grumble, "What? I don't get asked out on dates. Not my problem if you didn't want to go with him first."

I give myself a quick rinse in the shower—no need to shave or primp. This pussy isn't going for a spin over brunch. Any guy who expects that within the first hour of knowing me and after hash browns isn't going to get to eat my dessert taco. I've been there and done that, and it doesn't work out happily in real life… at least, not for me.

Honestly, dating never works out great for me. Maybe that's why I retreated to the world of romance books. I'm safe within the pages. I always get my happily ever after or my happy for now.

*No one can break my heart.*

Okay, that's not necessarily true. Sometimes, I cry like a baby with some scenes I read.

But I don't plan on falling for this sexy cougar-chasing fuckboy.

*However…* I plan to enjoy myself and flirt. I will make notes so I can use our conversations for my book inspiration.

I don't usually wear much makeup, but I put on some blush and tinted lip gloss. He's already seen me at my worst and asked me out anyway. Playing it up now seems freaking silly and pointless. Fortunately, I've been blessed with naturally dark eyelashes, so it already looks like I'm wearing eyeliner or mascara.

I slip on some comfy jeans and a lightweight sweater. Quickly, I make sure all my fur babies are fed and watered.

I frown when I see the dog didn't eat any of the steak I

chopped up. Or the kibble I threw in there. I open the back door to see if he will go outside and relieve himself, but he doesn't take the hint.

As I saunter by the dog, I say, "Don't wait up." And I give him a saucy wink.

He goes from lying down to sitting up and glaring at me.

"Fine. Do what you like, just don't eat the furniture. Or my friends. If you're good, I'll get you a doggy bag."

I want to reach out and pet him goodbye, but when I step closer, he ducks his head and trots away. So not as standoffish as last night, but close. We have a way to go, but I don't expect I will have him long enough to win him over. His owner will come to claim him soon.

# 7

# BRUNCH MISTAKEN

## MAXUM

*W*hen I hear her shower running and the sound of her stepping inside it and water crashing over her naked body, I take a brief moment for myself and imagine the hot water pouring over all those tantalizing curves. Down the slope of her—

Snapping out of my lust-filled thoughts, I rush across the small porch. Crouching down, I peek in through her living room window. I motion for Arran to come closer.

His wolf shakes his head at me.

*What in the ever-living fuck?*

I want to mind-dive him to find out what the hell he's thinking, but I promised him and the other guys I wouldn't do that. I can't break their trust. I can't even cheat. They would know I was invading.

I wonder if the witch would sense it was me if I did. I suppose I could just scramble her brains and call it a day.

Instead of fucking up Arran's brains with a mind dive, I mouth the words: *"What are you doing in there?"*

His head flicks in the direction of the witch's room.

*Yeah, no shit, asshole.*

I wave him closer again so that even with a low voice, we both can talk through the glass window because of our exceptional hearing.

He trots up to the window and shifts to his human form. With how I'm crouched down at his waist level, I get an eyeful of wolf shifter dick.

*Ugh.* I can't deal with his crap right now.

I glower up at him and say in a low voice, "What the fuck are you doing?"

He squats down and answers, "Investigating." The bastard has the audacity to look perturbed with me.

Out of anyone in our group last night, I'd have thought he'd be the last to willingly infiltrate a witch's home. And he's probably the last one who should. I'm surprised that he hasn't turned into his true beast and attacked her.

But I suppose he hasn't learned his lesson yet. He will, when either this woman or some other mortal magic weaver kills him.

I don't sense any wards around her house, but I'm tempted to risk being zapped just so I can storm in there and wring Arran's damned neck for being so reckless.

"Does she have you under a spell?" I ask. *"Trapped?"*

He shakes his head but looks unsure. "I think she really believes I'm a dog."

I picked that up too. I didn't dive into her mind. But from what I was able to pick up from her on the surface, she doesn't seem to know his true nature.

However, I don't trust a casual assessment. She could be skilled at blocking her thoughts and be able to project only innocent ones.

Although the few stray thoughts I caught on the surface might not be categorized as entirely *innocent*. She seems to be attracted to my physique—not that I blame her. Most find my body pleasing. Even without my glamour to make me appear human, I look almost the same.

But I need my glamour because without it, I have crimson skin, horns, and some other special bits that must be hidden from norms and witches.

She might not be so inclined to fuck me if she saw the actual complete package.

*Wait! Why do I care if she wants to fuck me?*

I shouldn't be sliding down this line of thinking.

But this crazy witch who invited a wolf into her home intrigues me. Even if she doesn't get that he's a shifter, Arran is a fucking huge beast of a dire wolf. And she just let him in and *protected* him. From me.

The witch doesn't appear to be dumb, so why is she behaving this way? She allowed herself to be caught spying on us last night. She invited Arran inside. And now she is going on a brunch date with me.

What's up with this woman?

I have to know. Hence, the date…

I hear the floor creak as she moves out of the bathroom to likely get dressed. Arran shifts and sits down to appear casual, waiting for her to return. I quickly return to the spot on the far side of the small porch and attempt to appear calm.

However, I'm anything but relaxed. I've lost my best friend and occasional lover, and this woman is already under my skin and inside my head.

I sense an insignificant amount of power coming off her. I wonder what sort of affinity this witch has. Is she a green witch —tied to nature and the elements? Is she into potions? Or is she more powerful than I understand and is able to hide it from me?

I have to stay alert.

The witch flings open the front door with her eyes wide, looking upset.

I hate to say that my first instinct is to protect her. I remind myself that she's likely my enemy.

She covers her face in embarrassment. "I can't believe I agreed to go out with you, and I didn't even find out your name!"

"Maxum," I answer truthfully. If she is a spy, she already knows my name. It's probably why she *forgot* to ask me.

"I'm… uh, Jade—" she then mutters, "Uh, never mind me."

Curious now, I ask, "Do you have more than one name?"

Ironically, *I* have two names, my sacred summoning demon name and my common use name that everyone calls me —Maxum.

"Uh, yeah." She locks her door behind her.

I grin to myself at her safeguarding measure. She already has her enemy inside her home.

"I'm an author," she explains. "I've been so immersed in that world and marketing that I forget my other name sometimes."

"Would you like me to use your real name?" I fish.

"Let's see if you earn it." She playfully quirks her full lips.

And… my heart flutters. *Flutters!*

That hasn't happened to me in… six hundred years, when I was just a teenage spawn. Not even Osen's power used to make me feel this ebullient attraction.

For the second time today, I am lost for words in front of this witch. This is not something I am accustomed to.

"I like my author name better anyway." Jade glances up and down the street. "Did you bring your car? And where are we going to eat? Do you have any special dietary restrictions?"

She looks ready to ask me another series of questions when I answer the first. "My car is back at the bar on the corner. I was canvassing the neighborhood," I lie. "Should we take your car?"

Nervousness plays on her face. She bites her lip. She points to her sensible tennis shoes. "Maybe we can walk down to the place just past the bar? It's not far."

"You're a smart woman." I nod appreciatively. "You don't know me. I'm glad you take precautions and don't give in."

Why does it please me that she knows how to claim her boundaries?

"I've learned that being polite can get a woman in trouble." She cocks a brow at me. "Are *you* trouble?"

Even if she is ignorant of my true identity, deep down, she must instinctively know that I am dangerous.

"I suppose anyone can be trouble." Giving a shrug, I take a step toward the sidewalk. "A walk sounds perfect. It gives us time to talk and get to know each other on the way."

Her eyes travel up and down my body, cautiously appraising me. Does she sense how much potential danger she is in being around me?

If I wanted to, I could scramble her brains right now until she didn't remember her own name. It wouldn't be the first time, and I doubt it will be the last. I had to do it for an old acquaintance just the other day.

I take up most of the sidewalk with my bulk, so I move as far toward the street as I can to give the witch some space. I want her to feel safe... for now. Once I determine what her intentions are, I'll likely have to destroy her.

But until then, she gets the nice, charming Maxum.

"Should you call your friend?" the witch asks as she nods to my pocket, thinking that I have a mobile phone.

"I don't have a phone."

She stops in her tracks, eyes widened, and places a hand over her chest. "Someone *your* age *doesn't* have a phone?"

I chuckle. Someone *my* age never even dreamed we would have cell phones. Sure, we had magic mirrors to communicate hundreds of years ago, but those are becoming rare and now don't work over long distances because of the failing magic in our worlds.

"That's surprising, huh?" I cock my brow and study her.

Odd. It shouldn't be surprising to her. She *should* know that a supernatural being's magic kills electronics.

Hmm. Is she really that oblivious of that basic fact?

"I figured you'd be some social media celebrity posting thirst traps every day."

Now my eyes widen. *"Thirst... traps?"*

I've heard of a lot of magical traps, but not these. The only traps I've had to worry about are demon-summoning circles, since they can trap me if someone knows my sacred name.

She doubles over with laughter. "Your face! You really don't know what I'm talking about?"

"Explain." I want to be angry with her for mocking my ignorance, but my lips can't help curling into a smile instead of a snarl.

Jade covers her face and blushes. "You know... when an attractive person posts themselves all sexed up to get attention."

I turn and stand directly in front of Jade. Towering over her, I ask in a low voice. "Do I look like someone who seeks attention?" My hands itch to touch her soft skin, but I keep them firmly at my sides.

Her mouth opens into a little O shape, and I want to fill the tempting opening with my tongue, then with my cock.

She sucks in a breath and gulps, maybe reading my mind as easily as I can read others. Her voice is soft with awe as she says, "No. You seem like you should have plenty of attention just by existing."

I resist the strange urge that overcomes me, making me want to pull her toward me, seat her on my growing cock, and claim her. My attraction might be a lust spell, and I won't fall for another one of those. It's one of the few magics that work on a demon other than a demon trap.

With blown-out pupils indicating her attraction, her hazel-green eyes drop to my lips. Then she snaps out of her naughty thoughts and locks gazes with me.

Surprisingly, she doesn't back down or avert her eyes.

I want to run my fingers through her gray-streaked hair and fist it while I claim her delicious body. I admire that she doesn't hide her silver as it reveals her hard-won life experiences. But since witches hardly age over their mid-thirties, I idly wonder how old she really is to have earned her gray. Not as old as I am.

I'm so close I can feel the heat of her luscious body. And I'm sure since I run much hotter that she must feel my heat caressing her curves. All I have to do is reach out and touch her, and I could destroy her—with my mind or with my body. It would be an easy thing to do.

But right now, I want to destroy her pussy with my cock.

*Focus!* Has it really been that long since I've been with a woman that I'm succumbing to the first female in my proximity?

Yet, I haven't been attracted to a female in years.

It must be a spell. Although, I can't deny what she offers on the surface isn't tantalizing all on its own.

I step back and raise my mental shields again.

Jade exhales, and her knees shake. Is she scared or turned on? Or both?

Worrying that she might actually be as innocent as she projects, I say reluctantly, "Sorry. I can be—"

"*Intense* as fuck?" she finishes for me with a bit of humor and relief in her voice.

"Yeah, that." I bite my lip and turn my face away as I walk again. Why does she have to be so damned... *cute*?

"So... no phone," she continues, as if my show of dominance never happened. "Are you anti-technology? Or just don't like to be tied down to a phone?"

"Technology and I don't really get along."

"I hear you. I remember the days when you weren't on someone's shit list because you didn't call or text them back within ten seconds. And since I'm an author and I work from home, people in my life don't always respect that I might be working on a scene. But if I were at some corporate job, it would be okay that I'm not answering for basic chitchat."

Okay, I'll bite. She's claimed this author's persona as her cover. "What sort of books do you write? Would I know your work?"

"Uh…" Her ears turn pink. Her heart beats wildly, more so than when I was looming over her. "I don't think you've read my stuff."

"Because I don't look like I can read?" I deadpan.

"Oh, geeze, no!" She covers her mouth in embarrassment. "I just… I write romance. You don't really seem like you would be into that."

"Because I don't look like I enjoy romance?" I joke but continue my serious tone.

She turns bright red now. "No! Oh, man, I'm turning this conversation into a shitshow. It's just… my audience is ninety-nine percent women, so I don't expect you to have heard of me or the genre I write."

"Is it… what do they call it?" I ask. "Steamy?"

Her eyebrows rise with surprise that I know something about romance books. "Uh. Yes, there are *detailed* and explicit scenes." Her aura tightens around her body, and she seems agitated.

Why is she nervous now?

"I didn't know you would be ashamed of your writing," I offer. "We can move on from this subject."

"I'm not ashamed of my work," she says, straightening up. "I just don't talk about it with people I only met five seconds before. And being a guy, I thought maybe you'd belittle me somehow."

"Does that happen a lot?" An urge to rip body parts off anyone who has mocked her rushes through my system. What is this protective instinct about?

"Well, I've had all kinds of responses. I've had guys hit on me and tell me they can help with inspiration, then send unsolicited dick pics."

I figure out that reference on my own—modern-day flashing. From this day forward, these dicks will now be burnt sausages.

Jade sighs and wrings her hands.

"But it sounds like there is something else?" I prompt.

"My ex tried to make me stop writing. He was jealous of imaginary guys."

"Truly?" I shake my head.

Humans are so strange.

"It doesn't matter. You don't want to hear about my ex." She brushes it off and changes the subject. "So, what do you do?"

I don't tell her I don't have to work for a living. She doesn't need to know about my finances or that I'm basically a soldier in the brewing war with her kind. So I go with a version of the truth of what I do in my spare time. "I run a disadvantaged youth outreach program."

"No shit." Jade grins. "That's awesome. How does that work?"

"I help high-risk teens to develop coping skills for life." More like teaching them to control their magic and training them in self-defensive combat magic to protect themselves. But she doesn't need to know that either.

"I imagine that would be so rewarding," she says, impressed with my pursuits. "I volunteer at the animal shelter, walking dogs, petting cats, and stuff. But I'm not great with people."

"Really?" I give her a look of disbelief. "You seem like you would be. I mean, you don't appear uncomfortable around me. And I don't necessarily put people at ease."

She frowns as she takes that in. "Yeah, well, I'm definitely not a fan of crowds. But for some strange reason, I feel okay being around you, even though you look like you might break me in two."

I could split her in two... with my cock. *Nope, stop it. Bad dick.*

We walk for a few minutes in comfortable silence.

In my mind, I go over what she's said so far. My senses didn't detect any lies about her feeling okay around me. Which is funny. If anything, her instincts should tell her to run—far, far away.

We get to the restaurant that's located just past the bar where she watched us last night. In the bar's parking lot, I see Flint and Calder sitting in Calder's vintage 1962 Rambler. I step faster to block Jade's view of them and point down the street. "Looks like it's not too busy at the Spud House this morning. That should put you at ease."

She hums her agreement, and we cross the road.

My senses tingle. Someone is watching. I want to shrug it off as if it's only my friend's attention, but I know better. I'm familiar with the weight and texture of their gaze. Maybe her witch associates are now preparing to kill me.

And my friends are probably wondering what the hell I'm doing with our enemy.

Hell, I'd like to know that too.

8

---

## SCRAMBLED

JADE

*M*axum is probably the most unusual man I've ever met, and that's saying something. He's sexy and intense, but also sensitive. Why he hasn't been snatched up by someone already is beyond me. But perhaps he's just a player who dislikes being tied down. Or, maybe he likes to *tie* people down and torture orgasms out of them. Maybe I'd let *him* play like that…

My mind ponders that kinky scenario for a lovely moment. My wrists and ankles are bound and stretched out. His dark, hungry gaze travels over my body as he calculates how he will make me beg for his cock. How long will he torment my nipples and clit before he gives in and wrecks my pussy?

"Jade?" he calls me as if he's concerned.

Oh geeze, I switched to full fantasy-author mode, zoning out, my eyes likely glazed over. Can he hear my heart pounding in my clit?

"Sorry, author moment," I joke.

He winks at me and opens the door to the cute little restaurant.

It's fine if he's only a fuckboy. This isn't going any further than this awkward brunch, so I can play along for a while as he flirts.

We sit at one of the empty tables the server points us to. This place is nice and cozy, but not fancy. When I'm not feeling like cooking, which is more often than not, I come here or to the bar if it's late and this place is closed.

I don't need to look at their menu already sitting on the table since I've memorized it.

Maxum grins at me, giving me a blast of sexy heat with his perfect teeth. His perfectly white and oddly sharp teeth.

Why did I not notice that before? I must have been overwhelmed by his size and sculpted physique.

His gaze skims over the menu, and he sets it down. His elbows are on the tabletop. He rests his chin on his fists and leans forward. It could be taken as a feminine gesture, but somehow it's all masculine. His corded forearms are huge and end in fists that look like they were made to bash skulls, but are just as ready to pull my hair as he shoves his cock down my throat.

I'm in danger of zoning out and writing a new scene in my head.

Moving my attention from his arms and fists, I look up at his handsome face. It doesn't help my need to fantasize how he would be in bed.

Being caught in his intense gaze throws me off. His eyes are obsidian, with just the palest smokey quartz around his pupils. His raven-black hair is so glossy it seems fake.

And his skin has an undertone of crimson. When I write about his character, I'll say he is a demon in disguise.

Alas, no, he's just an unusual beauty. He likely has a bit of a sunburn under his deep tan and it was probably brought out from walking around the neighborhood this morning.

Breaking my reverie about my gorgeous companion, the server comes up. "Whatcha having today?"

I hand her my menu. "I'll take a coffee and the Mad Scramble."

Maxum raises his eyebrows slightly. Maybe he expected me to appear like I don't have an appetite and order a cute little salad for brunch? Fuck that.

But I drop my hasty conclusion when he says, "The same for me. Thanks."

I fiddle again with my protection pendant and study this guy as he goes right back to watching me.

"So, how did your friend lose his dog?" I ask.

"Oh, sometimes my friend just doesn't think things through. And the gigantic beast got away from him."

"He seems like a well-behaved dog otherwise." Then I remember how he broke my picture frame. "If not a bit clumsy."

"Clumsy? Really?" Maxum perks up. "How so?"

"He knocked over a picture of my ex. Didn't seem to like him either." I laugh to lighten the subject.

"Well, sometimes I think Beast likes to get into trouble."

"He's been no trouble. I'll be sad to see him go."

Maxum grunts at that for some reason.

The server brings over our coffees. I pour some cream and add a spoonful of sugar, whereas Maxum drinks his black.

"When do you think your friend will come and get him?"

He stares at me over the rim of his coffee mug while slowly taking a sip. Then he says, "Beast should be out of your hair by the end of the day. I hope."

That sounds shady. I don't like that he sounds like a neglectful owner. "Uh… Why *wouldn't* your friend come get his dog?"

Maxum shrugs. "He has an on-call job that is sporadic. I'd take the mutt off your hands, but he didn't seem like he wanted to leave just yet."

"Okay." Something's odd about all of this, but I can't put my finger on what it could be. It feels like Maxum is skirting some truth. I wonder if the owner's unavailability has something to do with what made them all tense last night.

I really want to ask him, but I'm worried that might be too invasive, especially over a brunch date. But I think I might be part cat, and curiosity gets the better of me.

"I've never seen you or your friends at the bar before."

His eyes narrow just a fraction, and while he recovers quickly, I still notice. Coming from a volatile upbringing, I'm ever-vigilant for signs that I've displeased someone. Not that it's served me well at avoiding someone's wrath since I don't often stop whatever I'm doing to piss them off.

"I'm not trying to pry." I play off my curiosity. "It's just that I go there all the time. I was only wondering if one of the guys you were with owned Beast."

He takes another sip of his coffee, and it appears as if he's debating how to answer me. Which, again, is so weird. "He's one of my friends from last night," he says cryptically.

I try to lighten the mood. "Let me guess... the guy on the end bouncing his knee?"

Maxum stiffens his shoulders. "And why would you guess it was him?"

"He seemed sort of... upset, distracted," I explain. "If anyone was going to lose their animal, it would be someone who was distracted."

"True," he agrees succinctly.

I can tell now that he's not enjoying our conversation anymore.

"I shouldn't have pried, but I was curious who I should expect to show up on my doorstep."

The server places our plates in front of us. "Two scrambles. Can I get you anything else?"

"I'm good," I say.

But Maxum asks for hot sauce and relaxes in his seat again. "Why were you staring at us last night? Taking pictures?"

Dammit. I was hoping he wouldn't call me out like this.

"Uh. I don't think it comes as a surprise to hear that you are good-looking. And your friends are as well." I clear my throat. I won't be able to eat until I deal with this.

Did he wait until after we got our food to ask me about my gawking? So I couldn't just leave? But if I have to leave without eating, that's what I'm going to do.

However, I feel compelled to explain my behavior. "I feel like the biggest creep. You all are hot enough that you should be on the covers of romance novels. I've been a bit stuck in my writing. And it was as though you were some divine inspiration. I'm sorry if I made you uncomfortable. Anyway, none of the photos even came out!"

I pull my phone out to show him the pics and confirm I have nothing to show my friends or the internet in general. But my phone instantly dies after I show him the first blurry image. "Huh, I thought I charged my phone all the way last night."

He stares at the dead phone, looking guilty, and then gazes into my eyes.

His presence is so big and imposing that I almost imagine that his energy presses into me—into my mind.

I hurry to explain further, "I shouldn't have taken the pics. I wasn't going to share them. Just trying to remember you for inspiration. But I guess that still sounds sleazy, huh?"

Maxum finally blinks, and I fall back in my seat. "And what did you write about me in your notes?"

"Um, just your appearance. Nothing much."

He takes a bite of his scramble and watches me, waiting for me to break and tell him more.

I crumble under his gaze. "Don't be mad. So... as you know, I write romance... well, *paranormal* romance. And I imagined you could be a demon in disguise, and the broody leader of a ragtag group of mythological beings."

He stops chewing, appearing shocked that I've cast him as a monster.

*So much for my flirty date!*

"But you're a hot demon. A bad boy, but you could also really fall hard for the heroine. Touch her and die vibes. Believe me, it's a compliment in the romance world!" I cover my eyes, waiting for him to get upset and lecture me.

"You're not wrong," he says quietly.

I peek through my fingers. "And you're not mad?"

He shakes his head.

I finally feel settled enough to eat, but while I do, I can't help but wonder why he agreed with my assessment. "What part did I get right? Do you fall hard when you fall in love?"

"I don't know if I've ever been *in* love." He picks at his food with a fork.

"Oh... Then what part did I get right?" I cock my brow and grin. "I see... you consider yourself a bad boy. Or would you be possessive and protective? Or both?"

"All of it." He flashes his dazzling and almost frightening smile.

*Is he a psycho?*

He has dark red tattoo lines peeking out from under his long sleeve shirt where it pulls up at his wrist. The ink probably covers his arms and chest. He would probably look *fucktacular* if he were shirtless, posing as some promo model for a dark mafia book.

So I pegged him... well, ahem, not pegged. I hop onto that caboose to travel to my imaginary scene and wonder if he'd be into a woman strapping one on and going to town on his perky ass. Fortunately, I quickly jump off the sex train of thought.

Goodness, I'm worse than a teenager.

*Where was I?*

Oh, yes, I *guessed* correctly. Maxum is a possessive bad boy.

"Good to know." I take another large bite of my eggy scramble.

"And the others? Do you have any *guesses* as to what they are?" he asks. Why the question sounds so loaded, I do not know.

"They aren't guesses, just musings. Creating characters, you know?" I really hope he doesn't make me answer this question. It's not like he doesn't already know I'm a perv. But admitting my list of perversions and kinks to my object of lustful desires is a whole other level I'm not ready for. "Wouldn't you rather we talk about you?"

"No. I'd rather talk about you," he states firmly, with a stern look that makes me want to obey.

He's giving off dominant, master of the dungeon vibes, and my panties are officially flooded.

He continues, "It sounds like getting to know you means understanding your life as an author."

Well, isn't he fucking smart. And dang, he's called me out. I sort of have to answer his question now.

"Don't laugh?" I chuckle. "Okay, at least don't laugh much."

"I'll do my best." He doesn't look as if he plans to laugh. His smile is completely gone as he waits for my answer. His seriousness gives me pause.

Why do I keep getting the odd feeling that everything I say will come back to haunt me? Maybe because I expect the worst from people, especially the love interests in my own life.

I shake off my nervousness. It's so much easier typing this naughty stuff into my computer. "Um. So... the one guy at the end of the booth who seemed agitated? He felt like he'd be a wild animal. So I thought he could be a shifter in my story." Then I realize Maxum might not understand my lingo, so I explain. "A shifter is human and can change into an animal form, but usually they only shift into one kind of animal—most often a wolf, bear, or large cat. However, they don't have to only be these common types. They can be other smaller animals or mythical creatures like dragons, too."

"I get the general idea," he smirks at me.

So at least he's a bit amused with my explanation.

"But your friend can be a bit of an alphahole—a bossy jerk."

"Again. Not wrong."

"The guy with the pale hair and eyes? He was so still that he reminded me of stone. So I went with a gargoyle. I didn't get far with his personality other than quiet and brooding, since he didn't give much away. And the last guy? He confused me, but he was like fire *and* ice. So I thought he might be a cold-hearted dragon in my story? But under all that, he is very passionate about the few things he cares about."

Maxum almost tosses down his fork. "You have to be kidding me." He asks with disbelief and a heavy dose of condescension, "Are you for real?"

I blink. "Huh?"

He shakes his head. "So all that spying on us last night was for your…" Then the jerk has the audacity to use air quotes as he says, *"Novel?"*

"Excuse me?" I sit back and glare at him. "You might not think much of what I do, but people enjoy it. Paranormal romance is a huge and legitimate genre. You don't have to be dismissive." Without another word, I pull some cash out of my purse, throw it on the table, and head for the door.

I will not put up with some punk belittling what I do, no matter how hot. Just because I include magical beings and sexual moments doesn't mean it is worthless drivel. Women have been belittled about their sexuality for far too long. They've been brutalized for it. I'm proud that I celebrate women, and sometimes bisexual men, having choices and claiming their sexual selves. And I will not sit there and make apologies for empowering myself and possibly others.

Fuck him. And not in a fun way.

Am I triggered? One hundred percent.

Storming out of the restaurant feels great until I sense his presence right behind me. I walk faster down the sidewalk. Not that his stupidly long legs can't catch up with my much shorter strides.

"Bugger off," I say over my shoulder.

"*You* were spying on us, remember?" he spits out.

"Oh, I'm sorry that I was looking at you." I glare at him. "Did it hurt?"

"That's what I intend to find out," he mutters.

*What in the upside-down-cake hell?*

"Okay. Fine. I took some crappy pictures that didn't even come out right. I'm sorry. I get that I'm an asshole. Move along. Date's over… Or whatever this game of yours is."

"Game? *I'm* the one playing games?" he snaps.

I turn and scowl at him, and he stops in his tracks, almost looking nervous. "I'm calling animal control, and your friend can pick the dog up at the pound. Go away now. Bye!"

I spin back around and head toward my house.

As I pass by the bar, I see his two sexy friends in an old car, watching me. This is getting weirder by the minute. Fortunately, Maxum abandons his pursuit and heads toward his friends' car.

Thank goodness, I was worried he would follow me home. And he knows where I live.

I cross the street to my road. Calming myself slightly, I realize I'm still taking stomping strides, so I relax into a slightly less agitated power walk.

What was his deal, anyway? He *really* didn't like some woman watching him and his friends. It seems like a bit of an overreaction. Is one of them famous or *infamous*?

What's he hiding? Did I stumble onto some actual mob meeting?

Is the dog really his friend's?

Oh, shit! What if it was all a lie?

The dog wanted nothing to do with Maxum. If he was truly a friend of his owner, then the dog should have acted like he recognized him.

I glance over my shoulder as I get a few doors from my house. I don't see anyone, but I feel eyes on me.

A shiver races up my back. I run to my front door and unlock it. I crash through as soon as it's open and slam the door shut, locking it.

The dog races over to me, sniffing me. He appears concerned by my dramatic return. At least the dog isn't a complete asshole.

# 9

# PARANORMAL INACTIVITY

## ARRAN

*T*he witch crashes into her front door like the demon is on her tail.

Her panic is real. I can smell its authenticity. Fear is flooding her mind. I wonder if Maxum found out something and threatened her.

Everything I found was odd, but not incriminating.

Is he pressing into her thoughts now, bending her consciousness to allow him access to all her secrets?

If she resists, he might scramble her brains. He might do that anyway for fun. The thought of her collapsing in front of me terrifies me. That realization alone is upsetting. I should want her gone just for being born a witch.

But the notes I found don't suggest that *if* they sent her to spy, that she knew anything about us. The only thing that I'm fairly certain about is that she seems to have an untapped psychic gift. This ability is not surprising. Most witches have some sort of psychic ability. Depending on the witch, it can be premonitions, psychometry, mind reading, mediumship, empathic ability, or sensing nature. There are others, but the list is too long to remember.

But that she doesn't even know she has an actual affinity? That *is* unusual.

Thanks to Maxum taking Jade out of the house, I was able to study her computer and tablet in more detail. No longer worried she was in the next room, I could keep my nervous energy to a minimum so I wouldn't blow her computer's circuits.

What I found makes me guess Jade has another gift too—writing. Her notes about us last night from the bar did actually seem to be notes for a book. She does write romance books about shifters and other supernaturals. There are physical copies on the shelves.

If it was a coincidence that she was at the bar, studying us for a book idea, I find it uncanny that she was able to intuit so many details.

However, for someone without training to be able to do this is unlikely.

The whole situation confuses me.

Does she know about us? Or not? And is her writing not just her witchy cover story, but also her day job? Is she a lust witch who uses her powers to sell romance books?

Maybe the Witch Council wanted her to get something more from us? Or she's supposed to seduce us... that definitely won't happen. Well, at least not to Flint or Calder. I am slightly concerned about my resolve. And Maxum released a scent indicating his attraction.

I need to rule out that Jade doesn't live a double life. I need to make sure they have not sent her to kill us off one by one.

I need to know if she killed Osen.

But right now, she appears panicked and leans against the door as if she's just been chased.

I sniff her but don't scent magic, blood, or Maxum's scent. So what happened, and where is Maxum now?

Deciding to lean into the dog cover story, I whine to prompt her to talk… she *loves* to fucking speak to animals.

"It's okay," she tries to comfort me. Fortunately, she doesn't reach out to me. She holds her chest and breathes hard. "I think that guy earlier might be a psycho."

*No shit.*

I trot over to the window to see if Maxum is outside, but I don't see him. But I get an eerie feeling that someone is watching us.

I slowly back away from the window.

"Oh, my god. Is he out there?" She crawls over to the window and peeks out. "You feel it too, don't you? Like someone's eyes are on you?" She glances back and forth down the streets. "I don't see Maxum, if that's even his real name. Or his friends in that old car."

Hmm. Interesting that she noticed Calder and Flint.

I study Jade while she searches for whoever is after her.

With every interaction, I become more convinced she doesn't know what is going on. If she's acting, she is outstanding—even fooling my senses.

I can smell fear in her. Sure, it could be that Maxum scared the pants off her. He could frighten almost anyone he sets his mind to scare.

Jade mumbles to herself. "I'm pretty sure you aren't even his friend's dog. But why would he come here? Could he be that weirded out that I was admiring him and his sexy friends?"

*She really thinks I'm sexy?*

After another few minutes, she gives up searching for the source of the eyes on her. Instead of getting up off the floor, she turns and leans against the wall. Her hands cover her face. "What was I thinking? I should have never gone with some random guy. Geezus, the red flags were flying. I should have known he only wanted to be an asshole. I mean, come on…"

She looks at me, her eyes filled with hurt. "That hot, young treat? And *me*? Sure, I knew it wasn't going anywhere, but…" She sighs, picks herself up, and closes the curtains to the big picture window facing the road.

She thinks Maxum is young? I have news for you, sweetheart.

One more tally in the she-doesn't-have-a-clue column.

Jade frantically rushes around her house, checking the window locks and closing all the blinds.

"I guess I should call animal control and see if anyone has asked about you."

Jade pulls her phone out of her bag and curses. "Why does this thing need charging? Great, I need a new phone too."

Agitated, she pulls a taser and a can of mace out of her purse.

Part of me approves she was prepared for her date with Maxum.

But I'm stopped short when she draws out a small gun.

She tucks the weapon into her pants' waistband at the back.

Well, now… what makes her feel like she needs a gun for protection?

She doesn't live in a dangerous neighborhood. My mind flashes to the Witch Council, then Rob. It's also a wickedly smart weapon for a weak-powered witch to use against most supes.

The witch plugs in her phone and paces the living room. Mumbling to herself about always getting herself in trouble, saying this is why she's a homebody, and people aren't worth the pain.

I get it. My heart softens toward her just a little.

Jade shivers and glances at me. "I hear animals can be sensitive to spirits. Can you see anything? Because I swear, it's not just you witnessing me lose my mind."

I lie down and attempt to look innocent because, no, I can't feel spirits. Maybe if I could, I would talk to Osen, and I'd find out how one of my best friends died.

Her phone dings, and she races over to use it. She calls the pound, but no one has been looking for a huge-ass wolf. Big surprise.

After a disconcerted frown, she sets the phone down, checks on her critters, and sulkily sits in her office. She stares at the computer screen for a long beat.

"That's weird," she mumbles. "I didn't think I had that file open on here."

Whoops. I fucked up Spy Craft 101: leave things as you found them.

A moment later, I hear her clicking away on her computer. It occurs to me she might communicate with the Witch Council, so I quietly enter and sit where I can read the screen. She gives me a soft smile of welcome and turns back to her computer.

She's on some social media website... Facebooked? She has a screen open and is telling other people how she had a weird day. And she might have a new creeper boyfriend.

One of her associates says to be careful, but to channel all her nervous energy into her new book. Another friend tells her to fill it with smutty good times.

And she does... I watch in amazement how she twists the events of the last day into a completely new story.

She probably thinks I'm the weirdest dog ever for reading over her shoulder. But so far, she's been lost in the words and hasn't paid attention to me.

Hours go by, and Jade finally slumps in her chair. She yelps when she feels the gun in her pants pressing into her back. She pulls it from her waistband and sets it on the desk.

Then her gaze lands on me, and she grimaces.

I'm nervous for a moment. If she's ready to end this charade and she uses the gun, I'm likely a goner.

Instead of popping a cap in my ass, the witch opens a

drawer and sets the gun inside. "We don't want you to knock it off and hurt yourself, do we?"

Don't worry. I'm not fond of guns.

She feeds her animals and gasps. "Oh no. What the hell is wrong with me? I just realized that you haven't needed to pee or poo in a whole day! God, I hope you aren't sick." She gets on her knees in front of me, and her hand moves to touch my belly. "Please, I just need to see if your stomach is bloated. I'll have to take you to the vet if there's something wrong."

Oh, crap, *literally*. I had used her toilet when she was gone.

I move back and then hurry to her front door. She follows me out and shakes her head. "No. Out back." She opens the door and points. "It's fenced."

I race outside and pretend to pee to make her happy. I trot around and pretend I like the outdoors. I do, but that's beside the point. What I need is for her to leave me alone out here. I'm not taking a dump as a wolf while she watches.

Oh, Goddess. Am I going to shit in her yard and make her clean it up?

There is no chance of redemption after I do this.

Where has my life taken me?

I've made poor choices.

*I did not choose wisely…*

Hanging my head as I come back inside an hour later, I shuffle past Jade through her back door by the kitchen.

"Good boy," she coos when she spots my *gift*.

I'm strangely conflicted by this praise. My wolf loves it, but I'd rather get that while I was between her legs.

I'll show her who's a good boy.

When I was outside, I found Maxum had left my discarded clothes behind a bush in her yard. I suppose he didn't find Jade too dangerous if he allowed her out of his sight and didn't come back and demand I go with him.

*So the verdict is still out.*

"Will you eat for me tonight?" she asks sweetly.

I am fucking hungry. I probably will eat kibble if she offers it to me.

*Please don't offer that crap to me...*

"I had to throw out the bits of steak I gave you last night. I suspect you didn't like the dry food mixed in? Maybe you are used to a different brand?"

I'm seriously going to need to go on a bloody, vicious hunt after this is over to heal my bruised ego.

"How's this?" She places a measly amount of chopped steak in front of me on the floor. I sniff it but don't scent any poison or potions.

I understand her offering me a small portion. She doesn't want to waste food if I refuse it again.

Fuck it. I close my eyes and imagine I'm tearing the meat from the bones of my enemies and not out of a bowl on a witch's kitchen linoleum.

She squeals happily when she sees me eating.

My wolf pants happily and smiles.

Ugh. Why do I crave her approval already? She must be messing with my emotions, and I just can't sense how she's delivering the spell.

Jade chops up some more meat and waits for me to finish before dumping the rest in a clean bowl. "I'm so happy you're okay. I was getting worried."

I stare into her hazel-green eyes and truly wish she wasn't born a witch. Even if she doesn't know she is a witch and isn't aware yet that we are enemies, she *is* our enemy.

She *will* turn on us.

Jade says goodnight and locks herself in her room… again.

I sniff the door to scent for magical warding to prevent my entry, but I don't sense a thing.

A lock won't help her much if a supe or witch, or even a strong human wishes to get inside. It might slow down an attacker for a moment, but that's all the time Jade will need to grab her gun and put a bullet between someone's eyes.

I remind myself that I likely wouldn't heal from that.

She gets ready for bed, but I don't smell her arousal tonight. The witch must be done with her lust games, or, if she's innocent, isn't in the mood.

My wolf is rabid with the thought that Maxum scared her the way he did. Logically, I know I shouldn't be upset. But she has ignited protectiveness in me. Perhaps it's just my recent loss that makes me want to protect. Maybe I shouldn't have gotten this close to her.

But my wolf doesn't seem to believe she killed Osen, and I have a strong inclination to agree. She might know nothing about Osen, even if she is a pawn for the Witch Council.

Or…

I shiver… if she's part of the ASO—the Anti-Supernaturals Organization. Their goal is to get rid of supes by brainwashing supes to kill their own kind. No one knows who runs it, but our money has always been on an underground movement of fanatical witches and warlocks.

Witches are bad enough without being part of the elitist crowd. Supes had hoped that at one point, we had a tentative peace brewing between our kind. And on the surface, it appears the Witch Council was playing nice. But we know they aren't as friendly as they like to pretend.

The terrorist group, ASO, is likely who killed Osen. And the Witch Council is probably pulling their strings through secret channels.

Thank goodness the supernatural disappearances have

stopped. But now we know some of the missing weren't from that horrendous magical scheme.

No, from what we understand, ASO uses unwitting supes against their friends. Osen had been investigating along with my small group of friends—the same friends that Jade was spying on.

I wonder if Osen didn't submit to ASO's brainwashing techniques and died because of it.

If that's true, it means he died to save our quirky little family.

Standing outside of her bedroom door, I contemplate what to do next. I've already snooped as much as I can in the house.

Convincing myself that it's only because someone was watching her, and I might catch them if they come after her, I stay close to her room. I can also hear if she communicates with someone during the night.

Dozing in her hallway, I wake to hear her whimpering. I immediately know this isn't the same sound she makes when she's climaxing.

Right now, she sounds scared. But I can't scent or sense anyone else in the room with her.

Is it a nightmare? It must be.

Even so, I stay alert, just in case someone is able to fool my senses.

The Witch Council might have come after Jade, thinking she has been compromised by my continued presence and Maxum taking her to brunch.

Her breathing becomes ragged. She's more panicked. She's reliving a painful moment.

I hear her drop from her bed with a thud. Then she crawls along the floor.

What the fuck? Is she being attacked?

I still don't scent anyone. She sounds as if she's crawling into the closet.

I almost break down the door so I can understand what's

happening, but this will only blow my dog cover. Shifting instead, I race into her office and grab a thick paperclip to pick her bedroom lock.

Within seconds, I unlock her door and crack it open. I shift back into my dog... ugh, *wolf* form, before fully entering.

*Goddess, has this woman domesticated me already?*

As my animal, I crawl on the ground army style, making myself a smaller target, as I don't want Jade to shoot me. I don't see her, but the door to her walk-in closet is open.

The entire room is laden with the scent of fear so potent it burns my nose. It smells as if the person knows they are about to die. But not yet pissed themselves.

When I get close to the closet with my 'night' vision, I can see Jade curled up on her side. She's shivering, no longer whimpering, but is grunting in agony, like a soldier might do after being shot.

Relieved that I don't see her gun in her hands or on the floor, I glance back and see it's on her nightstand. Odd. If she had woken up and been frightened, she would have taken that with her. She must have been sleepwalking.

Without the threat of the gun, I venture inside the tight space and peer down at Jade's face.

It doesn't quite look like her—much like how actors can change how they look from role to role by engaging different muscles in their faces.

She's holding her stomach as if she's been injured. She has her knees drawn up protectively, from what, I am not yet sure.

Her eyes pop open. The irises are now a dark charcoal, no longer their pretty hazel-green.

"Arran? Is that you?" she asks, her accent and tone much different as well.

Is she possessed? And who has taken control?

"I can barely sense anything. Are you there?" they ask. "It feels like your energy."

I'm in my wolf form, so... not answering. And I'm not sure if I should.

"Arran... It's me... Osen."

What the fuck? No way. It can't be. Can it be? But this is impossible.

"Tanil is after me. She fucked me up real bad." Jade-Osen moves their hands as if to show me the damage. "She dosed the wound with iron. Help me?"

I shake my head in disbelief. This is an echo of exactly what happened almost fifteen years ago. Tanil was an evil witch Osen had fooled around with. Of course, he didn't know she was evil at the time. She seemed to be a sweet and kind witch, but she had seduced Osen and then tried to kill him.

It's just another horrific example of why I resist trusting Jade's innocence.

Which makes me wonder if this is some trick.

Is this really Osen's spirit? And is his soul stuck in the past?

But supes don't connect with the spirit world and work through mediums. We don't see or communicate with ghosts. Although hellhounds, a particular race of demons from the Underworld, can capture souls.

But witches are a different sort of magical being. Communicating with spirits is a talent witches sometimes have. However, most aren't spirit *mediums*, able to host a disembodied soul. Now, I suspect Jade might also have a talent for mediumship.

Yet, I had never heard of a witch channeling a *supernatural* soul before—only humans and other witches.

This is suspicious.

"Arran?" they call again.

Risking my cover, I shift into my human form, now on my hands and knees next to their side.

"Osen?" I whisper.

They jerk and look at me, squinting to see me in the dark closet.

"Goddess, I'm so happy to see you," they say, grabbing me around the neck and pulling me to Jade's chest.

I almost pull away. But the magic behind the touch feels faintly like Osen's energy, so I allow myself to sink into the embrace.

"What happened to you?" I ask, my voice cracking. I missed the jerk.

"Tanil," he says with confusion.

"No," I sigh. "You went to check out the old foundry building. You didn't…" I don't finish and remind him I found his dead body, stripped of all magic, even the usual residual amount that clings to a corpse. Bizarrely enough, there were no physical marks to indicate how he died, either. Nothing to tell us what happened. Only a void of energy.

"Foundry?" Osen asks, then he shouts as if he's being attacked.

Jade's arms and legs flail, and she vibrates.

Suddenly, I realize Osen is being expelled from her body, and I quickly shift back to my wolf.

With no hesitation, Jade clings to my furry neck, crying into my fur. For a moment, I worry she's cursing me with her tears.

But the emotion I scent on her is pure terror and fear.

A few minutes pass, and she pulls back. I'm guessing she realizes I shouldn't be in her room.

"Beast?" she whispers Maxum's name for my wolf. Her eyes widen, and she slowly removes her hold, a lingering worry in her eyes that I might bite her. She glances around the closet and rubs her eyes. "What happened? And how did you get in here?" Frowning, she looks at my foot that touches her leg. "Why are you allowing me to touch you?"

She doesn't expect answers. But I wonder if she is a medium, a psychic, if she could pick up my thoughts. I send her an image of her shivering form in the closet.

"You were worried about me?" she guesses, sounding

uncertain. "Thank you. But we should get out of here, but... uh, I don't want to upset you by moving into your space again."

Looking at our surroundings, I find I'm blocking the exit.

I take the hint, trot out to her bedroom, and sit near the foot of her bed.

Jade climbs out of the closet and stands. Noticing that I didn't crash the door down to get to her, she shakes her head in confusion. "I swear I locked it." She bites her full lower lip. "I suppose if I got into the closet without remembering, I could have unlocked the door, too."

I'll say one thing about her rambling mouth. I don't ever have to wonder what she's thinking.

I follow her closely when she goes out to the kitchen and drinks a glass of water.

Her hand shakes as she lifts the glass. With her other hand, she holds her forehead as if she has a headache. "I haven't had an episode like that for... well, since I was dating Rob." She sighs. "Maybe it's because I had a messed up day? I'm sorry I upset you, Beast."

When she returns to her bedroom, I stay at her side. She allows me entry, but shuts and locks the door behind her. "Thanks for coming to my rescue." She offers her limp hand for me to sniff and accept.

I do because I need her to trust me. And I'm beginning to trust her.

That trust will probably bite me in the ass.

# 10

# WAKING DREAMS

## JADE

*L*ast night was one of my more intense *episodes*.

Episodes... such a light and fluffy word for feeling like someone or something is invading my mind. Sure, I often dream what feels like another person's dream. Heck, I've used some of it in my stories.

But these episodes are more than the unusual dream of places and people I've never seen before. I've had odd dreams my whole life. But the intense episodes started almost two decades ago when I turned twenty-one.

The severity of the nightmares has made me wonder if I should be on medication for what feels like a paranoid delusion.

I rarely remember what happens to me and why I ended up somewhere odd... in this case, my closet. Another time, I ended up in my backyard. Once, I even woke up while walking down the sidewalk.

One day, I expect it's going to get me hurt or killed. I'll set my house on fire or I'll wander into traffic, and bam.

This time, though, I remember more than I usually do.

In this dream, I watched as a woman threw a curse at me, or more accurately, the person I was supposed to be.

Then the woman poisoned me with powder and terror hit me when I recognized what it was: ground-up iron. For some reason, I was afraid of the iron.

Thinking about it now, I had read that fae are supposed to be allergic to the stuff. Myths and legends. I wonder why I'm dreaming of fantasy beings. Especially since this vision felt all too real.

Then I recall another strange part of my vision.

"You want to hear something odd, Beast?" I ask as I chop up some more meat for the huge lug.

Beast is finally warming up to me after my episode. It's sweet that he was trying to comfort me when I was scared. Animals can be wonderful that way.

At my question, he stares up with his strange golden eyes that sometimes seem to glow, waiting for me to continue.

"Last night, I must have been really desperate for some hunky snacks. I thought you were one of the guys from the bar… He was holding me—shirtless, no less." I shake my head, amused. "But fortunately, I realized it was you right away."

Beast seems to visibly gulp. I swear this dog isn't normal. Maybe he does have a human soul.

"Don't worry, sweetie. I know better." I wave off the projected concern I've assigned to the poor animal. "It's just… I felt so at peace in his arms, like I belonged with him. And not just because he's hot, I mean, it definitely doesn't hurt. Anyway, I wonder if that's what genuine love will feel like. The feeling like I've found my true home. Safe. Cherished." I sigh dramatically, brushing away the few tears. "Oh, well, of course when I woke up it was just you, a dog. And even you will probably leave soon, out of my life in a day or so."

After I fill his bowl, he stares at me for a long beat, watching me. Perhaps he senses my sadness. But finally, he eats.

I show him out the backdoor so he can enjoy the pleasant weather. "I'll be writing for a few hours. But if you need anything, be sure to bark."

He bumps my hand, and I pat his head softly. My heart warms with his acceptance of me. Like I've won the skittish doggy lotto.

"Maybe if you let me put a leash on you, we can go for a walk later." The uncomfortable memory of someone watching crashes back over me. It can't be Rob again, could it? "Or maybe no walking. Maxum or whoever might still be lurking. I won't risk you getting hurt, too."

After letting him out, I settle into my office and begin to write.

The story pours out. It's a continuation of the one I started about the guys. There are some baddies who want to kill supernatural beings. And my harem are trying to stop them.

Witches show up in the story.

I often write about witches and warlocks. They can be morally gray at worst, but now, some witches in my story are downright evil.

Not to say that shifters and other magical people aren't also jerks.

In my mind, I see that there's a war on the horizon. It's over magic, and who should wield it. Neither side trusts the other. Both sides have legitimate reasons for their hatred and blame the other faction for the loss of magic. But my gut tells me the loss isn't about either side. Something cosmically is afoot.

Leaning back and stretching, I take a breather from writing... and let my fingers rest. Checking my email, my blood runs cold, and my heart rate picks up.

Rob emailed me.

It's his only mode of communication left since I've finally blocked him on my phone and social media.

My first instinct is to delete the damned thing without

opening it. But with my strange interactions lately, the sensation that I have a stalker, and my nightmare episode—which I haven't had since Rob was around—I open it up instead.

It reads simply: "You should be more careful who you go on dates with."

Yeah, no shit. Like you, for one.

Then my second reaction is to freak the fuck out.

Has he been watching me? Or did he just happen to see me walking with Maxum? He doesn't live that far away, so maybe it's just a coincidence?

Perhaps someone from the neighborhood ratted me out and relayed what they saw?

No matter how he found out, he has no right to email me and tell me who I can and can't go out with. It gives me creeper sicko vibes. But unfortunately, he didn't do enough that the police would take an interest in my complaint. He's smart enough to never document any of his actual threats outright. This could be seen as 'friendly' advice.

Cursing. I'm pissed that I have nothing on him. He's been extremely careful to never get caught doing anything to me in public or in front of our friends.

I soon realized our friends were truly his when we broke up. All of them sided with him when we split. He painted me as the neglectful girlfriend who only cared about her career. Well, someone had to care about my career.

Staring at the sentence on the screen, I cycle through all the emotions, finally landing on wariness. He's watching. He's still invested in me—feels he owns me.

If I hadn't already shuttered all the windows, I would have done so now.

I hate how unsafe I've felt over the last day, ever since... Maxum's date.

Too bad my dream man from the closet hadn't been real. The actual guy is likely a jerk, just like Maxum. But at least I'd have someone's hand to hold and assure me that I'm not crazy for being worried.

I've been through worse. I can face this alone too. Whatever *this* is.

## 11

# NO GO

MAXUM

Since Jade stormed off from the restaurant, I've been incapable of getting the feisty, curvy seductress out of my mind.

I offended her. I truly upset her about her writing.

From my mind-reading affinity, on the surface of her thoughts, I picked up that she really didn't understand my snarky insinuations about her spying for the witches and their nefarious plans to eliminate our kind.

She might actually be oblivious to everything.

So what the hell is Arran still doing snuggling up in her house? Has he found something I didn't? Is he falling for her wicked yet sweet smile and her dirty mind?

And *who* was watching us?

I was so preoccupied with her anger that I couldn't pinpoint the source.

For some blasted reason, I hate that she is pissed at me. Which isn't like me. I usually revel in pissing people off.

It's a professional-grade hobby. After hundreds of years, one does get bored with the day-to-day, even with a war or two thrown in for shits and giggles...

I certainly wasn't bored yesterday.

She intrigues me with her protectiveness over Arran's wolf, then she draws me in with her passion for her career. Her ability to stand up to my gruff and her naughty mind sealed the deal.

I've been casing her house throughout the night and most of today.

Fortunately, Ms. Jade lives on a corner, and I've just watched as she lets Arran outside so he can take a dump.

Oh, this is precious.

When I sense she's moved away from the back of the house, I stroll up and can easily see Arran's wolf over the fence.

He snarls at me. Defensive much?

I want to taunt him about his new lifestyle choice, but I need to convince him to get out of there while I don't sense anyone currently watching.

Arran perks his ears up, confirming Jade has walked away. Then he shifts and glares at me.

He's naked and has his hands on his hips in defiance. And while I would enjoy having Jade walk out to see his glory displayed in her backyard, it occurs to me she might not find a naked man in her yard as funny as I do. But I don't doubt she would check out his package and muscles before she called the cops. Maybe take some of those *thirst trapping* photos.

"What do you want now?" he growls.

Something in his tone concerns me. "Does the witch have you under her spell? Why are you still here?"

"No, she doesn't even know what she is. But there is *something* going on."

"I know. Come on, put your clothes on, and jump over this fence. Someone has eyes on her, and conveniently, I don't sense them now."

"Dude," he huffs. "Slow down."

Ugh. I hate SoCal lingo.

Arran continues, "I think she's a medium."

"Big fucking deal. Stop sniffing her panty drawer, and let's go, you idiot." I turn toward Calder's car down the road.

A pile of shit hits the back of my head.

*What. The. Fuck?*

I slowly turn back, wondering how I will kill him and how fast I should make it happen.

"Was that *your* shit?" I ask. "Did you crap in her yard like a common dog?"

His face is red with embarrassment. I didn't think he'd stoop so low as to actually shit in her yard.

*Oh, oh…* this is too much… I can't take it. This is hilarious. No longer mad at his tantrum, I roar with laughter, knowing that I'm going to roast him for decades over this. "You took a shit in her yard like a pet, and then you threw it at me like a damned monkey in a cage? What happened to you… *dude*?"

Arran paces the yard. "I don't know. But I can't leave her. She channeled Osen."

"No way." I wave him off, but I am worried he doesn't feel he can leave her. "Supe spirits don't speak through witches."

"But Osen did. And you know he was… special." Arran's voice is soft.

He's not wrong. Osen captured all of our hearts at one point. And he was powerful, even for what he was.

"So… what?" I shake my head. "You're going to be her sweet puppy from now on? We don't know where her allegiances lie. She's a fucking witch, for fuck's sake."

"I don't think she knows she is. Even her pets don't think she knows."

"Her pets?" I scoff. "So, has she captured other dumb shifters like you? Does she keep a menagerie in her basement? You want to join her collection?"

I should know better than to antagonize him. He's unstable and a legit monster when he's really pissed. Right now, he *should* be riding, or at least close to crossing that line with my comments.

He's proven in the past that he can't cope when one of his pack dies. And he considered Osen his pack, even if he wasn't a wolf.

Idly, I wonder if Jade's presence has calmed his beast. Stranger things have happened. She is unusual.

"Not shifters. It's a magical creature—a guinea pig. He fancies himself her familiar."

"A guinea pig familiar?" I blow out a puff of air. "That's it. I've heard everything."

Arran turns serious. "Something even bigger than Osen is going on here... which in itself is pretty big. By the way, I'm not happy with you. You frightened Jade out of her mind after your date yesterday." Deep in his throat, a growl rumbles. He really is becoming attached to the magic mortal. "What the hell did you say to her?"

"She was rambling on, claiming she mysteriously guessed all sorts of stuff about us. *My flaming red ass.* She knew I was a demon, and you were a shifter, and she pretended it was her imagination."

"She isn't playing. She believes that's where the stuff in her books comes from."

"She actually writes?" I rub my chin, pondering our brunch conversation in a different context. "It doesn't matter. Get your clothes on and let's go."

"No." He snarls at me. His skin ripples with his monster. "I'm not leaving Osen."

I cross my arms, highlighting my brawn. He won't make me cower, not even with his berserker beast. "Did Osen's alleged spirit tell you who killed him?"

"Not yet."

"Did you ask?"

"I think he was having a hard time possessing her. He didn't seem to grasp that he was dead. But he might next time.

I have to give him at least another night to see if he can remember."

"Fine. One more night. But if you aren't out of there after that, I'm dragging you out of her house and melting her brain if it comes to it."

"Shut the fuck up. You aren't hurting her." His beast's teeth elongate, and fur erupts over his body.

"Oh, yeah?" I step menacingly toward the fence.

We both know a fight between us does not end well. For either of us.

Pulling back his beast and losing the fur, he glowers at me, daring me to lie. "Yeah. Don't try to hide it, you like her too. My wolf scented it."

I give Arran a deadly glare that makes him take a step back. "I'll end her if I have to. Don't think I've gone soft just because I can play nice. She isn't part of our pack. Understand?" I jab my finger toward the house. "But for some confounding reason, you are pack to me, asshole."

Arran shakes his head, shifts into his wolf, and barks at the door.

Well then, I guess I've been fucking dismissed.

Angrily walking back to the car, I almost rip the passenger door off its hinge and slam it shut after shoving myself in the passenger seat with a huff.

"What's up with Arran?" Calder asks. "Did he find something?"

"Osen, supposedly," I grumble.

They both come to attention. Funnily enough, my violent car entrance did not even faze them.

Flint frowns at the house and asks in a low, rumbling voice that sounds almost like granite churning, "How?"

"Arran claims the witch is a medium." I hold up my hand so I can cut off their arguments. "Yeah, I know. Can't happen. Arran claims it did. I don't know if it's wishful thinking. Or maybe she's actually psychic and picked up on some memories

Arran has of Osen? I don't fucking know. But I'm allowing him to have another night there to prove me right. That this is a hoax. Then I'm dragging him out of the house. Consequences be damned."

"We all might be damned." Calder scowls at the house like it's offended him personally. A bit of flame simmers in his ice-blue eyes. "My senses are confirming what yours picked up before… things are going to get ugly real soon."

And if anyone can sense when death is near, it's a phoenix.

## 12

---

## GHOSTING

JADE

*B*east was more friendly with me today, following me around and letting me rub his soft ears. He's no longer giving me indignant glares when I offer him food or let him out to use the yard to stretch his legs.

It's cute that he enjoys being in my office and watching me write. I tease him and ask if he likes my latest plot twist or what a character did in my dreams. I swear he's reading over my shoulder and sometimes looks scandalized by some of the sex scenes.

But perhaps he can just read my nervous energy. I see his owner in some of the scenes and feel guilty about including the hunk of perfection.

I do love that I combined Beast and his owner into a wolf-shifter, though. It feels right, as if I'm just plucking these characters out of the ether, and they've always existed.

However, it troubles me that Beast has a hard time trusting me. Did his owner neglect or abuse him?

But if he's a wolf breed mix, or an actual domesticated wolf, as I'm beginning to suspect, they can be standoffish with strangers or anyone who isn't their alpha.

So I'll defer judgment about his owner's behavior until I know more. Perhaps it isn't his current owner who might have mistreated him.

When it's time for bed, Beast trots after me, so close he's almost on my heels, into my bedroom. He has his head cast downward as if he expects to be kicked out. But his solid presence brings me comfort, so I'd rather he stay.

I don't know if I want him on the bed. He strikes me as the type who will claim the entire space. So I grab an old, soft blanket and place it at the foot of my bed on the floor.

"Here you go, buddy." I kneel down by the makeshift dog bed and pat it, trying to entice him to use it.

He glances at my bed, then his offering, and concedes. Stepping onto the blanket, he sits and rests his head on my shoulder. His sweetness is almost enough to allow him on my bed. I sink my fingers into the thick fur at his neck and give him a nice massage. Apparently, I'm growing on him.

"I wish you didn't have to return to your owner." I give him a quick ear rub, and he settles down on his blanket.

When I walk away, he stares at me as if he wants to say the same thing. Boy, my imagination has been running wild lately.

I change into my sleep shirt in the bathroom. Mainly because no matter how I brush off my anthropomorphizing as my intense imagination, it still feels like there's a human inside that dog. The dreams about him being the guy from the bar haven't exactly helped.

Sometimes, I think I can see that man behind Beast's eyes.

Ugh, it's just that I'm writing and dreaming about that idea.

As soon as I crawl into bed, Beast abandons his spot and hops up, curling at my side.

But I don't mind the company, so I sigh and close my eyes.

Between Rob's alarming email and Maxum being a jerk, I could use the comfort of having someone nearby.

Would Beast help me if shit were to go down? I don't know, but maybe just his presence would deter someone... especially Rob.

I become lucid in my dream state, which is a fairly common occurrence for me. I'm often aware I'm dreaming in my dreams. Most of the time, it's because they don't seem like my dreams at all. Sure, it could be that I just read a lot and have picked up random scenes and scenarios. But if I do have a magical ability, it would be this... I'm almost convinced that I dream other people's dreams.

Now, I'm currently in a strange landscape that feels like hyperrealism. The colors are more vivid and brighter. It looks like a painting of a fairy world.

The sun sets, and a portal opens in front of me. The alphahole from the bar and Maxum walk through the portal and shake my hand.

I glance down and see my hand looks to be masculine. I'm tall, but not as tall as Maxum, but really, few people are over six-foot-five.

"Did the witches see you?" Maxum asks.

"Nah. I think we're good," my persona says with a deep voice that reminds me of whiskey pouring over ice. "The tracking spell should lead us right to their hideout."

"Perfect." Then the broody alphahole wolf-shifter warns me, "Don't go by yourself to check it out. Okay?"

"Sure," my avatar says, but even I can hear his lie.

The scene fades, and I'm outside of a large mansion. Not sure why it feels familiar, but maybe it's the sense I have in the dream. I'm supposed to have been here before.

Then the male voice I used earlier speaks directly into my mind. *"Who are you?"*

"Excuse me?" I've never had someone realize I had invaded their dreams. "Who are you?"

*"Answer my question, witch,"* he says with a firm tone. By the way he spits out the witch nickname, it's obvious that it isn't meant to be cute. It sounds like a curse.

"Might as well just level up and call me a bitch, because I'm not answering you until you answer me."

*"You don't want me rummaging through your mind. I won't make it pleasant."*

"I'm in your dream. Not the other way around." I wave my/his hands around at the scene.

*"This is... no. This isn't a dream. It's a memory."* He sounds disoriented.

I feel bad invading his mind, especially if I've made him confused by my presence. I sweeten my attitude and suggest, "Hey, I'll help you out if you help me. Okay?"

*"I won't betray my friends or my kind for the likes of you or your kind, witch,"* he snarls.

It seems his favorite curse word is *witch*.

I don't want to keep dreaming about this irritating guy and his drama, so I try again to smooth things over.

"Listen, I don't want to hurt anyone. As a measure of good faith, I'll help you work out your dreams, and then we can come back to you telling me why we both know Maxum."

*"Yes...,"* he says, as if he's straining to remember. *"You were spying on them."*

"I didn't mean anything by it. They were just hot!" I grumble.

*"As if the witches or ASO didn't send you to kill them."*

"Is this part of your dream? What is your trip with Wiccans? Are you sexist?"

"Wiccans?" He sighs. "Witches, you witch!"

Well, this is lovely.

"I'm picking up some signals that you don't like witches, and you believe I'm a witch," I say dully.

*"How else do you explain you are speaking to a spirit?"*

"Because I'm dreaming that you're dreaming you are a spirit," I reason.

*"I can't get back into my body. So I'm dead."*

I decide this conversation thread isn't getting us anywhere, so I surrender. "What do you want me to do? Tell me how to help you so I can end this dream and escape this nightmare!"

*"Tell me who you are."*

"My name is Jade. I'm a romance author. That's it, buddy. No top-secret dossier. No coven membership. Just Jade."

He grunts at that. *"Was it the witches or the ASO who killed me? Or are they one and the same?"*

"You don't know who allegedly killed you?"

*"Was it the Witch Council? Is that why they sent you to follow my associates?"*

"I don't know any witches! And I don't even know what ASO stands for. And when you say your associates, do you mean Maxum and his buddies?"

A shadow circles around my throat, closing in around my neck. A shadowy ghost of a figure stands in front of me. *"Did you kill me?"*

"No…" I wheeze.

Why does it feel like I'm really being choked?

*"Are you tasked with killing my friends?"*

"No… I'd never…"

He loosens his grip around my throat, having heard the truth in my words.

*"I saw Arran. Why is he in your house?"*

"I have a new dog in my house. He's supposed to belong to Maxum's friend."

He chuckles at that. *"Do you not remember what happened before? In your dream, with the 'dog'?"*

"I had a nightmare of being hurt, stabbed, and poisoned

with iron. And then the scene changed, and I dreamed the dog was a man in my closet," I say softly, wondering how fucked up my mind really is. "But this is all just a dream. My dream, right?"

*"It's not."*

"But—"

*"Time to go to sleep, witch,"* he says ominously, and everything goes black.

## 13

---

# NIGHTMARES

ARRAN

"*A*rran?" Jade's voice comes out gruff and masculine.

*It's not her…*

Where I rest next to the sleeping witch, I shift into my human form. Crawling closer to her face, I look into their eyes.

Similar to the closet last night, her sweet hazel-green eyes, have been replaced with Osen's dark charcoal ones. "Osen?"

"What the fuck are you doing here?" he snaps. "With a filthy fucking witch!"

"I'm talking to you, you asshole!" I growl. "You can't figure out why I would be here?"

"But I'm not the only reason, am I?" Jade's small hands grab my throat. "By the way, she's going to put it together. She might be playing innocent about my murder, but she has enough hints to realize what you are now. You need to kill her while you have the chance—while you have the upper hand. Or you'll be next on her hit list."

"No," I argue. "I'm certain she's ignorant of all this—her gifts, supes, witches."

"Listen to me, you reckless fool." He clasps the sides of my head and presses our foreheads together. "I don't know if I can hold her back much longer. End this now."

"I said no." My anger rises. My beast is being tested by his request. He doesn't want to see the witch dead either. Hoping it will jar the memory loose, I demand, "Tell me who killed you, and then I'll leave her alone."

"I don't know. It took me watching you all at the bar to even realize I had died. All I know is that I was alive, and then I wasn't. I don't know who killed me." A thumb brushes over my cheek, just like Osen used to do when we were together.

"How are you able to speak through her?" I ask.

"Maybe because of what I am?" He shrugs. "I'm getting stronger the longer I'm connected to the *witch*." He spits out the last word.

"I think Jade could help you. Could help us."

"Why are you going soft on me? Now?" Shaking his head, he collapses back on the bed. "Fuck... She's fighting me. I have to go."

"Stay close to her. There must be a reason for this connection." I cling to him, not wanting him to fade.

"You were never much for fate." He chuckles lightly, and his eyes close. "Torture her, get the information you need, and avenge me."

"Don't leave," I whisper.

My instinct is to kiss her mouth and maybe call him back. But that's a no-no. It's bad enough that I'm an uninvited naked male in her bed.

Jade lazily flutters her eyes open, and she catches sight of me hovering over her. She must be more than half asleep because she smiles instead of screams. "Arran, is it?"

I return her smile but don't answer. I'm afraid my voice might be enough to break whatever spell this is over her mind.

Her hand reaches for my face, and her soft fingertips graze the stubble on my chin. "You're very handsome for a man, or even when you're the dog... *wolf*," she corrects herself.

Gazing into the depths of her green eyes, I wish things were different.

The desire to kiss her is more than I expected in my human form. I wouldn't have expected it to be so overwhelming without Osen's presence to lure me in.

However, at any moment, this beautiful exchange is going to degrade into chaos.

She will come to her senses, find her gun, and shoot me.

And I won't stop her. Sure, I'll run, but I won't hurt her for protecting herself.

I've seen she's been in battles of her own—personal battles.

Her fingers trail over my bottom lip. "It's too bad you only exist in my fucked-up head. I'm probably just feeling up my pillow like a pervert in my sleep."

I haven't moved other than my smile. But I'm tempted to suck on her fingers and see what the steamy romance author would do with that.

Would she pull me down for a kiss? Would she reach down and stroke my hardening cock? Would she open her legs and attempt to take my knot? Would she let me bite down on her delicate neck and claim her?

Goddess! Snapping out of my fantasy, I find I'm practically on top of her, my mouth ghosting over hers.

She closes the distance and presses her sweet lips to mine.

*Keep it chaste, asshole!*

I have to go before she asks me to fuck her. Because she believes this is a dream. And it wouldn't be right.

*But would it?*

*No, bad dog! WOLF! Ugh.*

I let the kiss linger before pulling away slowly.

Jade's hand skims down my neck to my chest. Her eyes are half closed, looking as if she will fall asleep any second.

If she feels me up, is that my fault? Because her hand on my body feels so amazing that I'm tempted to let her explore.

Would she wrap those lush lips around my dick? Would she ride me, her big tits bouncing in my face, and come when I rubbed her clit? Would she take all four of us at the same time? Would she let us fill her up with our seed?

Whoops... I shouldn't have read her why choose romance. *Naughty witch.*

Sleep, my sweet. I give her a kiss on each eyelid, and she drifts off to sleep.

I shift into my dog form and rest my head on her shoulder, staring at her pretty face.

She snuggles me closer, her fingers tangled in my fur.

I fall asleep peacefully. It's the first time I've had a good night's rest in years.

I wake to Jade's groan and gasp of surprise that I'm basically on top of her—in my wolf form, unfortunately.

Her eyes are shadowed. I'm worried that Osen harmed her with his possession. Is his spirit draining her life force?

"What a weird night," she moans. "Sorry if I made out with your nose last night. I thought you were someone else." She chuckles to herself, but sounds depressed. "I had some strange, upsetting dreams."

I don't want to move away so she can get up. I want to snuggle with her longer, because today, I'm supposed to disappear from her life.

My mind scrambles to find any excuse to stay. But Osen doesn't remember his death, and Maxum will drag me out of here, and in the process, possibly hurt Jade. I can't have that. Besides, the longer I stay, the more likely she will catch me. She won't be happy with me. I'm betraying her trust by being here. And I'm beginning to feel guilty.

"Beast?" She gently strokes my neck. "Are you okay? You aren't usually this clingy."

Realizing I'm acting the fool Osen accused me of being, I stand up and jump off the bed.

She stretches, and her sleep shirt lifts up, revealing her belly. When she walks to the bathroom, her tiny sleep shorts highlight her full ass.

How I want to sink into that soft heat.

I'm falling for a witch? When the fuck did this happen?

Does it count against me when she doesn't know she's one?

When I hear her groan at her reflection, I'm upset by Osen's behavior last night. He had always skirted the morally gray area, but now? Maybe death changes a person.

What am I saying… it does.

Yet, Osen was always anti-witch, ever since he was a young man and had been tortured by one. That was well before he had fully come into his powers. He let his guard down again with Tanil, and that backfired. I don't blame him for being anti-witch.

I have my own painful history with witches. But Jade doesn't seem like she would ever hurt me… not on purpose, anyway. She really is different.

Wondering what I should do about Osen, Jade, and all these lies, I contemplate leaving and coming back in my human form to date her. But I'm afraid Maxum fucked that up. She won't trust me after he upset her. Nor should she.

Besides, she definitely won't trust me if she finds out about the supernatural world and realizes I've been masquerading as her pet doggie.

I'm screwed.

If that weren't enough, I can't trust my monstrous beast to leave her unscathed—physically or mentally. She might read and write monster fucking books, but that doesn't mean she actually wants to be in danger.

And she would be in danger.

Jade comes out of the bathroom, freshly showered, with only

a small towel wrapped around her voluptuous body. I contemplate tugging on the cloth. She slips into the closet and wisely shuts the door. Her instincts must sense something isn't quite right with me. After all, she does *dream* that I'm the *alphahole* from the bar.

Fully dressed, Jade comes out of the closet and heads to the kitchen. "I have to run some errands and get some food for all of us." She snatches up her keys and purse and opens the back door. "Be a good boy, and I'll bring home some yummy treats."

As soon as she closes the door behind me, I realize what I need to do.

Beast must run away.

# 14

# DOGGIE DADDY

## JADE

*H*eading out my front door to my Mustang, I feel a tingling, and not in a good way.

Someone is watching me.

Casually, I glance up and down my street to see if I can spot Rob's car, Maxum, or his buddies. No one.

My car rumbles to life. I briefly wonder if someone put a tracker on it. My spy slash writer's mind is hyperactive again.

Yet is it so far out of the realm of possibility? Not really. I received an ominous email from Rob. I had the sense that someone was watching me, even before that.

My first stop is the pet shop. I grab some special food and treats for my little guys. Then I picked out a masculine black leather collar for Beast. It has a bit of a BDSM vibe, which makes me grin and my mind wanders.

Would Arran look hot in this? Duh, he'd look good in anything, I'm sure. Well, if Beast refuses to wear this, maybe I can find a guy who will.

As I head over to the grocery store for some human food, I have that same unnerving sensation of being watched. While at the store, along with some of my own food treats, I buy a long-handled mirror.

After driving off, I find a quiet residential cul-de-sac and wait several minutes to see if someone follows me here. Again, no one shows.

I hop out of my Mustang and use the mirror to check under the car frame to see if there are any tracking devices. Nothing.

I sit back down in my bucket seat. Then I allow my vision to blur, staring into the distance through the windshield. Wistfully, I wonder why I can't just have a normal life where I dream up fancy peens all day without interruption.

Starting up the engine and driving home, I worry Rob will escalate to violence. Again.

Oh, well, maybe it's time I sell my house and move. But I can't really afford the time off to deal with all that—not with my packed book release schedule.

However, if things get any crazier with Rob, I will just have to disappoint fans by pushing back my release dates. Hopefully, they'll understand.

Driving down my street, I see a man on my porch, facing away from me and waiting.

My heart thumps wildly in my chest, because my first thought is that it could be Rob.

I slide my gun into my pocket for easy access, because I don't know what's going on.

But as I get closer, I can see clearer. The man turns, and I quickly recognize my gentleman caller. Now, I'm even more freaked out.

I grab my frozen food bag. It's the lightest bag for ease of movement if I'm attacked. Besides, I need to bring them inside after my tracking device check detour. This is partially self-defensive and ice cream-melting defense.

*I am woman. Watch me multitask.*

I glare at the man as I slowly approach. "What do you want?"

The male I've dreamed up the name Arran for, stands with his hands in his pockets and his head dipping down, looking timid. "Uh, hi. I heard you had my dog. I'm sorry for showing up unannounced, but I didn't have a number to call."

I huff that this guy shows up *after* I finally buy Beast treats and a collar. It shouldn't piss me off, but it does. Not to mention how long it took him to make his appearance.

But honestly, I just don't want to let the big lug go. We bonded last night. Emotions well up in my chest.

Ugh... do *not* cry in front of the hot guy. Shove the pesky feelings down, Jade.

He will probably just tell Maxum all about my breakdown.

Stiffening my spine, I brush past the man and eye him the whole time I unlock my door. Fortunately, he is conscientious enough to stand back at the edge of my porch. "Just give me a second to put my food in the fridge, okay?"

"No problem." He nods. "And thank you for taking him in. That was kind."

I don't respond to that. Let's see if Beast wants to go with him any more than he did with Maxum. I quietly lock the door behind me as soon as I'm inside.

Tossing my food into the freezer, bag and all, I hurry to the back door and expect to see Beast standing right there as he had done every other time. But he's not there. I step out and scan my small backyard.

"Beast?" I call. But the bushes aren't big enough to conceal his massive size.

My stomach drops.

He ran off because I left today. I glance at my six-foot-tall fence and see scratch marks. I thought it would have been high enough to contain him. I guessed wrong. Maybe for a Shih Tzu or medium-sized dog, but for Beast, it was a small hurdle.

He left me. Why does that hurt just as much as a boyfriend

abandoning me? Maybe I really do need to find someone to love.

Getting over my pain, I remember that his owner is here. Crap.

Will he believe that Beast ran off? Or will he insist that I've hidden him and demand him back? Will he storm into my house, searching for his beloved pet?

*Take a breath, Jade.*

Sometimes my author-mind gets away from me, contemplating every scenario.

I race throughout the house, checking to be sure that I didn't imagine letting him out before I did my errands.

Centering myself, I head out the front door and step out onto the porch, but on the opposite end from this man, so he can't easily push me back inside. For all I know, he's been the creeper watching me.

His eyebrows rise in confusion, reminding me of his dog.

"Uh. While I was out…" I wring my hands. "Your dog escaped. I'm so sorry!" I start waving my hands over my face as I heat up with nerves. I'm worried for Beast, and I'm concerned about what this guy's reaction is going to be. *Is* he an alphahole? "He might still be in the neighborhood. I'll put the rest of my food in the house, and I will make the circuit with my car. We'll find him. God, I hope he's okay!"

"Hey," the man says softly. "It's not your fault. He does this. He's a bit of a free spirit and takes off. He's probably headed to my place. I don't live that far away."

"You believe me?" I ask, sort of shocked he took my claim at face value. Especially considering how his friend Maxum acted so suspicious of me.

"You seem like a caring person." He comforts me, even though it's his animal missing. "I don't think you would steal someone's animal."

"Tell that to Maxum," I grumble under my breath.

"Maxum?" The guy shakes his head. "He can be… intense.

And sometimes distrustful. I'm sorry if Maxum bothered you when he saw you were taking care of Beast."

I chuckle lightly. At least I'm not the only one who thinks Maxum's a bit much. Unfortunately, it doesn't diminish how sexy he is.

"Beast was pleasant company. I'm sad to see him go," I confess.

"If you give me your number, I can give you a call and let you know when he shows up at my house."

"How about my email?" I counter, because I don't like how stalkery things feel in my life right now.

"Is it odd that I don't have an email account?" he asks.

"Yes. Yes, it is." I crinkle my brow. "Are you and Maxum part of some anti-technology movement?"

He smirks, and damn if it isn't a classic book cover model pose. The dominant mafia man is here to rock my world, and maybe tie me up and teach me how to be a good girl.

And… I'm a goner again. I imagine his strong, rough hands gripping my hips as he thrusts into me. He tells me I'm his and demands I come around his cock over and over.

Returning to the real world, he says, "We just don't jive with the computer fad."

"It's a damned cult, really," I agree with a laugh. "I'm sure the whole technology gimmick will blow over any day now."

"Exactly." Mr. Fuckolicious chuckles. "But we aren't anti-tech fanatics or anything." He shrugs casually.

Then he studies my face like I'm the most fascinating thing on the planet.

Did I accidentally fall into a vat of pheromones this week? I try to sniff my armpit casually, but abandon the attempt for later.

"Oh, I don't even know your name." I grab my other bags and carry them to the door.

He reaches out to help me.

I check in with my douche-o-meter, and I sense he's just trying to be helpful. But I pull back anyway. "I'm good."

"Of course, sorry." He takes a step back. "I'll let you be. But could I have a pen and paper? I don't have one on me. I can give you my number in case you want to check in about Beast or if he shows up again. My number is a landline, so don't text it."

"Uh, sure. Give me a sec." I rush inside, put my groceries down in the kitchen, and check the backyard on the off chance Beast has returned. Nope.

I snatch a pen and slip of paper out of my office.

Once again, I'm struck by his gorgeous features as I return. He has the kind of face that sucks my breath away.

Why do I feel like I could sink my fingers into his dark brown hair and he'd let me?

Centering myself, I offer the pen and paper to Mr. Hunky, who is waiting patiently outside. I don't know why he's being so insistent about this. Maybe it's because Beast might return. Or he's being considerate that I took care of his pup.

When he hands me back the paper, I see that he's written 'Arran' on it.

My world spins. I'm sure Maxum never mentioned his friend's name. How is it that I guess his name?

I stumble back a step, my heel snags on a plank, and Arran catches me as I fall. A surge of electric heat travels from my back, where he's touching me, to my heart, then immediately to my clit. Dammit. And that's just from a hand on my back?

What pleasure could he bring me without clothes and time to explore?

Geeze, is this guy a walking radiator? Heat pours over my body. I'd like other things pouring all over my body...

Arran pulls me upright and hesitates before letting me go, but he doesn't step back. Instead, he towers over me, with his amber eyes, much like his dogs.

That's weird, right?

I've heard people often look like their pets, but this is next level shit.

Do men have amber eyes outside of romance novels? I'm pretty sure they don't.

"What's wrong?" he asks, his voice soft, as if he's worried he will spook me.

"Your name is Arran?"

"Do you hate the name? I can change it." He jokes.

"I don't hate it. It's just… I don't remember Maxum mentioning your name, but strangely enough, it's the name I associated with you." I shake my head. "I must be losing my marbles. I'm sure he said it, and I must have forgotten. I'm not *that* psychic."

Arran still is all up in my personal zone. "Just a little psychic?" he asks, teasing, but also with interest.

"Nah. Intuitive at best." Reluctantly, I step back, making sure not to trip again.

"What does your intuition say about me taking you out tonight for dinner? I want to thank you for taking care of my Beast… urm, my dog." His voice is full of innuendo. That must be accidental, though. Right?

I remember how Maxum behaved. Do I want another Mr. Hyde situation?

"I don't know if that's a great idea. Your friend was…"

"Maxum screwed up my chances, didn't he?" Arran steps back too, now realizing he's not getting anywhere with me.

"It's nothing personal. You seem cool enough, but I've been having other issues, on top of Maxum. You don't need to risk having problems just for a thank you dinner."

The eerie feeling of someone watching again crawls up my spine. I glance around the neighborhood to see if I can catch my voyeur.

Arran turns too. "Do you have someone bothering you? Because I've been getting the vibe I have eyes on me. I thought maybe it was only a nosey neighbor. But you appear unsettled."

YVE VALE

For some reason, I feel like I can confide in him. Like I know him already. "You shouldn't take me to dinner because I think my ex has been watching. It's nice of you to want to thank me for Beast, but I don't need it. He was no trouble," I confess instinctively.

I move toward the door to end the conversation and get out of sight. I don't want to linger on the porch with Arran, fearful that whoever is watching might get angrier. Knowing that if it is Rob, he will just get crazier.

Arran moves with me—not blocking, but not letting me just dismiss him, either. He drops his voice low. "Are you in danger with your ex?"

How much do I tell a stranger? And does this random hot guy really care about my problems? "I appreciate the concern, but—"

"Call me if he shows up." He grimaces. "I'm guessing the cops don't do much to deter him if he's still bothering you?"

"Not really. But I'm not going to drag you into the middle of it."

He presses closer again. Not invading my space, but damn near. "It's what I do. I'm a personal bodyguard... mostly on-call."

"Oh." I wave my hand toward his huge, muscular shoulders and arms. "That explains all this."

Preening, he flexes ever so slightly. Guys are so cute when they get a compliment.

Not giving up, he asks, "Maybe you can meet me at the bar tonight at seven? We can casually run into each other. We could sit at the bar so it doesn't look like a date?"

"Do *you* think it's a date?" I ask, my eyes wide. "I thought it was a thank you."

"It's a *'thank you slash I want to get to know you better'* date?"

I never thought I would feel this drawn to someone. But maybe it's a sign from the Universe that I'm meant to go out and have a bite with this guy. What are the odds that I would see him at the bar *and* his dog would follow me home? Also, that I would dream up his name?

"Fine." I grin. "It's entirely conceivable that I might drop into the bar for a drink tonight."

His handsome face lights up with a smile. It does things to me. Specifically, my nether regions.

"Then I look forward to *maybe* running into you." Looking victorious, he skips away down the street in the bar's direction.

As I put my groceries away properly, I'm in a daze.

How is it that I'm going on a second date this week? I usually don't leave the house that often.

Finally, I get to sniff my underarm. Nope. Same smell. No magical pheromones. I check my reflection in the chrome toaster. No, as per usual, I'm the same warmed-over mess.

I could write off Maxum's interest that he was paranoid about me watching him and wanted to prove a point.

But Arran? It didn't seem like the case. I sure hope that isn't what this is.

Now that I've been around a couple of attractive guys, my crotch engine is idling hot, waiting for a spin around the block.

# WITCHES GONE WILD

## ARRAN

"What in all things unholy are you thinking?" Maxum growls.

The entire bar goes silent with Maxum's commanding energy. When I laugh it off, everyone relaxes and returns to their drinks. I need this dickhead demon to take the hint and take a hike.

I hiss my answer. "I need to get closer to her."

"Osen told you to back off," he says, using my own report against me. I knew I shouldn't have told the guys about that. They always blindly followed Osen's orders. I sometimes did, but I knew he was fallible. I'm fairly certain his stubbornness and obsessive need to fight the Witch Council is what got him killed. He had tunnel-vision when it came to them, and they likely used it against him.

"Osen's dead." I lower my voice. "And if I can still talk to him, then maybe we can work this out. He was getting stronger. Maybe he'll eventually remember something."

"So, you are going to use this woman to get close to him?" Maxum huffs and pounds his whiskey. Not that the human-made stuff could affect him. "That's fucked up. I know we hate witches, but *if* she is as innocent as you believe, then that's not cool."

"It's not like that," I grumble. I don't want to admit that I want to get into her bed for a whole other reason. That I'm falling for her.

"So it's *not* like you are going to fuck around with her, risking your beast killing her, then wait until she falls asleep, and talk to your former lover? I swear I thought I was the most fucked up one of us during our date." He scoffs and rubs his face. "Not even close."

I grip my glass so tightly I'm dangerously close to shattering it in my grip. "I want her. Okay?" I confess. "Even if Osen never comes back, I want to be with her. But if he does return, I can help her understand what's going on. Maybe if I got him to work with her instead of fighting her, he could think clearly. Besides, I think Osen's power is messing with her—draining her. And there is something else…"

Maxum perks up when he hears my hesitation. "What's that?"

"Her ex sounds like a jerk."

"Has your wolf claimed her as part of his pack?" He raises an eyebrow.

With a heavy sigh, I lean back in the booth and check the clock. I have five minutes until my witch is supposed to show up for our non-date date. "No, my wolf hasn't technically claimed her… yet." I glower at him. "You don't have to control every aspect of my life. Can you just fuck off and let me be for once?"

"Well, I *could* just chain you up and fuck your ass." He leans close. "Make you forget her pretty face."

My cock responds despite my frustration. "Wait. You are attracted to her too. That's why you want me to back off!" I glare at him. "You know, we could both pursue her. If her books are any indication, she might be up for a three-way, four-way... I don't even know how many ways. One book she wrote had six guys for only one woman. Some guy-on-guy stuff, too. So she's probably cool with that... as long as we are open with her."

"Just because she—*allegedly*—writes that doesn't mean she wants us all sticking our dicks in all her holes, filling her up with our cum."

The vision of that very scenario gives us both pause. Our eyes glaze over with lust at the image of the four of us and her.

As we abruptly shake our heads to bring us back to reality, Jade clears her throat and walks up to the table.

Did she hear Maxum's comment?

My face turns red. Almost as bright as the demon in his natural state.

She icily stares at Maxum for a long beat. It impresses me that she can handle the intensity of his gaze. Even after all these years, I can barely do that.

Then she dismisses him with an eye roll and says to me, "I think I'm going to pass on accidentally meeting up now or in the future. Good luck with Beast."

I scramble to stand up and stop her, but she has already spun on her heel and is walking toward the door. "Wait!" I rush after her. "Maxum was just leaving."

Jade gives a cold, calculated glower that travels up and down my body, as if inspecting my worth. Goddess, I hope my erection isn't too obvious. With the combination of imagining her taking all of us, Maxum's dirty mouth, and what I know he can do with it, I'm impossibly hard. I'm quickly deflating as I see my chances of tasting Jade's lips dwindling with every beat of my pounding heart.

Jade crosses her arms and glares at the huge demon, daring him to fuck with her. I'll give her props for sheer boldness. Not many would dare to do this, whether they know his true form or not. He's intimidating no matter what.

Maxum stands up slowly and locks eyes with our witch the entire time he walks past her.

Jade doesn't even blink.

Damn, when it comes down to it, she's a fucking badass. It's making me hard again.

When Maxum finally turns away and heads to the door, Jade looks at me with a cocked eyebrow.

Over her head, I see Maxum nodding his head in approval. He likes someone who isn't easily quelled.

She would fit in nicely with our group. If she doesn't run screaming for the hills when she discovers what we are, that is.

I hate that this dive bar is our first official date, but I wanted to pick a place where she felt comfortable.

"Sorry about him. He doesn't mean to be an ass," I say.

"Oh, so it just comes naturally to him, does it?" She grins as she slips into the booth where she had watched us that first night. Her eyes widen when she feels the heat of the seat Maxum left behind. He runs even hotter than I do... usually.

"I'd say a bit of nature *and* nurture." I flag down our server with a quick wave so we can get Jade settled with a drink. "Not that I'm defending his dickishness, but he's not always quite this paranoid."

Thankfully, the server comes up to interrupt our conversation, so Jade can't ask more about his paranoia and why he is especially touchy lately.

"Hey Jade, what can I get you tonight?" The server's eyes are alight with mirth.

"Paloma," she orders.

"You want another whiskey?" the lady asks, eyeing my empty glass.

"Yeah, since my friend drank mine." I chuckle. Maxum is such a dick.

The server hurries off after a little wink at Jade that I pretend not to notice.

"So, how's Beast?" she asks. "Did he turn up?"

"Hmm?" I take a beat before I remember her name for my wolf. "Oh, yeah. He was right where he was supposed to be!" I shake my head with a grin like he's a scamp. And right now? I fucking feel like one.

"Oh, good. I was worried about him today. Missed him too." She frowns, picking at her nails.

"I hope you don't mind shared custody, because he's likely to come knocking at your door at some point again."

Jade chuckles at that. "As long as he doesn't break into the house if I don't answer the door."

I can't promise her we won't do that.

When our drinks arrive, she raises her glass and looks me in the eye when we clink glasses together.

"To new connections," I toast.

She echoes me with a wry grin and peruses my defined, broad chest. "So, a bodyguard, huh? I might have to quiz you on that so I can write a bodyguard trope."

"Is that a romance thing?" I rub my face in embarrassment. "Uh, I guess it makes sense. Feeling safe and protected is something people want and need." I laugh. "Too bad it isn't as sexy as in your books."

Her face flashes with surprise. Whoops. I hope she doesn't quiz me about romance books. I only know how steamy her stuff gets because I peeked. And wow, she described things that made me blush.

"Well, that's the job of the author, isn't it?" She rubs the condensation off her cold glass. "We must take a mundane relationship or situation and heighten it until it's extraordinary. Life is messy. It's not like passionate romances with happy little bows at the end happen all the time. Most of us don't get scorching sexual tension that winds up being amazing, earth-shattering sex with syncronized orgasms with a perfect partner that completes us, heals our emotional wounds, and makes us better people."

I study her for a moment. "You're not wrong. But you're not completely correct either."

She laughs heartily at that. "Oh, boy, I know what you're going to say."

"Do you?" I lean forward, drawing her in with my intense gaze. She unconsciously leans toward me. "Tell me then," I dare her.

"You were going to say something like passion and romance happen all the time, and it's not that bleak." She lifts her glass, points with her index finger, and waves it at me, as if it gives weight to her argument. "But I'm sure you get all kinds of whirlwind hookups and torrid nights of passion. Except, not all of us have the supermodel thing going on. Or are we extroverted enough to go out and stumble upon someone who wants to be with us. Some of us are introverts. And we don't go outside where all the people are."

I nod my appreciation for her compliment. "Thank you for the vote of confidence concerning my sexual prowess, but I'm not getting laid every time I walk out the door—"

She interrupts, "Just every *other* time."

Laughing at her playfulness, I explain, "I was going to say… we can *easily* find romance in books, but that doesn't mean we can't have the same passion in our lives. Or true love. And yeah, sometimes love is messy. But when you find someone to connect with on a soul level, it's…"

Jade sets her drink down, waiting for me to finish my thought, but I can't. It's too much to think about Osen being gone. Or about my other loves who hurt me. I don't want to think about how she'll react when she discovers my lies, my secrets.

"You've lost someone?" she asks softly.

"Yeah, but enough of that. I'd rather talk about you." I try to change the subject. "On that note of the past, I wanted to ask if you're okay. Is your ex still harassing you?"

"It was just a one-sentence email." She waves me off, and I watch her energy tighten and shrink.

"Don't dismiss your feelings," I encourage her to arm herself with her natural Goddess-given gifts. "Your instincts and intuition are there for a reason. My instincts tell me that you are more worried than you are letting on."

"I've been getting this vibe lately that I'm being watched. All the time," she confesses, glancing over her shoulder. "Rob must have seen me walking with Maxum, because he said: 'You should be more careful who you go on dates with.'"

I sit up and go on alert. His language might suggest that he knows exactly who and what Maxum is. "Anything else?"

"No. He's always cryptic in his threats, so I can't use it against him with the cops or the courts."

"Is he a physical threat as well?" I dare to ask… on a fucking date. So much for fun banter.

Jade bites her lip, and it's all the confirmation I need. He's hurt her in the past, and he will die. I'll make sure of it. That will solve the stalker problem.

"Rob was more connected than I realized. So no matter what my complaints or reports I try to file, they all seem to be ignored or disappear into thin air." Jade rubs her temples like a headache is coming on. "I wish I never fell for his nice guy act."

He sounds like someone who can put a spell on the authorities. My best guess is he's a warlock. But the guys and I will find out for sure. It behooves us to follow him as a lead, since he might be our enemy. Besides, if I know what he is and how to end him permanently, it will be easier for me to remove him from the realms.

"Would you give me his full name so my security buddies can run a background check? I don't like leaving this alone."

"Just a background check. I don't want you entangled with this." I nod, and she acquiesces, "Robert Holden. He's forty-one. Lives in the city." She waves her hands in a stop motion.

"Okay, enough about him. I never go out, so I'd like to enjoy the little time we have left together."

"That statement sounds ominous. Are you about to whack me?"

"Whack you?" She blushes. "Do you mean to smack, jerk off, or kill?"

I smirk, running both my hands through my short dark hair. I enjoy her playfulness. There's been so little in my life in the last decade I have enjoyed. She is the sunlight after a never-ending storm. Sadly, Osen was often part of the storm.

I lace my fingers behind my neck, flexing my arms a bit to highlight my musculature.

Her eyes dilate, and her breath quickens.

My cock hardens, knowing I am tantalizing my witch. "What would you *like* to do to me?"

She eyes me seriously for a moment. "Can we circle back around to that after the evening is done?"

"Fair enough." I chuckle, drop my arms back to the table, and take another sip of my whiskey. "How long have you been writing?"

"Since I was a kid. But I've been an indie author for about ten years now."

"Does indie mean you publish your own stuff?"

"Yeah. It also means I'm responsible for everything: from book covers to editors to constantly promoting. It's a list so long you don't want to hear it. And if the books don't sell or people pirate our books, we eat all the costs of production and ads. On top of that, we can get our books banned on the online bookstore gods, if someone steals them and puts them up on pirate sites. I've been lucky to eke out a semi-comfortable living. But it's always a hustle. I work twelve-hours a day, every day."

I know that's true. I've seen her spinning all her metaphorical plates. She doesn't have time to be a spy.

"Sounds like you could do with some relaxation." I waggle my eyebrows playfully.

Jade chuckles.

I ask, "It sounds like a lot, so why do you do it?"

"Because I love creating new worlds, new characters, and I love getting lost in my own stories. And when a reader connects with my work, it's the best feeling. It sounds silly, but reading is true magic. When someone reads a book, they join me in my world. I tell them there's a handsome man with a cocky grin sitting across from me, and they are there with me. They get to fill in everything else about you. In a way, the reader and I can become co-creators in that world. And then the characters really take on a life of their own. They become real. In a way."

"It does sound magical." I find her choice of words interesting. "The way you explain it, the mundane can transform into a mystical experience."

When she sees I understand her, Jade's smile lights up the room.

We talk for hours about life, her writing, and how she has a habit of rescuing strays.

It feels like she's rescued me. Is that what we are searching for? Someone who will truly see us and take us in—into their hearts—and accept all the broken pieces.

When we finally walk out to the parking lot to our cars, she is practically dragging her feet, like she doesn't want the night to end.

"Would I be able to buy one of your books to read?" I ask.

Or maybe I should have asked to borrow one, so I have a reason to come back.

"Uh, yeah." She unlocks her Mustang's door, and I have to admit I'm a bit jealous. My old 1980s Toyota pickup is no muscle car.

"I suppose you could follow me to my place, and I can give you one," she suggests.

"Perfect!" I say with a bit too much enthusiasm. I jump in my car and follow her on the short way home.

She rushes inside and meets me back at the front door by the time I get up to the porch. She has two books in her hands. "One is steamy. The other is very steamy. Which would you like?"

I lean against her door frame, moving in close so that our bodies are brushing, and I pretend as if I'm studying the covers. But I'm watching her.

With my proximity, her skin flushes with arousal. Her heart rate increases. She's gripping the books as if they are ropes, and she's dangling off a cliff. I can scent that I turn her on.

I have to say I feel the same way, but I don't have something to hold on to... yet.

"What would *you* like me to read?" I ask suggestively.

She finally turns to look up at me. We are so close that I only have to drop my head just a few inches to kiss her.

She glances at my lips and then back to gaze into my eyes.

I wonder if they are glowing. I feel like my whole body is glowing.

This is the moment where everything can change... the moment of possibility. Or the moment she destroys my hopes.

"May I ask you something?" When I nod, she presses her lips together briefly. "Why does it seem like you're hitting on me?"

"Because I am," I answer simply, but tilt my head in confusion. "I know I'm rusty, but I thought my flirting skills would be sufficient enough for a romance author to do something with."

"So, is this part of your thank you for taking care of your dog?" she asks with a smirk.

"No. I like you... a lot. You're beautiful. Smart. Kind. Sexy." I lift my hand to cradle her cheek. "If you need a reminder of all you have to offer, then I'll make it my mission for the foreseeable future."

She gulps at the word *future*. My witch thinks this is just a fling for me.

"I don't have casual one-night stands," I say. "So if you like me too, and you want to take this slow, I'm good with that."

Jade drops her books to the ground with a thud. She grabs the back of my head and pulls me in for a passionate kiss that makes my dick inflate instantly. Damn, her alpha assertiveness is making my wolf perk up and howl.

My introverted witch continues her boldness, grabbing the front of my shirt and pulling me inside.

I kick the door shut and flip the lock, but I don't dare break our kiss while I do.

Her tongue tangles with mine. She wraps her hands around my waist, then slides them up my untucked shirt. Soft fingers caress my back as I guide her slowly to the couch. I don't presume I will get her into bed tonight.

Nor should I.

If I'm correct, she doesn't know about supernaturals, so she definitely doesn't think that dick knots are real.

I'm also afraid of my beast—my true beast. Not the one that Maxum jokingly called my wolf... no, the monster I now become when my emotions are riding too high, or when I'm in the throes of passion. All because of that evil witch from my past.

I'm honestly surprised I haven't shifted into my berserker with the weight of everything I've been feeling. Osen's death. Walking into a witch's house. Finding out she's my mate.

Is she my mate? Fuck, I think she is.

There's a light on in the hall from when she went to grab her books, but the living room isn't bright with ambient lighting. However, if I shifted into my monster, there would be no hiding it.

*Do I risk taking this further than kissing?*

I capture her head and waist as I settle her back onto the long couch. Placing one leg between her splayed thighs, I hover over her, caging her in.

Her hand skims down my muscled abdomen, and she hums

with approval. Fingers slide along the edge of my waistband, testing me.

The beast inside wants to burst free and claim her.

My kisses become more frantic. Soon, I'm biting and sucking along her jawline. Jade's body undulates, grinding her sex over my thigh that is wedged between her legs.

Her fingernails claw up my back. Just that alone is enough to make me unravel.

I pull up her shirt and suck in a breath when I see her ample breasts heaving and ready to burst out from her pretty bra. I know this is the sexiest one she has. I've checked. I'm a perv.

My cock swells even more, knowing she wore the pretty item for me. Maybe she was not expecting this, but she wanted to feel sexy because she hoped this was a date and not just a thank you for the dog.

*The dog…* I almost growl that I can't tell her yet. That I can't fuck her as I want to.

I gently bite the soft flesh of her breast. My teeth are sharper with a barely contained shift.

She gasps, but arches her back to encourage me to continue with my play.

I pull down the edge of her bra to reveal her large but rock-hard nipples—perfect for sucking.

I run my tongue over each nipple, then blow gently over them.

Jade is biting her lip, watching me like *I* might be magic.

Staring into her hazel-green eyes, I suck on her tit harder and harder until she squeaks. With one hand, I massage the other breast, teasing and plucking the nipple.

Her heart is pounding, and I smell another wave of her arousal—blackberries and a hint of lilacs.

Maybe I *could* fuck her if I flip her over just before my beast is unleashed?

"I need to taste you," I rasp, kissing her sweet mouth again and hooking my fingers at her waistband. I wait for her consent. I watch for any hesitation, but I see none.

"You sure?" she asks, like this is some sort of task for me.

But her thumbs hook at her waistband, and she helps me pull down her pants as she lifts her hips.

"Babe, you don't think I want to taste your sweet slick and savor every drop of you?" I ask as I fling her pants away, grasping her ankles and throwing a leg over each shoulder.

"I, it's just Rob never wanted to, and he wasn't the only one…"

"Then you've been with all the wrong males," I growl. "And I don't think I want to hear about those imbeciles right now."

I leave a trail of kisses down her inner thigh, torturing myself by delaying our gratification.

"Good plan," Jade agrees, but doesn't open fully.

Assertively, I pin her legs open and gaze upon my prize. "Fuck, that's perfect. You're perfect." I lean in and swipe my tongue over her wet, soft flesh, and she whimpers.

"Fuck, that is… yes." She allows her legs to relax as I explore her folds, and then I suck on her clit. Her body arches, and she grabs her own tits, pulling on her nipples. Now that is a sight I never want to forget. "Yes, Arran. Please."

My fingers slide over her wetness.

She cants her hips to encourage me when I near her entrance.

I dip one, then two fingers inside her and delve in slowly, licking as I take her pussy. I work her with my hands and mouth. Exploring and discovering all the places that make her light up. I watch every twitch and gasp, every flutter of her cunt. I will make it my mission to learn every inch of her body. Even if all I can ever do is lick and touch, I will willingly sacrifice my own release to bring her pleasure.

I will exist only to worship her body.

She's on the edge of an orgasm that I keep working her

toward. I rub the spot inside her that makes her tremble and palm one of her breasts with my other hand.

When I bite down on her clit, she bucks and cries out.

"Come for me," I command.

"Oh, god!" Her body flails, and she shakes.

I watch as her mouth opens, and she makes sweet groans and whines. I keep her climax going until she finally returns to the room.

Jade smiles at me with mischief glinting in her eyes.

"Come here," she calls me, clasping my head to bring me up to kiss her on the mouth.

I brush my slick-covered lips over hers and then delve my tongue into her mouth.

Her small hand cups the front of my pants. "Would he like to come out to play?" she asks.

Fuck. I have to be careful here. She wants to reciprocate, which I definitely want. But I can't with my monstrous self, and even if I didn't have that issue, I have a knot at the base of my cock. I know she thinks this is only some sort of mythological penis in her books, but it's very real.

She will freak out when she realizes supernatural beings are real. A blow job on a first date is no way to find out all that. I don't think we should have sex, because even if I agreed, I'd have to ask her to turn off the lights.

I don't want her to think it's because I don't want to see her luscious, naked body.

"I want to take this slow," I say instead.

"You just consumed my soul through my vagina. How is that slow?" she jokes, but I hear the concern.

"It brings me pleasure to give that to you. I didn't do it to get payback," I explain.

"I wasn't suggesting that you were. But I wouldn't mind sucking your cock or fucking your brains out."

I close my eyes to center myself so I don't jump her bones from her direct and sexy words.

"As much as I want to do both of those things, I promised myself that I wouldn't fuck on the first couple of dates with anyone. But I have something more intimate in mind, if you are okay with it. Can we do that here for a bit?"

"Uh?"

"I want to hold you." I feel the heat of a blush on my cheeks. "Snuggle."

She grins. "As long as you do it with your shirt off." She pulls a soft blanket from the back of the couch.

I stand and pull my shirt off. Jade's eyes drink me in, and she licks her lips. "You sure about that no-fucking rule?"

I chuckle. "Not really. But I need your shirt and bra off you, too."

She slips the shirt off, and I unfasten the bra and groan when her beautiful tits tumble free of their hold.

I slip my hands around her and pick her up easily, and she squeals with joy. I flop back down on my back with her on top of me.

"I haven't had anyone pick me up like that in a long time." She feels up my arms. "You did that with no effort," she says with awe. "You're strong."

I puff up with that compliment. Then I pull the throw blanket over us so she doesn't get cold. Not that she is likely to get chilly with my shifter body heat. We always run hotter than most.

Content, we both sigh together as if we had planned it.

I pray to the Goddess, let me have this. Give me one chance at happiness.

Let Jade forgive me for my secrets.

Please, let us move beyond our differences.

And if she accepts me, give me the strength to keep my beast at bay so I can bond with her how she deserves—with my complete mind, heart, and body.

## 16

POSSESSED

JADE

*P*lastered over Arran on the couch, I can feel by the enormous bulge in his pants that he enjoyed snacking on my pussy very much.

It's sweet that he wants to take things slow, but my author's mind is now imagining what terrible event happened in his past to make him want to take it slow.

Guys usually like to take it fast.

Hell, most people don't take things slow.

Unless someone has hurt them badly enough to make them cautious.

Speaking of which, I should be cautious and slow things down too. I know better than to fall so fast.

My pussy got away from me.

I breathe in Arran's cozy scent of lightning storms and sage. It reminds me of his dog, Beast, since he has the same earthy scent.

Arran hums happily as I run my hands up his sides. Under his silky skin, I feel muscles that flex with my touch.

My hand drifts up to his hair, and I tangle my fingers through his dark locks.

He moans and then sighs contentedly.

This is actually nice. I forgot how much I enjoyed snuggling. Rob wasn't much of a snuggler or one at all, really.

I still wonder why I was with him and for as long as I was. Objectively. Rob is handsome, but otherwise, he doesn't have many redeeming qualities—physically or emotionally... or at least none that I found particularly attractive.

Maybe I was just lonely enough to put up with his shit. I wouldn't be the first person in the world to stick around a jerk because I was more tired of being alone.

Arran's strong arms cinch around my body. He pulls me tightly against him as if he can sense the dark road my mind is traveling down, and he wishes to protect me from the memory of my ex.

I tuck my head under Arran's chin, and his naked flesh warms my skin. I feel more protected and cherished by this stranger than I have in my entire life.

I have no idea why.

Maybe it's the whole bodyguard vibes he gives off.

Could this be the beginning of something real? Could he really like me? Could I really want to be with someone again?

He's been funny, intelligent, and protective. He ticks all my boxes for a partner.

And some boxes he checks twice... such as his gorgeous physique, personality, and talented tongue.

He makes me feel good—not just attractive or desired, but in my heart, as though I'm at peace. I can't remember when a man elicited that feeling from me.

But am I someone he sees a future with?

It's not like younger guys don't date older women. I never

expected it to happen to me, not when he looks like a cover model for a fitness magazine.

I suppose we will have to see.

Comforted in his embrace, inexplicably feeling safe, my mind drifts into sleep...

I'm embodying the mystery guy again, the jerk from the nights before.

This recurring situation is so odd. I rarely dream I'm the same person twice.

And never have my dreams been so visceral. It's as if I'm actually living these moments, not just the vague, ethereal quality of most dreams.

Maxum and Arran are beside my avatar. We are storming through a dense forest at night, searching for something... or *someone*?

My eyes catch a gleam of light-colored stone in the distance.

"There!" we all say in unison.

Our steps quicken, but my head swivels back and forth, constantly looking for a threat or a surprise attack.

When we get closer, I realize it's Arran's friend that was at the bar that first night. He's the giant, quiet man with sand-colored hair and light gray eyes.

Lying twisted on the ground, he's mostly on his side. He appears to be nearly undressed, but wearing pants and a strange-looking robe glued stiffly to his back. His eyes are closed, but he doesn't look to be sleeping. No, this is far too consuming to be sleeping. He appears frozen solid. But it doesn't feel cold out here.

My avatar's heart races, and even Maxum looks concerned when I glance up at his face.

The crimson-skinned, demon-like version of Maxum crouches down and sniffs his friend.

"This is a witch or warlock's magic. He's stuck in his stone form," Maxum informs us.

I curse and spin around, scanning our surroundings for our enemy.

"We should get him out of this realm," Arran says, pacing back and forth and pulling on his short, dark hair.

Both my avatar and I want to reach out and soothe him. My male voice says, "We can't move him like this. He weighs too much, even with all of us helping."

"Someone needs to stay behind and guard his body while he's under the spell," Maxum suggests.

"What if he doesn't come out of this curse? What if it's fucking permanent?" Arran growls.

"I haven't seen a witch or warlock powerful enough that they could cast a spell that could make a stone form permanent in several generations," Maxum says, shaking his head but still looking worried no matter his assessment. "I doubt this will last more than a day."

"But that's long enough for them to distract us while they murder our entire crew. Or what's left of it now," I say. "Maxum, can you sense Calder at all now that you are in this realm?"

"No. He's not on this plane." Maxum stands up and gazes into the distance. "I will search for him in the Underworld."

"No. That's too risky to do alone," I argue.

"And who would I take?" Maxum challenges. "They've already killed anyone who would survive on that plane."

"Fine. Just go." I wave him off. "You're right. But be safe."

"Nowhere is safe... or haven't you been paying attention," Maxum grumbles and then waves his hand, chanting a few words under his breath.

A portal opens, and, unafraid, he steps through to an even darker place.

The doorway snaps shut, and I turn back to Arran. "Are you going to be okay?"

"If you are asking about my beast? No. I don't think we're okay." Arran palms his face with both hands and then rubs his eyes. "I'm on the verge of losing it. He wants to go on a wild, indiscriminate rampage. You may have to kill me."

*What the fucking hell? Please don't make me watch Arran get hurt...*

Feeling my shock and fear, my male avatar becomes aware that I'm dreaming with him again.

*"Witch?"* he asks in my mind.

This feels like something different from an ordinary dream. This doesn't feel like my dream. Or even a dream, really.

The scene fades until I'm only in complete darkness.

I would almost believe my avatar was a spirit possessing my mind and body.

"What's going on?" I ask, because now I fear that might be exactly what is happening.

*"How are you able to channel my memories?"* he asks, as if I had any answers to this craziness.

"This actually happened to you?" I ask. "But... it can't be. There's no such thing as realms, portals, and warlocks that can cast people into stone."

*"Are you really that ignorant?"*

"Are you really this much of an asshole?" I ask.

*"Yes."* He chuckles at his own answer.

"Well, thank you for being honest. And for my part, I don't know why I'm dreaming I'm you. Or what the hell is going on. I wish it would stop."

He hums to himself as if he's finally taking my word for it.

I feel pressure gathering around my mind.

*"You don't seem to be lying. But you might also have been trained to compartmentalize your thoughts."*

"I doubt my mind power skills are to the level you are estimating. I'm barely able to remember what I was supposed to be doing after I leave a room. But I appreciate the vote of confidence," I sass.

The pressure around my mind lessens, and I'm starting to believe that something paranormal is really happening in my life.

*"I don't know if I can stop you or your people from hurting mine, but just know if I believe you will hurt them, I will do everything in my power to stop you."*

"If I'm going to hurt someone unprovoked, then I don't blame you. But if you are talking about the guys from the bar… I like Arran. A lot. Maxum was a bit of a jerk, but I'm not planning on talking to him anymore. And I have nothing against the other two. But if they attack me, I will defend myself. Not that I'm likely to win, since they are all huge guys."

*"Guys?"* he chuckles again. *"They are more than mere men."*

"So they *actually* are demons, shifters, and gargoyles?" I laugh.

*"You really don't know you have witch blood?"* he asks, disbelief ringing in his voice.

"My grandmother claimed I was a witch like her. But my mother told me to ignore it. Said that she was crazy and dangerous. So I never took the claim to heart."

*"So, you have no powers other than the channeling of spirits?"* he asks.

"If that's what I'm doing right now, then I didn't even know I could do that. I half believed I could dream other people's dreams, but that's a far cry from being a medium."

*"You have dream magic?"* he asks with renewed interest. *"Fascinating."*

"If you really are a ghost, and you need me to get a message to someone, I could help." I say the next part primarily to myself, "If I had a validated fact, it would prove that this isn't just a dream."

*"Unfortunately, I don't feel I can trust you not to betray me."*

"Okay. Then how can I win your trust? For that matter, how can I trust someone who is supposedly invading my body and mind?"

"We can't trust each other. You are my enemy. Your kind hates my kind. We don't get to be friends," he answers, and I feel him fading from my consciousness. "Actions always speak louder than empty promises. And all your kind has ever handed out is lies."

I can't disagree with him about actions speaking louder than words.

I open my eyes and see the morning light filtering through the cracks of my closed blackout curtains.

And I've literally drooled on Arran's spectacular chest.

It's a chest that should be bronzed for posterity. Okay, ouch. Maybe not actually bronzed, but take a mold casting of it and make thousands of replicas. It should then be placed on display for others to drool over. But jealousy pinches my heart at the thought. I don't want to share.

Shockingly, this Adonis is still snuggled up with me.

Man, does he run hot. He's like a furnace. And where our bodies are pressed against each other, I've also sweated and now have moisture-stuck myself to Arran skin to skin.

I feel like wet velcro as I carefully pull away from him.

But he catches me as I try to lift myself off and presses us back together again. He gives me a sweet kiss on my forehead.

Finding that stupidly cute, I return his kiss under his chin.

"Where were you sneaking off to?" he asks playfully.

"Pee. Coffee. Clothes. Fur babies. Work," I list off.

"Would you like food?" he asks.

"It will probably be on the agenda at some point today."

His hand slides down my side to palm my hip. "How about you take care of your bodily functions and fur babies, and I can make you some coffee and breakfast?"

"Don't you have to go?" It sounds harsh, but I don't mean it like that.

I'm just a busy person, and I assume others have a full day

too. Besides, I'm not used to the attention. Rob never wanted to hang out and make my meals. Often, I felt like an irritating obligation. As if he was forced to put in the minimum required time to get his pension package.

"I have the day off, but if you want me to go—" he says with a tint of sadness.

"You can stay… But I thought maybe you'd want to do the walk of pity this morning."

"I thought it was the walk of shame?"

"Well, you have nothing to be ashamed of. Your performance last night was five stars. It's a *pity* since I didn't get to return the favor."

He pulls me back by the shoulder and looks me in the eye. His brow crinkles. "It wasn't a *favor*. I thought it was more than that."

I get this guy is more sensitive than most. But he acts like I've known him for days, and we have a developed relationship beyond our date last night and some fantastic cunnilingus.

Normally, I would take this as a red flag, but I feel our connection, too.

Is this the comfortable feeling people talk about when they say they found their person? And dare I say it and jinx myself… my true love?

"Okay. Sounds good. Coffee and breakfast. Stat!" I say with a grin and snag my throw blanket and wrap it around me as I race off to the bathroom.

I pee and splash my face with water to wash off my sleep drool.

Why does Arran have to be so sexy and sweet? With my track record, I'm nervous that I'm going to be broadsided by some horrible, dark secret.

I remember my crazy dream last night. And I wonder if it really is only a dream. Or is it a warning he might be a raging maniac underneath a kind facade? Or am I just trying to talk myself out of falling for him? Am I just damaged from all the jerks in my life—including family and boyfriends?

I pick up my phone and open my messenger app for my small author chat group. I update them quickly about my situation.

> Me: "He was eating my taco like it was his interview for his dream job."

> Mere: Proof of dick?

They want pics. Not really. Well, I *hope* she doesn't want me to send pics of my boyfriend's dick. Boyfriend? Can I call him that? Are we dating now?

Does Mere want a ransom's style 'proof of life' picture with a dick next to a newspaper with the date showing to prove this is a current penis situation?

> Me: Do you mean a picture to prove my hunky boyfriend is real? Not his actual dick, right?

> Nanette: These things are not mutually exclusive.

> Bekka: Send us whatever you got.

I laugh and close the app when I smell coffee brewing. I walk out to see a shirtless Arran scrambling some eggs. My heart pounds in my clit. Nobody has ever made me breakfast before, and definitely not looking as good as he does.

Can I keep him as my human hostage?

Do I have it in me to be a sugar mama? I'd need to write a few more books a year, and then I should be able to afford to pay for his membership to whatever magic gym he goes to.

Arran turns around and gives me a brilliant smile that

instantly makes my clit, I mean, my heart pound too hard. He might be the death of me.

But damn, I could get used to this. Forget fucking. If he does the dishes, I think I might spontaneously orgasm.

He returns his focus to his cooking as I walk over to him. I spot scars barely visible on his back. They look more like scratches. For a second, I worry I scratched him that hard. But no, when I get closer, I see they are old, faint lines. It appears as if he were sliced several times with a knife. Did one of his bodyguard jobs get ugly? Was he tortured?

Ignorant of my wild ride down imagination lane, he says, "I hope an omelet is okay."

"Perfect." I get out two mugs from the cabinet and set them down to fill them up. "Do you take anything in yours?"

"No coffee for me, thanks." He smiles and grates some cheese for the omelet.

"All for me?" I nod approvingly.

But I'll switch to my 'writing' tea for the rest of the day. It's time to channel all this craziness into my book.

# 17

# WALK OF PITY

## ARRAN

*I* cannot believe I was able to lick her pretty cunt and keep my beast at bay. Jade is a miracle. What if she is the cure for my curse that I've been looking for?

But I'm worried I will press my luck if I go any further with our explorations. I can't test my theory that she might help me control my monstrous curse.

Not yet.

Not until she understands what she is.

What I am.

I've been awake all this morning, basking in the bliss of having her naked flesh on mine.

I worry she had another unpleasant dream—if her grunts and whines were any indications. But just as I was ready to wake her or dare to call Osen's name, she settled in my arms.

I wonder if his soul still lingers around her, or if he has passed on through the veil.

Yet, I'm no longer here for Osen.

I want her. I want to protect her. My wolf wants to claim her.

He likes the ear scratches and tells me he wants to be around her again.

It's difficult explaining to your animal self that it's not as simple as all that.

I tell him soon, but I worry I shouldn't show my wolf until I confess my sins. I spied on her and pretended to be a dog to discover her secrets. She might not forgive me.

As she wakes, her cheeks turn pink when she realizes she's drooled on me. Beast loves it. Honestly, we both find it charming.

After convincing her to let me stay to make breakfast, she rushes off to freshen up. I hear her giggling before she comes out. Probably texting her friends about me.

I'm half-tempted to spy again and see what she says about my performance last night. From her facial expressions and body's reaction, I seem to have got the physical part right.

But does she see me as someone she might want for more than a few nights of fun? I felt her distancing herself already.

And last night, she appeared baffled that I would want to snuggle rather than get my dick sucked.

It would have baffled me as well, if I had been just a regular guy. However, I'm not a regular guy. I have a beast inside me. Besides, I secretly lived a dog's life in her house for the last couple of days. I can't take this too far without confessing what I am and what I've done. But first, I want her to get to know the person behind the supernatural curse and all my deceptions.

I start some coffee in her stovetop percolator. I love that she has an old-school coffee maker. Opening the fridge, I find there's enough ingredients to make an omelet, barely— dangerously close to expired eggs and a chunk of cheese.

This woman really needs someone to grocery shop for her. She can strategize an entire series plot line, but not what to eat for the next three days. There are tortillas with nothing to put inside them. Not much in vegetables, except for the stuff she purchases for her pets. Her frozen dinners are all she has for full meals. However, she's fully stocked with ice cream... and chips.

I realize she probably eats out regularly.

My alpha instinct to protect and care for my pack extends to making sure she has whatever she needs. And right now, she needs good food. Not that I think she needs me to help her, but she needs *someone* to help her. I want it to be me.

When she emerges from her bedroom, she wears a loose t-shirt and leggings. Both look soft, and I fight the urge to find out if they are.

I don't want her to think I'm clingy. She already accused Beast of that. I'm guessing she isn't used to a lot of physical attention... even when she has a significant other.

She's surprised I don't want coffee, but shifters can't usually stomach it. Not that I'm telling her that reason. She'll assume I'm a health nut, which isn't completely wrong.

"I'll be a few more minutes with the omelet if you want to check on your pets."

Jade raises her eyebrows and remembers telling me about her fur babies. "Good idea," she saunters off, sipping her coffee.

When she returns, we have a nice, simple breakfast filled with talking about her animal hostages, as she likes to call them. I laugh like it's the first time I've heard this joke. And I admit, it's funny now that I know she isn't *really* keeping abducted shifters.

"What are you doing today?" I ask.

"Uh, I've been goofing off too much lately, so I need to get my word count in."

"Is that your not-so-subtle hint for me to get lost?"

She finishes her omelet and clears her throat. Nothing good ever comes from a throat clearing when relationship topics are in play. "Look, I really enjoyed last night, but you said we should take this slow."

"Physically... sexually," I correct.

"Well, I suppose I need to take it slow *emotionally*." She looks me in the eye and waves her hands in my direction. "You seem serious about wanting to date me, which is lovely."

"*Lovely?*" I laugh without humor.

"I'm guessing I'm close to a decade older than you."

"How old are you?" I know this, but she doesn't know I do.

"Forty," she says with defiance, crossing her arms.

"I'm older than you," I tell her.

Her mouth drops open. She won't believe me. I know I don't look my age. Most supernaturals and many witches don't look their ages.

She gives me a distrustful glare and says, "That can't be. You don't look over thirty."

I grin and shrug. "It's true."

"Well, you look like a player—at whatever age you really are."

"Like I said before, I don't have flings." This is turning sour fast. She can't understand why I like her? She just has to look in the mirror. And her personality? I fucking love all her quirkiness. I frown and sigh. "Look… if you don't like me, then just say that. Don't make excuses. Tell me if you aren't interested in me. But please, don't assume I'm a player. I don't make a habit of what happened between us last night. I can't remember when someone has captivated me the way you do."

It's true. Not even Osen grabbed my attention as she did.

"You are very attractive, and… I like you… a lot. Probably too much." Jade rests her elbows on the table. She gives me a sad expression of grief and weariness. "I barely got out of a terrible relationship alive because I let him get too close too fast. I'm not even sure why I allowed it to happen."

"With Rob?" I ask.

"Yeah." She studies her fingers, unwilling to look at me while she shatters my dreams. "So even though I'm actually very attracted to *you*, I don't want to fall into another situation. I thought I was into him, but it quickly felt like he had tricked me. I'm not accusing you of that, but…"

This Rob person concerns me even more now. "You make it sound like you weren't very attracted to Rob."

"I wasn't… His looks, personality, and energy were all wrong for me." She shrugs. "I'm not sure *why* I was with him. Even the sex was bland and pointless."

I barely fight back a growl. I don't want to imagine Jade fucking that male.

Instead, I turn the growl into a hum, considering what she confessed. Rob is sounding more and more like a warlock.

"And it appears he's stalking me. I'm sorry, but it wasn't smart of me to let you stay last night. Or even hang out at the bar. You might have been dragged into my drama already."

"I'm not being dragged. I walked into this with you willingly. And if something happens, I want to be there to help you."

She hears the sincerity in my voice and clasps my hand as I offer it to her over the table. "I appreciate everything you are doing. You're being amazing, but I still need this to go slow. I can't make the same mistake. I hope you understand that."

"Understood." I grin. "So, in the spirit of open communication, I would like to know exactly how slow. When would you like to go out again?"

"Give me a couple of days?" Jade offers, "How about Saturday?"

Reluctantly, I leave Jade to her writing. I plan to meet with the guys at our safe house, which is a few miles from Jade's. She lives on the border of the supernatural side of town, not that she realizes it.

Between all our magical wardings, the safe house is

reasonably secure. We don't have much here, as we set this up for emergency use only. But we have a safe place to rest our heads.

I don't go directly to our hideout, since I worry that whoever is watching her could also be following me. I must drive all over town until I'm certain I haven't been tailed.

Pulling up to the single-story large ranch-style house, I appreciate how non-assuming it appears. From the outside, you wouldn't expect some of the deadliest supes reside here. The trimmed yard is basic and unremarkable. The house gives off grandmotherly vibes from the curb.

But inside, it's sparsely decorated and filled with weapons. Maxum invested in the basic furnishing of comfy couches and recliners. All five bedrooms have king-sized beds because we're all big guys, and in the past, we sometimes slept together.

If I hadn't been over at Jade's the last few days, I might have risked bringing more stuff from my house. But as it is, all I have is not much more than what was in my go-bag when Osen died.

When I walk in the wide door, all three guys give me a disappointed look.

"What?" I snap.

Surprisingly, it's Flint, the taciturn gargoyle who lectures me. "What are you doing with her? Your actions are dangerous, no matter how you look at this situation."

"Dangerous for who?" I growl.

"For both of you," he says, his tone even. "You know what your curse can do."

"Jade is in real danger, but not from me," I tell him.

"What do you mean?" Maxum's voice is tight and strained. He doesn't want to admit it, but he's soft for our sweet witch.

"Her ex is a threat. I'm starting to believe that Rob might be a warlock."

Calder throws his arms up in the air in exasperation. "Is she that dumb? How can she really be that ignorant of the supernatural world if she was fucking a warlock?"

I snarl again at the idea of that male's hands on her.

After a deep breath, I suggest, "Maybe he was able to hide it from her just as we can?"

"But why?" Calder prods. "It makes no sense for a warlock to hide his nature, to be with a weak witch. Witches outnumber their male counterparts. He would have his pick. So either your witch is more powerful than you can perceive, or this wanker is nothing but a normal, everyday human dickhead."

Maxum adds, "They're a dime a dozen."

I've been wondering what Rob's angle was in all this. "Perhaps he used her for her mediumship skills? Or maybe she had more magic before he came into her life? We know some supes are able to drain magical beings of their magic."

"Has he threatened her?" Maxum asks.

"Yeah, sort of. Rob sent Jade a message 'to be careful who she dated'... after her date with you. Which means he was somehow watching. It also indicates to me he might have recognized who or what you are."

"That doesn't mean we have to get involved," Calder huffs.

I notice the gargoyle is quiet. He's a protector by nature, so he won't like it if she's in danger. If I can just get him on my side...

"So what the hell are you suggesting, lil' doggie?" Maxum asks and crosses his arms, his classic demon move, closing me off before I can get out my idea.

"That we monitor her... like I've been doing."

"You mean fucking her?" Maxum raises an eyebrow. "You know I can smell her scent all over you."

"I didn't fuck her," I snarl.

"Yeah, I know." Maxum grunts. "Because if you did, I'd smell her blood from you ripping her to shreds, since you can't control your curse."

The guys know what could happen if I have sex.

"If you're going to kill her with your out-of-control dick, can we just get it over with?" Calder groans. "We have bigger fish to catch. We don't have the resources for you to do your pet play kink."

I growl at him.

The fucking phoenix shouldn't be poking me right now. I'm riding the edge with all this talk about me walking away from Jade.

"Does she put a collar on you, then tell you to be a good boy and lick her cunt?" he jabs again.

Maxum laughs and says to Calder, "You're just jealous, little bird."

He's probably not wrong. Calder hasn't been able to be with someone in this incarnation. His last death really fucked him up. Before that? He was a bit of a player.

"Can we just check this guy Rob out to see if he's got magic?" I hand Maxum the paper where I jotted down the information and the half-destroyed picture of Rob I pulled out of Jade's trash. "If he's a warlock, maybe you get to kill him for funsies."

Maxum gives me a wry grin. "And take out your competition for you?" he jokes.

"And your competition," I say to rile him up.

Maxum doesn't want to want her, but I'm not as oblivious as Flint usually is.

That poor gargoyle doesn't seem to understand romance or sex at all.

But he knows loss.

We all do.

Maxum grumbles. "So what? She has a feisty attitude, a fuckable ass, and a fascinating brain I don't want to scramble. That doesn't mean I'm interested in going steady."

I shake my head at his deflection. "I don't think people know what the phrase 'going steady' means anymore."

"It's not my fault the world moves too fast," Maxum mutters and glances at the paper with Rob's details. "I'll investigate this turkey because it makes sense to do that—for us." He becomes serious and stares into my eyes. It's not something he usually does because of my inner monster. "Prepare yourself. She might not be as innocent as she appears."

"I will not let my guard down," I promise.

*That's a damn lie.*

I've already done that.

# 18

# BACKGROUND CHECK

MAXUM

*I* have very few mortal human contacts. There are the rare non-supes who are not complete and utter nitwits.

I collect the good ones as if they are golden tickets to a chocolate factory.

Chocolate and brain scrambling are my small pleasures in life—my weaknesses. Deal with it.

After hundreds of years in the realms, I've realized decent and dependable people are like unicorns... so hard to find that they might as well be only a myth.

Almost everyone I've known—supes, witches, creatures, or norms—has betrayed me at some point. It's a surprise when I haven't been ratted out or used. That's why my ragtag group is so precious to me. They might be a pain in my ass, but over and over, they have proven, even through torture, that they are loyal.

That's why I have to discover who killed Osen. I owe him

that. It's why I'm allowing Arran free rein to have his *puppy* love, just in the off chance something becomes of Osen's channeling through the witch.

Besides, this Rob sounds like a menace. Warlocks are often a menace.

So, maybe I will get to scramble some magical brains after all if he turns out to be a threat to us... or Jade.

Knocking on the door to what appears to be an abandoned warehouse, I wait impatiently for the humans to answer.

A scrappy-looking young female flings the door open and cocks her hip. Mal currently has blonde hair streaked with a variety of bright colors, making it look like a unicorn farted a rainbow on her head.

She crosses her arms and gives me a perturbed glare. Her big ovary energy is packed into a tiny package. I *almost* find it cute, except for all the smack talk she usually hands out when I swing by. Okay, all of it is adorable, like a sassy little cousin.

Mal knows I'm a supe, but not what kind, how powerful, or what damage I could do to her both mentally and physically without trying.

"What do you want, *orc*?" she asks. Her favorite game is seeing if I'll react to being called different supernatural species.

I give her nothing with the orc comment. So far, she's never guessed demon. If she does, I'll give her the reward of shocking the crap out of her with a full reveal. Well, not the full monty. Her husband wouldn't appreciate that.

"I need to get some info on a potential mark," I say. When she looks as if she wants to turn me away, I explain, "Arran's girlfriend has a bad news ex. I want to know how bad he is before she gets hurt." I don't mention that I might hurt Jade if I discover she's the bad news.

"This isn't about the ASO?" Mal bites her lip. She's a good egg, but she worries about her and her husband getting caught up in this supe-witch drama.

She is not wrong to be worried. If what our supernatural

seers have *visioned* is accurate, we will soon be dealing with the renewed vigor of ASO terrorist attacks on supes. And our human allies and assets will become targets.

Just when I thought we could have a moment to breathe with the missing supes situation over.

Mal grumbles, "You know I'm a softie when it comes to jerky exes, so if this is a ploy—"

"Even if it was a ploy, I only come to you when I'm worried. And I don't worry about much."

She looks me up and down—all six-feet-five of me—and nods. "Ugh. Fine." She waves me to come in, and behind us, she locks five different bolts for the industrial door. "Remember to stay away from our gear."

"I know the routine." I must stand almost all the way across the room to keep their computer equipment safe from my magic.

"There are rumors, Maxum," she says quietly as we take the metal stairs. "ASO is upping their attacks. Osen was probably the first of many supes who will be taken down."

Mal and her husband are part of the small population of humans who know about supes, magical beings, and the existence of other realms. Approximately five percent of the population knows about us, and most of them end up as the supernatural's intermediaries to the mortal realm when we aren't able to cover up our magic. These humans span the cross-section of society—from hackers and thieves to government officials and first responders like cops and EMTs. They help keep the secret safe from the general population.

"I've heard the same rumors," I acknowledge her concern. "Unfortunately, I believe it's true. I'm going to be dragged into another war."

"Shit." She shoves open a door and reveals Dwayne typing away at his console.

"Really, man?" He shakes his head. "You better not have been followed."

"I wasn't, and I have a full payment." I pull a huge roll of hundreds from my pocket.

Mal's eyes widen, then she narrows them. "I thought you said this was a basic background check."

"I don't know how deep it goes," I explain. "I suspect this dickhead might be connected to the supe world or ASO, or maybe he's just a solo dickhead warlock."

I hand her the cash, Rob's name and details, and sit on a worn-out couch, waiting for my answers.

"Maxum." Mal shakes her head. "Is a woman really in danger?"

"Yeah. She's in danger from me if she turns out to be an ASO or Witch Council spy. Or she could be in danger because her ex-boyfriend is an abusive asshat and a possible magic user. I hope she is in danger because she's ignorant of her witchy nature. Because that's an easy fix. I just tell her what she is."

"I don't think that will go over very well," Dwayne says as he takes the note and picture from Mal and types in the info. "Humans don't react well knowing there is all this magic shit."

He's right. I've seen it a thousand times. I can't even count how many times I've outed the magical world to a norm. They deny it no matter how I reveal it to them. I've even removed my glamour right in front of them and shown them my true form. And they somehow block it out or claim it's a trick.

Humans are magical in that way. They can section off their brains to believe any belief they want to hold on to. If it doesn't belong in their worldview, it doesn't exist. They can be amazing as well as frightening.

"Hmm," Dwayne says as he crinkles his brow while squinting at the computer screen. It isn't a small screen, so this piques my interest. "Robert Holden doesn't exist... not in this area. And the ones in this state don't match the picture here. I'm expanding my search country wide. But my guess is that he gave her a fake name."

Arran's photograph has come in handy.

"What about police reports? I believe she filed a restraining order."

"Nada. Zip. He doesn't exist under that name in any local records. I tried all the variations of his name, too."

"Okay. So what now?" I ask.

"Even this picture doesn't help much. Sure, I could run an image reversal search. But that's time-consuming and rarely delivers results without something else to narrow it down. Besides, this picture is half destroyed." Dwayne pushes away his keyboard and spins his office chair to look at me. "It's a dead end until I have something more from you." He grabs the wad of cash I had just paid and tosses it back to me. "No fee for this."

"No. Keep it." I catch the bundle and toss it on the coffee table in front of me before I get up. "Buy some protection spells from my contact. Do whatever you need to keep yourselves safe. If I find something more on this guy, I'll be back."

I storm down the warehouse's stairs and hear the little human female following me with her light steps.

"Maxum, hey?" Mal calls to slow me down since I'm able to take two steps at a time.

"What?" I toss over my shoulder but don't slow.

I'm pissed. Arran was right to be concerned. I hate it when that mutt is right.

He's going to rub it in my face.

Something's off with Jade and her ex. And I need to know if she's lying about her ex's identity or if he lied to her.

I want her to be innocent. Then maybe I can have a taste of the sweetness between her legs as well.

Why would a guy lie about his true name unless he had a big secret to hide?

Hell, *we* didn't even hide our actual names.

"Maxum!" Mal shouts, pulling me out of my thoughts as I'm about to burst through their main entry door.

Whoops. I suppose I should unlock it first.

"What?" I barely keep back the snarl in my voice as I spin to face her.

Mal doesn't even flinch. She's a tough cookie.

"She's important to you too, isn't she?" Mal asks.

"Huh?" I shake my head. "She might be wrapped up in something bigger than herself. But she could easily be at the center of it and is fooling me."

"I doubt many people fool you," she says, worry clear on her face. "When humans lie about their identities, it isn't like the supes... it usually means they are running from the law."

"I've been around a decade or two," I say... more like centuries. I know human games. "But I also haven't ruled out him being a supe yet either."

"Be careful out there. The brewery got hit last night. They think it's ASO."

I hadn't heard about that. I was too busy watching the witch's house with Arran snuggling up with her all night.

I tell myself I was out there to keep Arran safe. But it was also to see who might be watching her. And perhaps I wanted to be there to stop Arran if he were to go into berserker mode. I wouldn't let him hurt her.

But no one showed up last night. If there was someone else outside Jade's house last night, I didn't sense them. It will be interesting to hear if she had any more messages from the ex. It would mean he could slip past my guard.

A lingering thought passes through my mind that she's innocent, and we brought this all down on her head by assuming her a spy, but I let it go for now. There are too many unanswered questions to assume or dismiss any possibility.

*Jade still might be our enemy.*

I make my rounds throughout the city and hop through a portal to the fae realm to check in with my contacts there. No one has heard more about the incident with Osen or who is behind the ASO.

The Anti-Supernatural Organization has claimed a lot of attacks, but they hadn't claimed Osen for some reason. And nothing at the scene indicated their involvement. Actually, nothing at his death spot made sense. That's why we haven't ruled out the Witch Council and the extremists among them.

If the whispers are to be believed, ASO aren't witches at all, but possibly other supes.

Honestly, I don't think anything would surprise me anymore.

If I didn't know the horrific magical draining operation had been stopped, I might think it was the people responsible for that who completely sucked Osen's magic from his body.

But he didn't look like how those other victims looked. The others were nothing more than shriveled shells, and it took weeks for the process to kill the victims. Osen was just gone... all of his soul and magic. We even had a hellhound inspect the body to confirm what I felt. Nothing was left but the physical form.

From what Arran said, if Osen is possessing the witch, his spirit was confused and likely didn't know what happened.

As I burst through the front door of our safe house, Arran comes to attention and sits on the edge of the couch, waiting for my report.

"Well?" he asks when I don't immediately give him a news report. I've been dreading this all day.

I pour myself some demon-brewed whiskey. It's the only thing that can give my kind a buzz. Calder and Flint appear from their rooms to join us. After savoring the burning sensation of the liquor, I address my eager audience.

I'm curious about what they will make of this mess. "It doesn't appear that a Robert Holden exists around here."

"She lied!" Calder shouts.

"I don't think she lied," Arran defends her. "Unless she's

been acting this whole time, even in her sleep, she doesn't know I'm the dog. And she's afraid of Rob. I can smell her fear, even if she tries to brush off how bad it was with him. She showed no signs of lying when she talked about him. Her heart didn't quicken. She didn't perspire."

"It just means she's a psychopath!" Calder paces the room.

I find it interesting that he's more riled than normal. I would skim the surface of his mind to discover why, but he's the best at blocking me. Besides, he would sense the slightest prying.

Is he also confused about his feelings for the witch, and he's overcompensating?

Am I compensating? Do I like her?

I don't *not* like her.

Focus up, asshole.

"We need more from her about her ex. And I think we should tell her what she is and see how she reacts." I throw out the idea like a grenade, waiting for Arran to panic.

Arran glares at me. "You just want to fuck up my chances with her."

"You've already accomplished that all on your own." I roll my eyes. "You have no chance with her if she doesn't know what you are. What are you going to do if she accepts your beast and forgives you for spying on her? Will you eat her pussy for the rest of your relationship? And hope that your beast doesn't literally eat her pussy with a killing bite?"

Actually, licking her pussy doesn't sound like a terrible way to pass the time.

Flint fidgets uncomfortably. Damn that guy. He needs to get laid. Too bad he never will.

Arran doesn't snap back with a reply. He knows I'm not wrong. He'll want more. She'll want more. And he can't give that to her the way he is. And she won't understand why he's denying her unless she knows about his curse.

"If there were any other way…" I say as my half-ass apology. "But we need to confront her about supes and witches.

If she already knows about it, and not her fake book shit, then we can cut our losses. We eliminate her and move on."

"You mean to kill her if she's been lying about her ignorance?" Arran asks.

"Unfortunately."

He glowers at me. "And what if she *is* ignorant?"

"Well, she will know the truth, and she can embrace her magic. Likely, she'll be pissed off at us for everything we've done… like spying on her as a lost doggie." I raise my eyebrow and pour myself another glass of demon brew.

Arran's face turns red at that reminder. She won't want to be with him after that comes out.

"Fuck!" he shouts, and his beast ripples over his skin. He tosses a heavy recliner, and it flies into the wall. "She's going to reject me."

"I hate to tell you I told you so." I down the fiery liquid. "But I told you not to stay with her. Or pursue her."

He whips his head around and stalks toward me. He wants to unleash his beast. It's been riding on the surface for days now.

I can handle his attack. All three of us could survive his beast. It wouldn't be pleasant to feel his claws and fangs, but I heal quickly. Arran would be hard-pressed to hurt Flint. Calder is the most susceptible to his attack if it goes too far, but he would just reincarnate. Unfortunately, he loses a bit of himself each time.

Not that I expect it to come to death blows. But one never knows what to expect from berserkers—that's their intrinsic danger. Unpredictability. Sometimes, we can manage him. Other times, he goes off the rails.

I jut out my chin, inviting him to fight. "Hit me if you need to, but this is why you can't be around Jade anymore."

Arran stops in his tracks. Shame colors his expression.

Without warning, he shifts, tearing his clothes as he does.

Suprisingly, he is a massive wolf, and not in his monster form. He races from the house and into the night.

I wish I could ease his pain and give him words of hope. But none of us have been lucky in life or love, so the words would be empty.

And this is just the latest example of life kicking one of us in the balls.

## 19

---

## NOT AGAIN

JADE

*I*t pisses me off. I miss Arran and Beast. How can they have gotten under my skin so quickly?

I remind myself over and over, like a mantra: *I don't need the peen.*

A casual hookup might be perfect for now.

But shockingly, Arran seems interested in more. He looks like the type who would prefer a young, sexy underwear model on his arm rather than a middle-aged, curvy homebody.

He claims he wants an actual relationship with me?

However, I don't know if I can ever truly trust someone again. How can I let someone inside my heart after the way Rob treated me?

Deciding to go to bed early since I haven't been sleeping enough with these strange nightmares, I crawl into bed. A sense of foreboding weighs heavily on me.

That's never a good sign. I definitely believe in my intuition. I've had too many confirmed instances to ignore it.

Anxiety rises in me, and I know my life is going to be turned upside down soon.

Exhaustion finally takes me after laying awake for too long.

*And I have another mysterious dream…*

The guy from the bar, with the ice-blue eyes and smoldering gaze, stands in front of me. We are in a cheap motel room with two queen beds. A outdated table lamp casts a dim light around the shabby room.

The place is a mess. It has blankets tossed about. Random stuff, like food packages and weapons, covers all the tables and dressers. Discarded, torn clothes are piled on the bed.

"We can't stay holed up here much longer," Mr. Blue Eyes says. "They'll narrow down our positions soon enough."

"I know what we need to do, Calder," my male avatar grumbles. "But we have to wait for Maxum to show up again. He's the only one who has a secret safe house. Everywhere else has been compromised."

"If he hasn't returned from the Underworld by now, he might never," Calder says. He looks worried and runs his hands through his auburn hair nervously.

"No. Maxum will make it," I stroke his face, soothing him. "He's smarter than any of the shitheads there."

"If he doesn't come soon, we should go after him." Calder gestures with his hand at one of the beds. "Flint is almost recovered."

Hidden in the bulk, I see a massive arm poking out from what I assumed was only a pile of sheets and blankets. His figure was so still, I didn't realize it was a person. From the strange light skin coloring, I assume it's their friend, the one I imagine is a gargoyle. And I had seen him frozen like a statue in my last dream.

*Flint*—that's a funny name for me to come up with for a being made of stone. The subconscious works in weird ways.

"His recovery took longer than Maxum thought. The witches are getting stronger as we are getting weaker," Calder says.

"No. We are just noticing how weak we've become," my avatar says. "The spells that once would have barely bothered us are now easily knocking us down."

"How are you holding up?" Calder asks, reaching out for me before quickly pulling back. For some reason, he doesn't feel comfortable touching me... but at some point, he has been able to freely touch. Maybe they are no longer together romantically. But I can feel our heart-wrenching ache to reconnect.

My muscular arm reaches out and captures Calder by the back of the neck. I draw him closer until our lips are only an inch apart. This close, I see the hot blue flames in his irises. Calder is not ice at all, even if he often displays a cold exterior.

He is barely contained passion and a powder keg ready to go off. The blue is not of ice but of the hottest kind of fire.

"As much as I would like to fuck you, I'm not sure you can handle me right now," I say and lace my fingers into the back of his auburn hair, fisting it.

He groans and bucks his hips into mine. His hard cock is apparent as he grinds into me, seeking relief.

"I can handle it," he pleads. "I need you."

Just by his desperate look, I know he's in love with this person I'm supposed to be. I wish someone would look at me like that—just once.

"I love it when you beg for me... for my cock. You know what that does to me." My mouth crashes down on his, and we tangle tongues. I feel I'm holding back some part of me. Some kind of magic power.

Tugging on his hair, I move him away. "Strip. On the bed. Ass up."

Calder strips and snarks. "I know the drill."

"Stop your sass, or you don't get your relief," I threaten.

Not wanting to risk it, he snaps his mouth shut and crawls

up the bed, pressing his face into the mattress. He's propped up by his knees, delicious ass in the air.

I unbuckle my pants and pull my dick free, stroking it as I approach.

*Oh damn, having a dick is nice.*

My dreams or imagination never felt so real before.

From a pack on the dresser, I pull out lube and grease up my cock. Then I drizzle some over Calder's asshole, and he sucks in a breath.

"I'm not going to loosen you up," I warn.

"Goddess, dammit." He tenses and then relaxes. His breathing becomes ragged as I position myself behind him.

I line up my sizable cock to his puckered hole. My vision dims as if my eyes are half closed.

Calder is unusually still as I sink into him. The only reason I know he's felt my invasion is from a moan he lets out.

I finally bottom out, *pun intended*. Grunting my satisfaction, I can't get over the intense realism of this dream.

"You miss this?" I ask. "You miss me dominating you?"

"I'm addicted to your touch," Calder confesses. "Use me if you must. But touch me. Please."

Without warning, I pump into his ass.

Calder remains motionless, with only his grunts and moans to encourage me to continue. My hands skim over his gorgeous flesh—his muscular back, his hips, his chest. I almost feel as if I could consume him with just this simple act. I want to consume him, make him mine completely, but I can't do that.

When I feel my peak is imminent, I release my hold on his hips. One hand brushes down his spine. Calder sounds as if he'll come from that simple gesture.

I wrap my other arm around to his front and finally take his girthy length in my hand.

The residual lube aids in my ministrations as I pump him slowly.

"Do you like that, my sweet bird?" I coo.

As I fondle his balls, Calder whimpers, "Yes."

I pump him faster, and I feel his testicles draw up. His energy swirls around my cock. Something akin to pure electricity tingles up my spine. It's as if I'm empowered by my partner's pleasure.

"Come for me," I command.

He spills his seed with a shout.

I continue to stroke him with the same rhythm as I finish in his ass. He pulses around my cock, milking me with his orgasm.

As I unload into him, my whole body arches back and trembles.

When I'm spent, I fall forward, and press my forehead to his back. In a moment of affection, I give Calder a kiss.

"That was fucking hell," the gargoyle grumbles from the other bed. "Couldn't you get your own room?"

"This is our room," Calder sasses.

"I just wanted to show you what you're missing," I taunt as I unashamedly free myself from Calder's tight ass.

*Geezus, I feel bad for Flint. He didn't like this.*

The man I'm dreaming I am becomes aware of me again, and the scene freezes in the moment. *"Witch? Did you enjoy the show?"* he asks with an edge to his voice.

"I didn't mean to… I just was here."

*"And you couldn't help yourself?"* he sounds a bit amused.

"This is my dream. I can do what I want," I argue.

*"No. These are my memories, and you are invading my sacred time with my lovers."*

"This is so weird," I mumble.

*"I'm tired of you poking into my thoughts."* He snarls. *"There is only one explanation as to why I'm connected to you. And I think I know what it is. You should have exorcised me when you had the chance. Good night, little witch."*

Suddenly, I'm kicked out of the motel room and stuck in complete darkness.

I try to will myself to wake up, but I can't.

# 20

## ALL WRONG

ARRAN

*I* shift and run the fifteen miles to my old house. My wolf gets there faster than I could in my other form. I needed to get out of the safe house. I needed to be alone and anywhere but there. I wanted to run to Jade, take her in my arms, and claim her mouth, her heart, and her body. But with Maxum's reminder, I realize my affections would be rejected when she knew the truth.

Out of habit or instinct, I stop a block away from my home and call upon my senses to see if any witches or supes are lying in wait for me. When I don't sense anyone watching, I slowly approach. My nose to the wind, I'm hoping I don't scent anyone in my space.

Finally, I shift back to my human form as I slip in through the hidden entrance on the side of my home. I double-check my senses aren't on the fritz by peeking in each room. Not that it's a large house. It's only a two-bedroom, one-bath of utter bachelor chaos. As soon as I'm sure I'm alone, I chug a large glass of water.

The fridge reveals that I'm not much better than Jade when it comes to taking care of myself. At least I have a stale loaf of bread in the fridge. I make myself a sloppy peanut butter and jelly and scarf it down.

I feel completely lost as I stand nude, forcing down the crappy meal. The sandwich sits in my gut like a brick. Pacing the tired, outdated kitchen, and I wish I was in my witch's place. But she's already pushing me away, and she doesn't even know all the reasons she should.

I'm pissed at Maxum. But he's right. We need to tell Jade the truth.

She should know about her true nature and about what I am. We all are. That Osen has been possessing her.

I have no right to prevent her from this knowledge, even if it will most definitely cost me my relationship with her. Our future.

I give the safe house landline a call.

Thankfully, it's Flint who answers.

"Can you come get me?" I ask. "I'm at my place."

"You okay?" His deep, grumbly voice carries a lot of concern for me.

I appreciate it and hate it in equal measure. I hate being so damned sensitive right now. But it's as if the threat of losing Jade has me more riled than I've been in years—since I was cursed.

"No. I'm not okay," I sigh. "But Maxum's right. Jade should be told what's really going on."

"I'll be there in a few minutes, brother," Flint says. He only calls me that when I need to be reminded that we're a family—a pack.

I dress in my cheap, tear-away clothes, which are pretty much all I have anymore. It's probably for the best. I have a terrible feeling that I will go into full beast mode and run off when she rejects me.

Flint pulls up in the Rambler. I chuckle every time I see him in a car. He always looks too big to fit inside properly.

Checking down the street, both ways, I put my nose in the air and there's no scent of anyone unfamiliar in the neighborhood.

Sliding into the passenger seat, I grimace at my gargoyle friend.

Flint gives me an empathetic nod. "You should all listen to me. Relationships aren't worth the grief."

I don't argue, because I don't want to get into it with him.

He has his reasons for feeling that way. For myself, I was hoping Jade would be different. That she would be the one who turned my lousy luck around. I hoped, even though she's a witch, we could have moved past that hurdle.

But that was the impulsive part of me that doesn't think things through. To be fair, that is pretty much my whole personality.

Maxum calls me foolish. Osen used to call me reckless. I'd say I'm spontaneous.

We're all correct.

Flint is pulling up behind Jade's green vintage Mustang much faster than I'm ready for. It's later than polite to drop by —nine-thirty at night.

"You sure?" Flint asks. "If she is tricking us and you call out her witchy nature, she might hex you. Or worse."

"If she does, I deserve it. I tricked her into thinking I was a dog. I shouldn't have let the ruse go on like that."

"The problem is you had intimate relations with her before telling her what you are," he reminds me.

I turn my head so I can roll my eyes. This guy and his awkwardness toward sex. But he's called out my unacceptable behavior. "Yeah. I fucked up, and now I'm about to pay for it."

"Should I go inside with you?" Flint asks, his large hand on the door handle, ready to jump out instantly—to follow me into the witch's lair.

"No. It might make her more nervous, having someone there she doesn't know at all."

He nods, but looks a bit disappointed. Is he interested in Jade, too?

*Nah, impossible.*

Not with his history.

His stubbornness.

*Not the 400-year-old virgin.*

Maybe he just wants to help me through this.

I knock on her door, but no one answers.

Now that I'm closer, I can peek past the blackout curtains to see that the lights in her house are off. Fuck. I will just have to fret until I come back in the morning. I won't be sleeping much tonight.

Then the curtains pull back briefly as someone checks who is out here. There isn't much light on the porch, so I'm surprised when her door opens without the porch light coming on.

This alone puts me on edge. I don't know Jade very well, but this doesn't seem like a move she would make. Not with her ex allegedly stalking her. Not with how freaked out she's been.

Unless she has her gun pointed at my heart right now.

I realize too late that I should step back.

Before I can react, a hand reaches out from the open door and yanks me inside.

I'm pushed against the wall. The wind is knocked out of me with the force of it. Whoever is attacking me is strong.

I stop panicking and see who my attacker is. I'm in shock.

"Jade?"

She's holding me against the wall with one hand fisted in my shirt's collar.

I quickly glance down, and she isn't holding a gun in the other hand. Thank fuck.

"Nope. Guess again," she answers in a deeper, more combative tone. And a faint accent that I recognize.

"Osen?" I grab her wrist, but not tight enough to hurt her human flesh. "Let go of me!" I snap because the longer he holds his aggression, the more my beast wants to be unleashed. Maybe that's what he wants. "I won't hurt Jade," I promise. "So stop provoking me, dickwad."

He lets me go with a shove, turns away, and paces the room. "This witch is somehow sifting through my memories, searching for names and faces of the people who are working to eliminate the ASO. She's a damned spy, and I'm trapped inside her."

"I don't think she realizes the dreams are real... that they are your memories."

"It's all an act," he says with certainty.

The confidence in his answer makes my heart drop into the acid pit of my stomach. Has he seen Jade's mind and uncovered her innocence as a lie?

But I refuse to believe that about her.

If it's true, she's dead. Not by my hand. I could no longer do the deed. But Calder has been itching for a reason. He would snap her neck in a heartbeat.

"How do you know it's an act?" I ask. "What proof do you have?"

"It's obvious!" he shouts, pulling on her long, silver-threaded hair in angst. "She ensnared my soul. I can't move on. I can't rest. No, she makes me relive all my memories—all my failures."

It sounds more like his own guilt is making him relive his past. I don't see the kindhearted woman I know doing that to him... not on purpose, at least.

"I don't think she means to keep your soul. She's been distressed about what she considers to be dreams."

"She's a witch! That's all we need to know." He charges at

me and gets in my face. With his spirit invading her entirely, I can almost see his masculine features overlaid on hers.

He is the most attractive and charming man I've ever known, but he now is downright demented. He was always obsessive… but now?

My heart aches for his condition, but he's not sane. And I won't have him hurting her or convincing the other guys to hurt her.

"Kill her so I can be free," he begs of me. "You'll be safe."

"She may be a witch, but she's not my enemy." I hold my hands up in surrender so he knows that I don't intend to hurt Jade.

"You really care about her, don't you?" Osen steps back, disgust written all over her face. "Enough to betray me? Me?!"

"I don't want her hurt," I agree, my voice soft.

"Even if she wants to kill us?" he asks.

Flint's voice rumbles from the open door. "We don't know that she has any ill intent. She doesn't feel like a threat to me. I would sense that much."

Osen huffs and falls back on the couch, sighing with defeat, giving up the fight a bit. We all know Flint's intuition about threats supersedes all of our senses, even Maxum's. It's built into a gargoyle's basic and primal nature.

Jade's hand rubs her face in a very Osen way. He grumbles, "You sure, Flint?"

"Yeah. There's danger around her, though." Flint steps into the house. "You're hurting the witch—draining her. Aren't you?"

Osen pshaws and waves him off. "Not you too."

"I don't like to see innocents hurting. I feel it in my own soul." Flint frowns. "If you're going to stay connected to her, you need to do so in a way that you don't harm her any more than you have."

Thank Goddess, it's Flint here telling Osen to do this. Because my request wouldn't be so kind and even-keeled.

"How do you have so much control over Jade's body?" I ask, since he barely seemed to be able to move before when he possessed her.

"I... I just took over. I've been feeding off her emotions, I think. It's helping me remember." Osen shakes their head as if confused.

"Then she can help you remember who killed you," I say. "But you know as well as I do that you don't have to hurt her to feed."

"Why should I be gentle?" He huffs. "She was spying on my memories, so I punished her. Pushed her into a corner of her mind."

That doesn't sound good. "She wouldn't be able to see your memories if you hadn't attached yourself to her."

"But *how* am I attached? I didn't do it. Why would I pick some random *witch*?" Osen puts her hands in front of her face and stares at them. "It makes no sense. I can't remember my death, and then I was attached to her. I don't think I *can* let go. I've tried."

"Are you suggesting someone created a bond between you two?" Flint stands in front of Osen, more intrigued by this claim.

"Have you all not been paying attention?" Osen snaps. He's more agitated than when he was alive, which is saying something. He had a temper. "I told you she had a hold on me. She must be lying about her ignorance."

"You need to back off, and we will watch her for signs of her involvement." I doubt he'll listen to me, as he often brushes my advice aside.

He surprises me and agrees. "Yes. To see who is working with her." He nods, thinking I'm devious.

Actually, it's to see who might be *using* her.

My plans to reveal the supernatural world must be delayed. I can't jeopardize our relationship and her pushing me out of her life because I betrayed her trust. She might need my

163

protection. And I need to prove to Osen that she isn't what he believes she is.

I need to stay close.

# SPLITTING FUR

## JADE

*I* wake up at nine in the morning feeling like I haven't slept at all.

My dreams last night were even more disturbing. I wish I could shake them. But this latest character has taken over my mind and my dreams.

I have no idea why I've created this crazy asshole as the dead friend of the guys from the bar, but I don't always have control over my imagination and muse.

Maybe it's my subconscious trying to justify not developing a relationship with Arran.

I've been lured into a sense of peace over the last few months. I haven't had as many disturbing dreams since Rob left, and I sometimes wonder if he had subconsciously encouraged the horrible dreams by being overly interested in them. It seemed to be one of the only things about me he was interested in.

Now, I know he's just a cruel fuckhead and enjoyed making me suffer.

So I wonder, why have the dreams returned now?

It's been several months since I ended it with him, and he's finally left me alone... or so I thought. But apparently, as his email would indicate, he hasn't completely exited my life.

I sway on my feet when I drag myself out of bed to use the bathroom. My vision spins. I stagger to the bathroom door frame and brace myself. Touching my forehead, I don't feel like I have a fever. And I don't have chills, per se. But my body doesn't feel right.

Am I sick?

I don't get sick often. Well, not until I met Rob, now that I think of it.

Being ill has been so rare for me that I've only been to the doctor a few times for unusual stuff. Although, when I think back on my health, it was only after I hooked up with Rob that I began to have any health issues. Nothing was ever dire enough to go to the hospital, but I was often under a strange malaise.

Why had I not realized that until now?

I suppose I brushed it off as depression from being in a crappy relationship or getting older.

This sensation feels like that funk, but several times more intense.

The fog begins to clear, just enough for me to do my business and wander to the kitchen to make my morning coffee.

I pause when I walk into the living room on my way to the kitchen.

Why does it feel like someone was here? Am I being paranoid?

I had the same eerie feeling after I broke up with Rob. I often had a nagging sensation that he had been in my space when I wasn't around or while I was sleeping.

One night... he came back. Fortunately, I woke up. It's why I lock my bedroom door.

That's why I bought a gun. I needed to feel safe. Not that it did all that much to make me feel safe.

Just because I can whack my side characters and torture my main characters with abandon doesn't mean I could easily pull the trigger if Rob were to attack me. I'd do it if it came down to him or me. But I worry I'd hesitate.

The idea of having Arran as a bodyguard sounds more appealing by the minute. I don't feel I have enough strength to hold a gun or fight someone off.

Yet, I like to think of myself as a strong, independent person. I've never enjoyed relying on people, and I don't want to start now. Jumping into relationships too quickly gets me into trouble. I've learned my lesson.

After I feed and give some attention to my fur babies, I practically fall asleep in there, holding my guinea pig as we snuggle. For some reason, my animals ground me.

Animals have healing in their very souls.

I'm jostled out of my napping with my phone ringing in my pocket. I fish it out of my sweatpants and see it's the number Arran had given me before. Interesting, I hadn't given him mine. I suppose he was able to hunt it down with his professional security skills.

"Hello?" I answer, sounding curious, like I don't know who it could be.

"Jade? It's me, Arran." He sounds sheepish. "Hey. I'm sorry I looked up your number, but I didn't want to invade your space and knock on your door whenever I wanted to talk."

"So, you invade my privacy in a brand new way?" I'm not that upset, but I need to state my boundaries. It's also a test to see how frustrated he gets with me stating them.

"Yeah. I shouldn't have done it. But I was worried about you," he sounds contrite, so I'll let it slide.

"Why are you worried?" I ask. I get up, head to the living room, and peek through the window, glancing up and down the street to see if he's in his truck, watching me from the street.

"I have a bad feeling about your ex," he says.

I roll my eyes, because that is a sort of weak excuse. "That's been established."

"So, I know you want us to take this relationship slowly. And I want to honor that, but please, will you call me if something feels off or something happens? Anything at all," he asks.

I realize my mistake... I'm putting Arran in harm's way. I need to end this now.

"I appreciate you wanting to look into Rob. But with him emailing me about going to brunch with Maxum, I can't get into a serious relationship right now. I'm sorry. I shouldn't have encouraged something between us the other night. Rob's dangerous. And I don't want to see you get hurt."

"Hey, sweetheart," he says softly. "I understand you aren't ready for a committed relationship. But I just want to be there for you." He sighs quietly. "But you shouldn't let Rob stop you from living your life. And if you wanted to date other people while we got to know each other, I wouldn't try to stop you. Maybe he'll back off if you have me and my friends around."

*Where is this coming from?*

He almost sounds... *hopeful*. Does he want me to hook up with Maxum or one of his other friends?

Are my dreams picking up on the fact that their group has an open sexual dynamic with each other?

Have I stumbled onto a free-range, all-male polycule?

*Have I stumbled upon a sausage queen's dream team?*

I grow heated between my thighs, thinking of Arran and Maxum fucking and begging me to join in. "Are *you* with someone else?" I ask.

"Not at the moment," he says with a hint of sadness.

Hmm. I'll wonder what that means later. I really need to pull away from Arran and his friends, so I won't be lured in with the fantasy where I'm spit-roasted by his buddies while he looks on.

Arran clears his throat and says, "Uh, back to why I'm worried... I have new information about Rob. I had a security associate look him up, and..." He trails off as though he doesn't want to tell me.

"And?" I prompt, my nerves vibrating with tension.

"Robert Holden doesn't exist... not with that name. Not in this state."

I collapse on my couch, my mouth dropping open. I cover my face and sit with that plot twist.

"Do you have anything more for me to find out who he really is?" Arran pauses, "Like maybe a workplace? Any relative's names? A copy of his ID, birth certificate, or passport?" He chuckles darkly with the last few suggestions.

"No..." My mind spins back to when I was with Rob. "But... I filed police reports."

"No police reports came up in the search," Arran informs me. "You're right. He must be well-connected."

"Well, shit." I wish Arran or Beast were here with me so I could hold on to them. Both would be awesome.

"Do you remember where he worked?" he asks.

A fog settles over my mind. Details about his past seem far away, as if I should know them, but they evade me. "He... uh, he was a real estate agent," I say, more as a question than a statement. I chuckle uncomfortably. "But every third person in California is a real estate agent."

Arran hums without amusement at my joke. "Okay. What about his last known address?"

"I don't remember going to his place... ever." This fact only seems odd now. "He just always showed up here."

"Friends' names?" he prompts.

When I try to recall his friends' names, I realize now I only got their first names.

My blood runs cold with fear. Am I losing my mind? "How could I not have known anything about Rob? I'm usually too curious for my own good."

"Nothing about his original hometown?" Arran pushes me to remember something he can work with.

"I think he said he always lived in the area." I shake my head, trying to rattle my brain into working. Panic begins to rise inside me, and it's like I can't trust my own mind or senses. What am I doing with Arran? He might be another creep. "Why are details about him so vague?" I ask, mostly of myself.

"I don't know, Jade." He sounds utterly concerned.

Unfortunately, I have a problem to deal with before I can explore things with Arran… and-or his friends. "I should probably call the cops about Rob."

"The cops are probably in his back pocket," Arran reminds me.

"Okay, fine. I'll let you know if something weird happens." I bite my lip, wondering if I should tell him about this morning. "I didn't feel right when I woke up. Like I was up all night partying, but it's been a while since I've done that."

"Oh?" He pauses and then says, "Anything else?"

"My nightmares have been getting crazier." I notice my couch pillow isn't in the spot I left it after cleaning up when Arran left yesterday. But my memory must be failing me. "I have this strange feeling that someone was in my house last night. But I can't believe that's true."

"You shouldn't dismiss your feelings," Arran says with tightness in his tone. Maybe he's worried that Rob is stalking me, maybe even breaking in. "Is it okay if my friends or I are in the area if we drive by and check the neighborhood out?"

"I guess." With him giving my fears validation, my anxiety ramps up more. "You think that's necessary?"

"I'd rather be safe than sorry. I'd rather be inside with you, but I totally understand your need for space… especially after hearing about Rob," Arran's voice softens. "I just want you to be safe. I care about you."

"You were going to drive by my house anyway, weren't you?"

"Maybe." He sucks in a breath, and I can almost hear him squirm over the phone. "I'm not doing great with boundaries because my protective side is being triggered."

"I get it." This sucks. I don't enjoy feeling out of control. But I'd rather Arran have my back than something horrific happens to me. "Is Maxum one of the people who will be swinging by?"

"Is that okay?" he asks, then quickly adds, "I don't expect him to be a jerk to you again. Well, at least not as bad as he was before."

I grin at that. I wonder if Arran told him to back off. Maybe Maxum realizes he was being a wanker.

"It's fine, but let Maxum know I won't put up with his sassy mouth," I taunt.

I hear a deep grumble in the background. Oh, my god…

"Is he there?" I say in a quieter tone.

"He's my roommate, so yeah, he heard. Maxum has exceptional hearing and is just as inquisitive as you are," Arran says with some restrained amusement.

"I wasn't spying," Maxum protests. "It's not my fault she talks so loud."

I know I didn't say it *that* loud.

"My threat still stands." I bluff. "I'll give it right back to him, if he gives me trouble."

"Promises, promises," I hear Maxum mutter.

A chill runs up my spine and into my low belly. But there is no way Maxum is into me too. I hate that Maxum has to be so sexy. If Arran and I end up together, his friends will torment me with their hotness.

There are worse ways to be tortured, though. My mind plays out fantasies of them tying me up and pleasuring me to the point of losing my mind. In a fun way this time.

"Jade?" Arran calls, probably not for the first time.

"Uh. Yeah?" I blush, as if he can read my thoughts.

"Do you think I can come by and see you soon?" His voice is so vulnerable.

Against my better judgment, because of my obviously horrible dating sense and the lingering issue with Rob, I give in a bit. "I'm not feeling great now. Can you check back in with me tomorrow, and maybe we can plan something then?"

"Of course, and be careful."

"Will do," I say and hang up.

Some spidey sense tells me there is much more to Arran, but I can't figure out what that might be.

I don't believe he wants to hurt me though. And that is what matters—for now.

My hopes aren't high that this is a long-term relationship, but he might have come into my life just when I needed a protector.

Whatever runs this universe might be throwing me a bone here—literally and figuratively. I'm going to bite down and hold on for as long as it makes sense.

I stand by the window and peek through the crack in the curtains. The blinding California sun lights up the scene outside. You would think the land filled with sunshine wouldn't have so much darkness, but it seems that there's always a balance.

I wish Beast was with me now. I wonder if he had sensed my need that night, as animals often do, and that's why he found me.

Or maybe humans just put way too much importance on circumstances.

I don't care if I'm doing that, because I like the world a lot more when the crazy stuff that happens has meaning.

After making my chai tea, I head into my writing cave, and the words flow, mostly from the strange dreams I've been having.

Can one plagiarize their own dreams?

I don't know, but I almost feel guilty writing out the hot hotel sex my avatar had with Calder.

## 22

---

## BETRAYED

FLINT

*I* won't lie. The odd little witch intrigues me.

She has peeked out several times to catch one of us, or maybe her ex, driving by. But she hasn't seen me, standing across the street yet.

Gargoyles have illusion magic. We can disappear into almost any background—like a chameleon or an octopus. A gargoyle can be so still it seems as though they aren't alive. Most people don't look beyond the obvious human form or movement to catch their eye. So I look to be just another inanimate object while I stand here. And yes, gargoyles can also shift into our actual stone forms when we need to protect ourselves from attack.

Our vision is also better than most supes. Perhaps it's to make up for our diminished sense of smell.

With my visual acuity, I clearly see Jade's hazel-green eyes while they pause their search when she gets to my general location. Can she sense my presence?

Would she panic if I were to drop my camouflage and show her my true form?

Arran and Maxum tell me she reads and writes about supernaturals. But it's one thing to dream up an image and another to have it standing in front of you. She wouldn't want to see a monster appear before her eyes in her quiet neighborhood, watching her.

As our gazes almost seem to lock across the street, she appears to be sensitive, gentle, and perhaps inquisitive enough to want to know a person under their stone.

Few have ever wanted to know me. Even my circle of friends don't know me as well as they think they do. Yes, they know the reason for my refusal to engage in intimate relations. But none of them know the details. No one asks how it feels to be this lonely. They claim loneliness, but they have had the comfort of each other's embrace… of another's touch. The only physical contact I've had in four hundred years has been in battle. And that certainly doesn't count.

My sexual nature, if I have one, has never stirred. But I sometimes crave to feel the soft touch of someone who feels connected to me.

Arran has that same craving with this witch. And I have to admit, I understand his attraction. She has appealing features and qualities.

Her hair looks silky soft with its streaks of silver, and I want to see how it feels in my hands. I never would touch a female… not again. Not even if I lived another four hundred years. I won't do that.

Not that she would accept my touch.

Arran teased me that she wrote about how attractive I was, but she only saw my human glamour. I'm not as pretty as my true self—not at all.

My monstrous appearance would frighten her.

Real gargoyles, living ones, are so rare that they frighten most of the supernatural world. Many supes and witches don't know what to make of my abilities. Most supes prefer the etheric beauty of their own faekind. To them, I'm an abomination.

She is too beautiful for me to claim. Other than her full curves, Jade has the look of a half-fae. She has a beauty that glows. Her clumsiness or the small laugh lines around her eyes and mouth only enhance her attractiveness. She's perfectly imperfect.

Not that I'm interested in pursuing her. It's not like she would see me as a compatible mate anyway.

No one does or should. I don't fit in with witches *or* supernaturals from Fae or the Underworld.

I am *other*.

I had always figured I would never fit in anywhere until I met Maxum.

He accepted me. Then the others did too. We are all outsiders in our own way.

Calder is almost as rare as I am. And Arran is one of a kind with his beast… that we are aware of.

Maxum himself doesn't fit in with his fellow demons, or supernaturals, for that matter. Most supernaturals rarely trust him just because of his species—never mind that he's been a more positive influence in the supernatural community than most. His own demonkind can't understand his desire to make the realms a better place.

If she really is ignorant of her witchhood, then when Jade discovers her true nature, she will probably feel like an outcast too. The witch won't be part of the human community anymore. She won't really be part of the witch world, either. She probably already feels like an outsider, sensing she isn't quite like her human friends.

I don't get the sense she means to be a threat to us, but danger surrounds her. We could be hit with the fallout from the situation going on with her ex.

Arran has entangled his emotions, and I worry for him. But

I'm not in danger of doing that, so I must be the one to keep a clear head about her.

Calder claims he doesn't want to be near the witch. However, I believe he finds her form attractive, and that's why he resists her so vehemently. Although, I understand his hesitation to go near her given his traumatic past with a witch.

I've been sitting here the entire day, just watching her place. A few times, I sensed a magical being, but that was in a passing car, but nothing that appeared suspicious.

Fortunately, she lives on a corner lot, so I can also watch her backyard from my vantage point.

No one has attempted to enter her yard or approach the front porch.

One of the guys is due to relieve me of duty for an hour or two so I can go home to eat and rest. I need little sleep or food, but maintaining this level of camouflage has been draining my magic.

Not only am I hiding from the witch so she doesn't get upset by my constant presence, but I'm also making it appear the way is clear to her house.

The setting sun is casting a warm glow over the world. Contentment settles in the hard bones of my primal nature. My ancestors were primarily nocturnal creatures, and most of my kind are still more active at night. I've learned to be flexible with my patterns since I've chosen a pack outside of my kind.

Twilight is my favorite time of day—the in-between time when all things are possible. Magic works differently at twilight and dawn. It's perfect for illusionists like me.

Speaking of illusions... a man is walking up to the witch's front door, using an invisibility spell of his own. A magical cloak around him compels a casual observer to turn away and forget his presence.

I, however, am not a casual observer. I'm a gargoyle. We see beyond that sort of magic. It's Rob, her ex.

Itching to move closer, I want to hear how the witch will

respond to his arrival. Yet, if I do, someone might see me lurking. Quickly, I cast my senses out to see if this male visitor has a companion waiting in the wings.

After a brief wait, the witch opens her door. I hear her ask, "Why are you here?"

"We need to talk," Rob says, his voice commanding.

"Then let's talk," she says and opens the door, stepping aside to allow him entry.

*Stars and Stone.* Why would she do that?

I thought she was supposed to be afraid of Rob. But I sensed no fear from her... none at all.

Something isn't right.

I'm on edge since I can't hear what's being said. I don't think even Arran or Maxum could listen in at this distance.

*Is the witch betraying us?*

I can't say for sure, but this doesn't look good. And I'm not pleased that she somehow tricked me. I didn't suspect this at all. If she is working for the witches or the ASO, it will crush Arran. She will die, possibly by Arran's hand. Calder would definitely eliminate her.

Just as I'm ready to bolt across the street, Arran's wolf form comes trotting up as if summoned. He's carrying a small bag in his mouth.

"Don't shift yet," I tell him. "I have some bad news."

He tilts his head, indicating for me to explain.

"Some middle-aged average-looking male just was invited inside. He looked like Rob's picture. He wanted to *talk* with her." I frown. "It almost seemed like she was supposed to report what she discovered."

Arran snarls. Ignoring my advice to stay in his shifter form, he steps around the cover of the house behind a large shrub and shifts. "You sure it was Rob?"

"He was using a cloaking spell to deflect attention, but I believe I saw his true face."

"And she just let him in?" Arran growls the question.

"I'm sorry. I really thought she was innocent. But if he was an abusive ex-boyfriend, as she claims, why would she let him inside without a hint of fear?"

"It doesn't make sense."

"No. It doesn't," I say, "Unless—"

We both say it together, "Osen?"

"Or does Rob have some spell on her?" Arran suggests.

"She's compromised… no matter what," I say aloud, so we can solve this riddle. "It was clear that Rob assumed he could just come over. She'd let him in without argument or hesitation. Something nefarious is going on."

When her door slowly opens, I duck behind the corner of the house I've been stationed next to and turn essentially invisible.

Arran peeks around my body.

The guy we assume is Rob shuts the door behind him and hurries away. Not quite running, but only slow enough not to draw unwanted attention.

"Follow him," Arran orders. "I'll check in on the witch."

This doesn't sound good for her.

She's back to being *the witch* in his mind. I hope she survives what wrath his beast intends to unleash.

As soon as my wings catch air, I soar far above the street to keep an eye on Rob—or whatever his real name is.

My first instinct is to rend his arms from his body—perhaps other much smaller body parts. If he is a predator of an ignorant female… as I suspect, that's the least he deserves.

And my instincts are rarely wrong.

I hope whatever Arran discovers back there explains her side quickly and effectively.

I hate leaving Arran when his beast can surface so easily.

Will he take a moment to make sense of things and not just react without thinking things through? My money isn't on that bet. He's too impulsive.

This is when cell phones would be handy for our kind. I could call Maxum and have him check on the situation with the witch. But when it comes to witches, would the demon be level-headed either?

Down the residential street, Rob jumps into a nondescript black sedan on the passenger side. The car pulls into the light traffic. I swing wide so I can dip low enough and see inside the vehicle and memorize the face of the driver.

When I do, I recognize the woman as a known witch rights activist and a likely candidate for ASO membership.

Well, this is a dreadful turn of events.

Jade is indeed involved (in whatever way) with our enemies.

They don't drive far, a few miles away to the business end of the city. They pull into a parking lot. Perched high on a ledge on the opposite side of the street, I watch as they enter a modern office building.

I'm close to our safe house, so I risk losing their trail to alert Maxum and Calder to the current events. If Arran or I were to be incapacitated, they would have no clue. I'm not allowing what happened to Osen to happen to me. He was a cocky bastard who thought he didn't have to check-in. Look where that got us.

He's dead.

And we're in the dark.

I make sure no one tails me back to the safe house and land at our front door.

Barging inside, Maxum reads my aggressive demeanor and is already poised for a fight.

"What is it?" Calder asks, faster than Maxum when it comes to using his voice.

"Rob paid Jade a visit. Not sure what happened inside. My instincts still say she's not behind all this, but perhaps she has been used. Arran planned to check on her. I followed Rob and Galiana Collins to 1020 Main St."

"Rob and Galiana, *together*?" Calder pulls off his button-up shirt, revealing his toned muscular upper body. He straps on his weapons holster that holds his Katana-style blades. The custom holster allows his wings to move freely, if he chooses to half-shift, and use them.

I'd never tell him, but he looks like a badass dressed as a warrior—which he is. Typically, he looks more like a rich, uptight businessman dressed for the weekend.

His back and upper arms have tattoos—wings made of fire —that look a bit too real… because they are.

"You go back to keep an eye on the building," Maxum orders. "We'll pop over to see if Arran's killed the witch yet." He chants and opens a portal in our living room to Jade's backyard. He waves Calder through and gives me a grimace. "Good luck."

"I think you three will need it more," I sigh as the portal closes behind them.

I hope she survives.

# 23

## LOST

### CALDER

*M*y fiery wings are desperate to unfurl. I'm ready to enact some vengeance. I've been ready for far too long.

Yet, I will stay my hand—only long enough to confirm that the witch is our enemy. Not that she isn't already *my* enemy by default. But Arran is sweet on her now.

I don't want to make an enemy of him. I've already lost a loved one this week.

I suspect I would be in the proverbial dog house if I kill the witch before he confirms her nefarious intentions.

Maybe he's already killed her himself.

Flint's normally calm exterior was ruffled when he burst through the door. That's no easy feat to rattle him. I don't think he's fallen for the witch's lure. So he's probably feeling what I'm feeling: worry for Arran's fragile sanity.

Maxum opens the portal to the witch's small backyard and waves me through.

My eyes lock on the back door of her house. I don't see any activity, but the blackout curtains are drawn on all the windows. Arran claims she fears her ex. Now, we know she allowed him inside. So it's likely what I thought all along... she didn't want *us* seeing inside.

I can't sense anything inside her home. But most magical beings and supernaturals have a minor magic spell that naturally occurs around their homes. It's where the whole vampires needing to be invited inside nonsense comes from. Just by claiming a shelter as their sacred place, a magical person creates a fragile protective ward around their homes.

Whether she knows it or not, this witch has definitely claimed her sacred place here. Since I'm not one of her chosen friends or family, I wouldn't be able to perceive much beyond her walls.

Maxum's magic works differently, so he could pick up brainwaves and bursts of magic beyond a barrier. He steps through his portal and seals it up. I glance over at him, expecting his quick assessment. He shakes his head, indicating he hasn't picked up anything yet.

I take another step and feel something soft stick to my shoe.

I lift my foot to see it's dog shit.

Without a sound, Maxum doubles over in laughter. His enormous body is shaking, and he points to my crap bombing. "Arran's," he wheezes out.

"You have to be fucking kidding me." I hiss and wipe most of it off in the thick grass. "I... don't have words for this bullshit."

"*Wolf* shit," Maxum corrects. Then he sobers, focusing on the house. "I don't pick up anything from inside. However, I sense Arran at the front, pacing and worrying. So she's likely unscathed... for the moment."

He frowns. I think Arran might be right, the demon has fallen for her charms too. But he's doing his damnest to cover up his interest.

"Why hasn't he gone inside yet?" I ask. But maybe he has, and he's panicking on the porch after ending his woman. I don't envy him. Not that I intend to have another female in my life—especially a witch.

We easily hop the tall fence and rush around to the front. Arran hears us coming, and his expression is one of complete devastation.

"Update?" Maxum switches to soldier mode to snap Arran out of his emotional state.

"She won't answer the door." Arran's half-shifted clawed hands are shaking. He can barely contain his beast. "Probably smart."

"Have you heard her moving around?" Maxum asks.

With this question, Arran focuses on the demon. Then his eyes widen. "No. I don't think I have."

"I'm not picking up brainwaves... not active ones." Maxum steps between Arran and Jade's door. "It could mean anything."

It likely means she's dead, and her brain is sputtering to it's final end.

Arran charges at Maxum, but it's only because the demon is in his way to get to the witch.

"I'm not going to hurt her. Hold on, Arran." Maxum pushes a bit of his mental influence at Arran.

It's not necessarily cool that he is using his ability on Arran, since he's not supposed to use his powers on us, but I'll forgive him for this one. We don't need the berserker version at the moment.

I glance around the neighborhood to see if anyone is witnessing our break-in.

Typically, regular mortal police don't get involved with supes *if* they know about us. But dispatchers will often call the Supernatural Enforcers if we cause a scene. If cops show up right now, we probably won't be able to hold Arran back if he freaks.

"Arran, I'm going to need you to breathe," Maxum says

calmly. "I'm going in first since I'm the most resistant to magic. There might be some sort of trap or ward."

He's always risking himself like this. One of these days, someone is going to spring a spell that can take down a demon.

Arran grunts instead of speaking. I don't think he's capable of using his human voice anymore. I'm surprised he hasn't sprouted furry ears and a jaw full of razor sharp teeth.

Maxum takes his grunt as a sign of agreement. He turns around and enchants a spell to unravel any wardings over her front door. The door clicks open.

With his shoe, he pushes it open. When the door swings wide, we see the witch on the floor, face down. It appears as if she was crawling away and passed out.

I clearly sense death now. As confirmation, I don't see her rib cage moving with a breath. I glance at Arran, but he's struck stock-still. Good thing, because Maxum must move forward first to see if the place has been rigged with any spells.

My senses don't pick up any magic, but that doesn't mean a damned thing. I don't have the keen perceptions Maxum has. My ability centers on death and rebirth—and, once upon a time, sexual pleasure. I hate that part of myself has been stripped away by an evil act of a witch.

Despite my hatred for witches, I discover I weirdly care that this woman is hovering near death's veil.

Maybe she put a spell on me…

Nah, it must be my concern for Arran's sanity. I love the jerk. Or that she might be the last connection to my love, Osen.

Maxum slowly steps inside the living room. He scans the entire room for magic traces. When no booby trap attempts to hex him, he crouches to study the witch's condition.

He holds his hand just above her shoulder, then proceeds to turn her over onto her back. "Still no brainwaves." He waves me inside. "Can you check her?"

I won't fucking touch her, but I don't need to touch her to do what he's asking.

Standing near her, I expand my scope of perception. I feel soul energy hovering around us. Hers... and another encasing it, probably Osen's?

"She's disconnecting from her body," I confirm.

Arran is inside the house and on top of her within seconds. He roars, rattling my bones.

Gripping her to his chest, his vocal cords change back so he can call her name. "Jade?" And then he adds, "Osen? Come back."

Energy swirls in my mind's eye, pulling down toward her body.

She sucks in a breath, but it isn't deep.

Arran somehow summoned her back.

"Thank Goddess," he says, lifting her into his arms. "Portal. Now."

Although I see it on his face that he wants to argue, Maxum doesn't. With a huff, he creates a portal back to our safe house.

Apparently, we've adopted a useless, half-dead witch.

Oh, joy.

## 24

# FOUND

ARRAN

On her porch, I work myself up into a frenzy.

I didn't want to intrude on Jade's space again, but I also don't want to leave her alone after her ex showed up.

My gut is telling me his visit isn't what it seems to be.

Thank Goddess Maxum and Calder show up when they do. I am about to lose what I have left of my fragile sanity.

When I see her on the floor, I know. I'm more certain than ever that she is a victim of all this. I don't know if the guys will agree. They might still think she is involved, and the ASO betrayed her. But they don't know her like I do.

Clutching her to my chest and hearing her take in a breath is the sweetest sound I've ever heard.

Stepping through the portal I demand of Maxum, I want nothing more than to carry her to my room so I can be alone with her. I want to symbolically claim her as mine to the males by taking her under my protection. I won't claim her as my mate until I have her permission. Hopefully, one day I can convince her to accept what I am.

Instead of hiding away with her, I settle down on one of our large couches so I can talk with the guys about what to do.

Gazing down at her sweet face, I have an uncomfortable thought. "What if it isn't Jade who returned to her body, but Osen?" I mumble to myself.

How will I deal with him taking her body?

As much as I want Osen alive again, I don't want it to be at the cost of my beautiful witch.

"If anyone could have ousted her soul and claimed her body for his own, it would have been Osen," Maxum confirms my worries.

"What if Osen killed her? Not Rob?" Calder asks.

"What did it feel like when she was outside her body?" I ask. "Did you sense both of them?"

"I did." He frowns. "At first, it felt like he was surrounding her soul."

"To contain it?" I wonder.

"I suppose it could have been like that." Calder pulls on his auburn hair in frustration.

"Osen could have helped her return to her body. His power worked in the astral realms. It's not impossible." Maxum rubs his face and curses. "But I also wouldn't put it past Osen to knock her off if he believed she was the enemy."

"She could have willingly met with Rob. Then Osen attacked her from within, after Rob left," Calder argues, unhelpfully filling my mind with poison.

"Stop it!" I shout. "We don't know a damned thing. We'll have to wait until Jade regains consciousness to find out what we can."

*Please wake up. Please.*

Maxum clears his throat. "Arran, we have some bad news. Flint followed Rob and saw him drive away with Galiana Collins after he left Jade's house."

"Fuck." I close my eyes to center myself before I go into full beast mode. I'm honestly shocked I haven't yet. "So Rob *is* a warlock."

"Appears so." Maxum shrugs. "Galiana doesn't mingle with humans or supes. So it appears Jade might know more than she lets on."

I shake my head. I hate that they doubt her, but the facts are stacking up against her innocence.

Glancing out the window, I see night has finally come. "Where's Flint?"

"At an office building, last we know. Might be ASO headquarters." Calder stands up and stretches his shoulders. "I'll fly over and see if he's still there, and if he needs backup. You good?" he asks me.

"No. But you know that much." I sigh. "Just don't let her ex slip away. I want to kill him for the hell of it now."

"You got dibs unless, of course, he comes at me. Then I'll take him down. I'm guessing he's the dick who's behind Osen's death, too. Or one of the culprits." Calder glares at Jade's unconscious body, his insinuation clear.

"Rob's probably part of Osen's murder." Maxum cracks his huge knuckles. "Go. Help Flint."

Calder gives us a nod and unfurls his giant red-orange wings from his back as soon as he's out the front door.

"How are her brainwaves now?" I ask Maxum as I stare down at her sleeping face. She almost looks peaceful.

"Getting stronger." With a growl, Maxum launches to his feet and heads into the kitchen to pour himself a demon brew. He downs a generous serving in one gulp, glowering at Jade the entire time.

Is he certain that she's a spy now?

Having her in my arms settles me some. I close my eyes to grab onto the small bit of rational thinking I have left. Even before she wakes up, I need to know what happened to her.

"It appeared as if she was attacked and was trying to get

away from Rob," I say quietly, but I know Maxum can hear me. He can hear me across a battlefield, because he has.

"That is how it appears," his tone is flat.

"Can you see if you can pick up what Rob might have used to kill her?" When Maxum doesn't move or respond, I remind him, "If Rob or his friends killed Osen, then he might have tried to use a similar spell on Jade."

Maxum grumbles but walks over and towers over us as I sit, holding her fragile form in my arms. "There's no magic residue around her, but we might have left any traces of that at her house." He grimaces.

"Should we... check her body?" I gulp because I don't want to undress her in front of Maxum. She wouldn't be happy about it. But I remind myself he's practically like a doctor, and she's an unconscious patient in triage after a battle. And we don't have to strip her of her underwear to see if she has any marks to indicate what hurt her. It might still be hurting her because she hasn't regained consciousness yet.

Besides, our inspection isn't sexual. Maxum doesn't want her like that anyway... at least not anymore.

I unbutton her cardigan and pull her right arm free of the sleeve. Trying to hold her and undress her is awkward. Gratefully, Maxum huffs, then helps.

His touch is gentler than I would expect. I wonder if he's doing it for my sake? Or does he realize how fragile her mortal body is?

He holds her arms above her head, and I brace her body as I slowly lift her t-shirt off. She's wearing a flimsy bra that isn't more than a thin, cropped tank top. Her nipples are hard and begging me to touch them.

But I'm not *that* guy.

It's her soft skin that almost undoes me. I want to howl at the moon. I only had that brief, beautiful night with her, and that is likely all I will get.

Maxum gently brings her arms down to her side, then

inspects each with care. He brushes her long hair to the side to glide a massive hand down her back. Instead of watching Jade, I observe the demon. He's invested... more than he lets on.

"No curse marks so far," he says. "I don't know what happened to her."

Usually, a hex or curse leaves some energy signature or even a physical mark on a body. I wonder what could have hurt her enough to kill her without leaving a trace.

"Should we?" I nod to her pants.

Maxum grimaces. "We've come this far as perverts. Might as well seal the deal."

We make sure to slide her jeans off without taking her underwear with them.

Maxum does a brief but thorough check, but discovers nothing. He grabs a blanket and places it over her naked form. "You really care for her, don't you?"

"If I thought it was possible to have a fated match with a witch... I'd believe she was my mate."

"Dammit." He flops onto his favorite chair.

He's a sucker for fated mates. It's one of the soft things about him. Although, I'd never say that feeling soul-crushing love for someone was weak. I doubt he believes that either.

We haven't been very lucky when it comes to relationships —especially with females.

"Do you feel a pull to her as well?" I ask, not sure what I want to hear his response.

"I feel... something," Maxum says just above a whisper. Then he crosses his massive arms and sulks. "But we don't know if that's part of her magic. She could have hexed us with a lust charm."

"I'm not feeling lust," I argue. "Well, I feel lust for her, but it's deeper than that. And I think you know that's true for you, too."

"No. Lust never felt this painful."

## 25

# COMING UNDONE

JADE

*I* don't remember falling asleep, but I must be dreaming.

I'm naked, and my limbs are tied down to bedposts. Arran, Maxum, Flint, and Calder surround me.

We are in a room filled with a soft, warm glow that only serves to accentuate their otherworldly beauty. Currently, they are all shirtless, wearing low-slung pants.

Calder's skin seems to glow orange-red, as if he's about to burst into flames. I might do that too if he keeps looking at me the way he is—like I'm his next meal. I wonder if he will be as skilled as Arran with his mouth.

Maxum has his horns from my previous dreams. His skin is a gorgeous deep crimson. His obsidian eyes dance with fire as his gaze travels up and down my body, pausing at my exposed pussy.

I heat only with his perusal. I'm getting wetter by the moment.

With a predator's grace, he steps closer.

My pussy clenches with excitement.

From the other side of the bed, Arran moves closer. His eyes are filled with more than lust. I see hope within his gaze. His eyes are wild-looking and he appears much larger than I remember in real life. As if he's on steroids... like he's hulked out. His hands look more like monster claws than the human fingers I'm familiar with.

But even with his dangerous monster claws, I crave his touch again.

Will he drag them over my sensitive flesh, marking me with thin lines? Will he use them to pinch my nipples and edge me with a bit of delicious pain just at the right moment?

Arran grins, and I see his canines have elongated as if he's part wolf.

Flint stands in the background. His huge, muscular body leans against a wall, as if he'd rather watch than participate. Maybe he's a bit of a voyeur. The idea turns me on even more. Large bat-like wings frame his broad, thick body. Horns poke out from the sides of his head. He looks like he's made of polished tan-colored marble. Would his cock feel as hard as a stone?

I wonder if he will stroke himself as his friends fuck me. His expression gives nothing away, and I want to know more about him. Who is this mysterious quiet male... *gargoyle*? What's his story? What is his dark secret that he tells no one?

I love that my dream is playing into the characters I've created for them.

Oddly, I wonder where my ghostly avatar is. Usually, it's him that actually interacts with these guys.

"Ghost?" I call.

The four guys glance at each other as if I've said something unusual.

"Are you calling for Osen?" Arran asks.

"His name is Osen?" I frown when I hear how fragile my voice sounds.

"Yes." Maxum leans over, just a few inches from my face. I can smell his smokey scent that warms my insides. "Why did you call for him?" he asks. His voice isn't seductive but demanding... as if I've made some mistake requesting his presence. Maybe I have. Osen seems to tolerate me, at best.

"This is my dream. And I want to know where my ghost is. He's the one to get all your attention." I frown. "I find it upsetting that he's not here, too."

"Why do you care where Osen is?" Maxum cradles my chin, and I feel tension building. His grip is growing firmer by the moment.

I sigh. I hate admitting that I want to know more about him, because he hasn't been the nicest person to me. However, I believe there is a reason for that. We just need to develop a connection, a bond.

Dreaming or not, these guys all love Osen. We must have gotten off on the wrong foot. "Because you care about him," I say simply. "Your hearts ache with his loss. And I want him to stop hating me."

"Why do you want him to like you? So you can pull secrets out of him?" Calder asks.

I narrow my eyes as I look at him and groan loudly. "What the fuck is up with this secret shit? It's all very interesting as a book idea, but I don't care for it in my dreams. I just want to experience the love you all feel for each other. I just want to resolve this tension so I can move on."

Arran's rough hand skims over my arm. "What about experiencing the pleasure we can give you?"

"Yes! I want that!" I nod. "I don't like this idea that we're enemies."

"And if we like to punish our enemies sexually?"

I raise my eyebrows and then grin. "Oh, well, that could work. But I don't want to be really hurt."

"Witch, you need to know this is actually happening," Arran whispers in my ear, but the voice is the ghost... *Osen*.

"But this is my dream," I say. "Or maybe our shared dream."

"It is in a way, but it's also the shadowscape. A very real place. One I can control," Osen speaks through Arran. "I'm a disembodied soul. But what these males do to you now is truly me."

"So you are a ghost... and you'll be fucking me as these guys?" I ask.

"Yes."

I frown. "No."

"No?" His angry voice resonates all around me. "I don't have to ask for your permission. I can take what I want."

"Why didn't you do that then?" I challenge him.

He pauses, then finally answers, resigned. "Because I promised these males I wouldn't do that."

"Why do you want to have sex with me at all? I thought you didn't like me." I ask, "And why are you using their faces instead of your own?"

"Because you're attracted to them." Arran's hot breath washes over my neck. "You want to fuck them. You don't like me."

I squirm with need. "And why do you want me to want them, or you, for that matter?"

"I need your sexual energy," he finally admits.

"Are you an incubus?" I ask.

"How did you know?" His voice is harsh again.

"I write this stuff, silly."

"Oh, that's right." Arran nuzzles into my neck, then his soft lips graze up to my ear. "Do you understand this isn't a dream?"

I feel the pinch of sharp canines on my neck, more real than I've ever felt in a dream.

"Stop!" I gasp. "I... I believe you."

He releases his jaw and licks over the marks. "I always wanted to bite someone like that—as a werewolf."

"Great. Achievement unlocked," I sass. Then I pull back as much as I can and study Arran's face. "Let's just say this is real, and you're trying to seduce me so you can feed off my sexual energy... why do you need it?"

"I've been feeding off your emotional energy for days, but it isn't enough. I need more so I can remember everything. But I had to drain my reserves to save you."

"I was sick..."

"It was more dire than that. If you are to continue to survive, I will need to feed you energy. You might even need outside help."

"I'm that bad?"

He nods. "And I don't like you rummaging through my sexual memories so I can feed."

"I didn't mean to invade your privacy."

He grunts as if he's still not convinced.

"I mean, the scenes were hot as a volcano, but I didn't realize it was real," I grimace. "Sorry."

He studies my face or energy, or whatever, for a long moment. "I sense you are only starting to understand. You really don't know about supes and witches?"

"I didn't... And you need my energy to become stronger?" I ask, nervous to hear his answer.

Osen uses Maxum's hand to wrap around my throat, pinching enough to make me feel how real this is. "Yes, and because your magic isn't enough to protect you."

"Why do you care if I stay alive?" I ask.

"If you die, I won't be able to avenge my death."

"Death goals. I get it." I realize there's more to his game. "Are you planning on taking complete control of my body?"

"I need to confirm you aren't the spy as I had suspected. But if you are innocent, I won't possess you permanently."

"Just for weekends and date nights?"

"You are a sassy one... even though I sense you now realize this is truly happening."

I don't know how I know, but I do... this is terrifyingly real.

He continues, his voice soft and thoughtful, "As long as you aren't the one who killed me, I'll leave when I know my pack is safe and my murder solved."

I feel the truthfulness in his words.

"If you want to sex me up, full disclosure... I hooked up with Arran," I admit, feeling guilty.

"You aren't exclusive, though."

"No, but..."

"I heard his conversation with you. He'd share your love with the rest of us. We all share our bodies. Well, except for Flint," he explains. "Having multiple partners is not unheard of with our kind."

He's right, Arran told me he didn't mind if we were with other people.

"Can you show me what you look like?" I ask.

"You really don't know?" He sounds skeptical. "You have no memory of seeing me?"

"No. When would I have seen you? I only inhabit your body during your memories."

"So you don't remember having something to do with my death?" he mutters, not really a question. Maxum's hand squeezes tighter around my neck.

"No! I could never kill someone."

"You have a gun," he reminds me.

"To shoot them in the leg or wherever I have to hit someone to slow them down, not *kill* them."

"To stop your ex? Rob?" he growls with Arran's voice.

"You know about him?" I'm surprised he is so aware of my waking life.

"That he's a threat? Yes."

"Will you protect us from him?" I worry Rob will hurt me.

Wouldn't having an invisible ghost who can help me be a good idea?

"I can help you if you feed me."

"Then show yourself," I demand. "I don't want to be with these guys if it's you touching me."

The four guys disappear. Next to the bed, a dark shadowy figure stands, staring at me, if what looks like eyes are any indication. He is almost transparent, like thick, dense smoke, but in the shape of a man. "This form is much easier to maintain."

"Were you wasting energy on the illusion?" I ask.

"I thought it might work you into a sexual frenzy faster," he explains.

"Maybe another time, but I need to know who you are right now," I say. "If this is really happening, I want it to be between us. Not through them."

He hums thoughtfully, "You are worried it will corrupt your feelings for them?"

"Yeah." Then I pout. "Why don't you show me what you look like?"

"If you want the real me, this is as good as you're going to get until I feed more. In many ways, this *is* the real me. Besides, I don't think I should show you the face my physical form wore yet."

"So, are you made of shadows in the dream world?"

"It's my incubus-feeding body in what you might call the astral plane." His arm reaches down and strokes my cheek. "You sure you want me to fuck you? This will solidify a connection between us. I will see further into your mind. Lines will be blurred."

"Are *you* sure?" I ask, my forehead wrinkling in confusion. "I didn't expect that you would want to bond with me. I'm a disgusting witch, after all."

"I'm looking past that."

I chuckle. "How sweet."

"Do you want sweet? Or do you want me to give you the best orgasm of your life?"

"Door number two," I joke. "If this is an either-or situation."

"When I feed, you will be under my complete control," he warns. "You won't be able to move. You'll only be able to talk, use your eyes, and come for me like a fucking nymph. Starting now."

I gulp. I try to pull on my restraints, tying me to the bed. But I can't move to do that. Glancing to the side, I can see now that my ropes are actually shadows.

My heart is racing. And my body is thrumming with fear and excitement.

I'm about to have astral sex with an incubus ghost. Feels like I might be forging new ground here.

I'm a pioneer.

A trailblazer.

Taking a shadowcock for the team.

Osen drags his shadowhand from my neck and over my breast. He squeezes and pinches my nipple.

"Oh shit," I gasp. I didn't expect the shadows to be so dexterous.

"That's just the beginning, little witch." I can hear the smile in his voice. "Open up to me. Give me all that lust, the desire, and the emotions behind your need."

"That will help you?"

"You actually *want* to help me, don't you?" he asks with awe.

Two shadow tendrils move up from both ankles, slowly climbing up my legs. Again, I try to budge but can't squirm.

"What do you like, little witch?" he murmurs. Now his shadowbody moves around the bed until he crawls up, kneeling between my spread legs. I feel his attention on my wet, exposed pussy. "You want me to fuck this pretty cunt?" The tendrils slide up to pull my labia open, further exposing me to him.

"Oh, god," I blush.

"I'll be your god," he chuckles. "But you should thank the Goddess for my gifts."

The tendrils continue their explorations up my body to my breasts, wrapping around and around each one, covering them completely, and acting as a living bra. He squeezes like he's milking them, and my arousal jumps to another level.

His hand replaces the tendrils at my entrance, sliding through my wet folds, working me higher with his attention. His thumb finds my clit and gently strums it with the rhythm he's now setting with the rest of his shadowy appendages.

"Has anyone fucked your ass?" he asks.

"Once. But he didn't know what he was doing."

"Well, I do. And if the guys claim you, you will know the feeling of amazing anal sex in the physical world."

"Are you going to do that with me now?"

"Let's work up to that, little witch." I notice the hate is dissolving around that nickname and becoming a phrase of endearment.

I breathe out, "Okay."

"Do you enjoy sucking on cock?" he asks. "You like a long, thick dick fucking your throat? Swallowing down a male's cum?"

"Yes."

"Good, because I'm going to take every hole during our sessions."

"Sessions... with an S?"

"Oh, yes, my troublemaker." He leans forward, his phantom tongue slipping over my center.

I cry out because it feels so damned good.

"Feel free to come as many times as you wish," he says off-handedly. This guy is confident. I'll give him that. But I suppose his power centers on sex, so he should be.

I laugh. "Guys rarely make me come, and if they do, it's once. Tops."

"But when you are alone? With your toys? And you don't have bumbling fools in your bed?"

"Well, yeah. But that's different," I argue.

"So am I." His shadowtentacles shoot out from his torso and wrap around my upper thighs, pulling my legs open more and folding me in half. My knees are almost touching the sides of my breasts.

I'm completely exposed to him and at his mercy.

One tendril tickles my asshole. And another fondles my clit. Then I feel a vibration.

I pant. "Are you… *vibrating?*"

*Okay, wow.*

This whole incubus lover has some serious advantages. All I can do is lay here and take all the pleasure he can dole out. I'm convinced this is only the beginning of what he could do with me.

His tendrils tighten around my breasts, massaging them, and I moan.

Something wraps around my throat and then drags over my lips.

I open my mouth obediently. His shadow feels like a thick cock in every way.

"Good witch," he coos. "Suck my shadowcock. Show me how much you desire this."

I swirl my tongue around the head and give it an experimental suck.

Osen groans with pleasure. Slowly, he presses it farther in until he's blocking my airway. He plays with my ability to breathe, as I feel pressure at my wet entrance below.

With my mouth full, I can do nothing more than hum and moan.

His body comes forward, on top of mine. I open my eyes to see the outline of his face, and a hint of what his human face might have looked like.

He thrusts the cock into my throat deeper. "You like choking on my shadowcock, witch?"

After deep-throating me and ratcheting up the tension, he pulls his shadow out for me to answer.

"Yes, I want more."

"So do I." The large head of his lower cock presses slowly into my pussy. "I need more."

I want to grind against it, make him shove inside faster. But he's in control. There is no mistaking that. With my consent, he means to do with me as he pleases.

"You want me to slam home hard, don't you?" he asks.

"Fuck me," I plead.

He shoves his shadow back down my throat.

A tendril sucks on my clit, and I cry out around the mass.

"I forgot how lovely females can be," he says, licking over the bump where his shadowcock is plunging into my throat.

It's too much. My climax hits me like a freight train.

Immobilized, I can't even move to show how it affects me. I can only feel my pulsing pussy, hear my muffled cries, and see stars behind my eyelids.

When I stop clenching around his shadowcock, I open my eyes to see Osen has a bit more form to him now. Crisper.

I'm helping him. Then I wonder if he's hurting me in the process, but I don't feel drained. If anything, I feel stronger.

"You come on my cock so perfectly. Let's see if you can take the whole thing." He pumps forward, and I feel the burning stretch of my pussy accommodating his girth and length.

The cock in my mouth slides out.

"Tell me how much you want this," he orders.

"I want your thick, massive cock. I need your delicious cum filling me up. I want you dripping from all my holes."

He pounds into me faster, turned on by my words. "I should have been fucking more romance authors all these years."

"The readers would have been a good choice too," I offer.

"And you want to fuck my friends, don't you?" he asks. "I'm going to love watching them destroy this pussy with their huge cocks. They will stretch you and use you so thoroughly that no man will satisfy you again."

"Yes," I shout as his ministrations work me into a fevered pitch.

His shadows are swirling all over my body. They're plucking my nipples, tightening their grip around my throat, and strumming my clit as he rocks into me. He's touching places I didn't know were erogenous zones.

"You're going to take my shadowcum. I'm marking you. You're mine now. My little witch." He hisses, as if he didn't mean to confess that bit.

My bliss lifts me to such heights I'm afraid of the fall. All I need now is a gust of wind, and I'll plummet off the edge.

"Come for me," he commands.

And I do.

A bomb goes off inside me—our energies merging and swirling, like a cascading explosion, echoing out farther and farther until I'm not sure if I'm alive anymore.

Heat fills my core and then reaches my fingers and toes. I'm filled with a strange glow.

A shadow curls around my light.

Osen curses but keeps coming inside me.

Then he collapses on top of my body, and I feel his shadow's weight.

"I wish I could have fucked you with a physical body," he whispers as I drift into total darkness.

Did he just kill me with his shadowcock?

*Worth it.*

# REBORN

ARRAN

*J*ade's body is wrapped up in the blanket like a burrito, but she wiggles and squirms in her unconscious state.

It gives me hope that she's returning to us.

However, Maxum's intense glare reminds me we don't know what will happen next. Is Jade working with our enemy, even unintentionally? Was she being used? Was it Osen who hurt her? Or did he save her?

We need answers.

I hold her on my lap and rest my head on the back of the couch. But I haven't been able to sleep.

Calder walks in the front door, returning from checking in on Flint. The phoenix glares at Jade's sleeping face. Then he glances at Maxum and me, reading our energies. He shakes his head in irritation and gives us his update, "It appears Rob and Galiana haven't left that building. Which indicates there might be sleeping quarters inside since it's about three in the morning now."

Maxum grunts quietly, almost dismissively. He doesn't move a muscle, only watching and waiting for a change in Jade's condition.

Perhaps he senses a shift in her brainwaves.

"You two just going to stare at the witch the entire night?" Calder cocks his brow and his hip. Sassy brat.

"Yes," Maxum answers with such resolve and determination that it brokers no arguments to suggest otherwise. Or it wouldn't be wise to comment.

Yet, Calder isn't always smart.

"She obviously betrayed us," Calder says, waving his hands in her direction.

"So why would Rob attempt to kill her?" Maxum asks.

I'm surprised he's the one arguing the point.

Calder huffs, "I don't know, but—"

"But nothing," Maxum cuts him off. "We need answers. And if Osen is still linked to her, we might get the truth of the matter from him. All we know is that Jade was attacked."

Calder softens with the mention of Osen. If anyone was *in* love with the incubus, it was Calder.

I loved Osen as well, but I had ended the sexual dynamic when he became increasingly obsessed. He only cared about fighting the witches and proving who was behind the ASO.

I was invested in stopping the threat, but Osen was a fixated maniac in the end.

Calder sees how I'm clutching Jade protectively to my chest. He sighs and offers, "Snacks while we await the verdict?"

"Sure," Maxum agrees.

"I can't eat," I decline. "Not with her like this."

The phoenix frowns, sympathetic even though he disapproves of how attached I've become. Then he rummages through the kitchen for something to eat. I know he only means to protects us all with his gruff behavior toward Jade, but I can't allow it.

I watch him for a moment, then I turn my attention to Maxum. "Are you picking up anything?"

"She's been dreaming, but the texture of it feels more like a shadowwalk."

I perk up.

So does Calder from the other room. He asks, "Osen? You think he's still in there with her?"

"That would be my guess." Maxum leans forward, watching her like a cat about to pounce.

Jade breathes in deeply and stirs, her head turning toward my chest.

My broken heart soars with the positive sign she will be okay.

But when her eyes open, they are not their normal hazel-green, but charcoal.

"Osen?" I dare to ask.

Jade turns her head and sees Maxum and Calder towering over us.

"Hey, assholes," Osen says.

"It's him." Calder smiles. Then he becomes instantly serious. "What's happened? Is the witch's soul still in there?"

He's asking what I need to know.

*Where is Jade?*

Calder's likely hoping for a different answer than I am.

I'm conflicted, because I also want Osen to be alive, but not at the cost of my sweet, curvy witch's life. Even if she never forgives me for breaking her trust, I want her to live a long and healthy life.

Yes, even if she knowingly betrayed us.

She doesn't owe me anything.

War is war.

"The witch is still here," Osen says. "I had to pull her soul back into her body, but the act drained my reserves."

"Why did you save her?" Calder sounds completely perplexed.

"It appears that she was under a spell and I need vengeance." Osen looks down at the tightly wrapped blanket around her body. "Worried she's going to hex you?"

"Should we be?" Maxum asks in a neutral tone.

Osen jerks in my arms and closes his eyes as if fighting off a pain.

Her body goes limp.

Then Jade's eyes open, revealing hazel-green irises.

"Jade?" I ask, wondering how much of her is aware and functional.

Osen could have fucked with her memories if he's gaining strength, as I suspect he is.

"Arran?" She blinks even though it isn't bright in here. She startles when she sees Maxum and Calder standing beside the couch, staring at her. "Where am I?"

"Never mind that for now, tell us what happened," Maxum orders.

I notice he's back in human glamour, but he still looks like an intimidating demon without horns.

My protective instincts are in full force. I pull her to my chest.

Encased like a mummy, she can't do anything but allow me to do it.

"Back off," I snarl at Maxum.

"I don't understand. Did you guys kidnap me? What are you going to do to me?" she asks, her fear and confusion ring clearly. Her eyes widen when she sees Calder's bare chest and weapons holster with the swords peeking out over his shoulders.

"Jade, listen to me," I say softly. "You were hurt. We want to know what happened. Let's start there." Fortunately, neither one of my cohorts chimes in that her answers could determine her future.

What will I do? Will I fight to save her? Will I have a chance against both of them while also protecting Jade?

I don't want to hurt them, but I won't let her be harmed again.

"I was working on my book. Then... I thought I heard a knock on my front door." She scrunches up her face, forcing her memory forward.

"And?" Maxum prompts.

She blushes and averts her eyes. "I... I can't."

"Why not?" I ask, gently before Maxum or Calder begins to threaten her.

"I'm pretty sure I'm losing my mind, and Maxum looks like he's going to tear me in half. He already doesn't think much of me."

"No matter how strange, tell us what you think happened," I plead.

Jade bites her lip and squirms. "Can you loosen this blanket? I feel like I'm going to have a panic attack."

I don't want her to realize she's down to her underwear, but I also don't need her panicking... But will she panic because she's only in her underwear?

Forewarning her, I confess, "We found you unconscious. We were worried you had been hurt, so we stripped you down to your underwear to see."

"Why didn't you call an ambulance?" she asks.

"Once we explain, after you explain, you will understand why we didn't."

"Okay." She wiggles again.

I set her down on the couch next to me with her sitting up and help loosen the blankets' stranglehold.

She pulls her arms free.

The guys tense their bodies and watch her closely as if she were about to cast a spell.

I don't think she has enough in her to stand up on her own, let alone use magic.

Jade cradles her face in her palms and tells us her story. "I think there's a ghost possessing me. I know, crazy. I've had dreams that aren't exactly dreams. I knew things I shouldn't have." She peeks through her fingers to see my reaction. "I knew your name was Arran before you told me because I heard it in my vision."

"Go on," I encourage.

"You don't think I'm crazy?" When I shake my head, she looks at Maxum and Calder to gauge their reactions.

"Not about that." Maxum cocks a brow. Is he trying to be playful?

"Keep talking," Calder demands, his arms crossed and his face stern. He's overcompensating because he doubts his position on the witch's guilt.

Jade sighs wearily and continues, "So, this ghost might know all of you. He finally told me his name right before I woke up. Do you know someone named Osen?"

"He was the friend we just lost," I confirm.

"He is?" Jade covers her mouth. "Oh, my god... You mean this *is* real?"

I nod and squeeze her reassuringly. "Continue."

"Well, I heard a knock at my door. When I looked out the peephole, I blacked out. And then the next thing I remember is Osen, um... *talking* to me in what he called a shadowscape."

"Talking?" Maxum says with skepticism. He suspects the incubus did more than talk.

Jade hears his disbelief. "At the start, it was only talk. He said I wasn't powerful enough to protect us from Rob. He said he was an..." She pulls the blanket to her chest, feeling shy about her confession. "That he's an incubus?" She tries to redact everything she's said, "I know, it's a weird story, even for me." The witch looks at all three of us. "So, can you tell me what really happened to me? Why am I here, almost naked, and being interrogated?"

"Flint was watching your house to see if he could catch your stalker ex spying on you," I tell her. "He watched as you invited Rob inside…"

"I did *what*?!" she shouts.

"That's what I said," I agree. "Flint followed Rob and some woman after he left your place. I knocked and knocked, but you didn't answer. Then Maxum showed up. Since I was worried that you weren't answering, we broke in. You were on the ground…" I soften the truth and say, "… dying."

"Uh… what?" Jade goes stone still, then finally, her body trembles.

She's probably going into shock—if not from the subject, from the trauma her body has just been through. "Don't fuck with me," she hisses. "Please."

"We aren't." Maxum crouches down. I believe in an attempt to appear less threatening. But he's fucking massive, and the effort doesn't really help. He's just closer to her now and more imposing. Then again, maybe he wants to get a reaction from her when he asks, "Jade, why would Rob want you dead?"

"Because he must be crazier than I ever imagined?" Her eyes are wild with fear.

I can practically see her mind questioning everything that's happening.

"Were you working with him to attack other supes?" Maxum asks.

"Me… attack?" She looks at me, imploring me to believe her with a desperate expression. "I wasn't working with Rob—at all. Wait, do you mean supes as in supernatural beings? Like an incubus?"

"Yes, supes, as in supernaturals," he confirms.

"I'm *not* losing my mind?" she breathes out, mostly to herself.

Maxum sighs and momentarily looks as though he will reach out and caress her hand. "And you… are a witch."

"That's what Osen calls me. Little witch." Jade waves her hand dismissively. "But I don't have magic. I would know, wouldn't I?"

"You aren't particularly powerful. Or maybe you've suppressed your magic for so long it barely registers," Maxum explains. "But you have a particularly interesting gift —mediumship."

"Spirits of the dead... like your friend," she says, not completely denying her ability.

I take it as a good sign that she will handle the transition from a norm to part of the magical community.

"Yes," I confirm. "Osen has communicated through you, which, as a supernatural being, he shouldn't be able to do."

"Wait..." Jade grips my knee.

My body lights up that she would want to touch me at all. But I remind myself she doesn't know about my deceit yet. She doesn't know I'm a monster.

"Are you suggesting that Rob is some sort of supernatural being?" Her eyes widen, and she looks like she's about to run if we tell her yes.

"Our best guess is that he's a warlock," I answer and clasp my hand over hers, hopefully comforting her.

She stares at our joined hands. "I'm confused. From what I've gathered from Osen and now you, you don't like witches and warlocks. So why do you care if I live or die? Is it only because I can talk to Osen?" She pulls her hand free from mine and tucks them under her arms.

"It's the reason we didn't kill you already," Calder finally chimes in.

*Thanks, dickhead.*

"So if I can no longer give you access to your friend, you plan on killing me?" Her eyes glaze over as if she's witnessing her future death scene. Maybe she is filling in the blanks of how we'd do it, recalling something from Osen's memories.

"We aren't going to hurt you," I promise.

Jade turns to me, tears welling in her eyes. "This was all a lie." Then she looks up at Maxum. "The whole dating thing was just a ruse to have access to your friend."

"Not for me," I say, but it sounds weak after all we've just told her.

"It makes sense now. You hate witches, meaning I'm your enemy. But you can't kill me, since I have a link to someone you want back. So you'll spare me... until Osen's spirit moves on."

I can almost see her emotionally detaching from this situation. It's a solid and proven defense mechanism.

"I don't hate you," I explain. "But yes, I don't like witches in general."

"We all *hate* witches," Calder grumbles.

"But that's only because witches have hurt us in the past," I say, trying to explain our stance. "Witches and warlocks have declared war on supes... over and over throughout the centuries. Well, the extremists have been the problem."

"You know the rest will fall in line when the battle truly begins." Calder paces the room in agitation.

Maxum is oddly the voice of reason and says, "Witches and warlocks are just as complex as supes. Not all of them will follow the Witch Council or ASO blindly. I have known some witches who have turned against their own covens and fought them when their covenmates' methods have gone too far."

Interesting that he rarely mentions these outlier witches. Why is he doing it now? Perhaps it's for Jade's sake, letting her know this doesn't necessarily have to be us versus her.

"I don't want to hurt anyone." She lifts her head in an act of defiance. "I even helped Osen when I wasn't sure if it was in my best interest. I fed him to give him power."

My monster is jealous as fuck that Osen has been with her. Rationally, I know it was probably to help Osen get stronger, and the act might be what saved Jade's life.

"You only fed him so he could protect you, since you're a weak witch." Calder has lost some of his steam, so it comes out as more of a fact and not quite an insult.

"Yeah, I don't want to die. But I also did it because it felt like the right thing to do to help him solve his murder." She frowns. "And I did it for all of you—because he's your friend. But the gesture is likely lost now, since I'm guessing I'm your prisoner of war."

Calder grunts in agreement.

Maxum narrows his eyes at the phoenix. "We need to keep you here, Jade. But that's as much for your sake as ours. If Rob finds out you survived, he will come after you again."

"Oh! My fur babies!" she gasps. "Did Rob hurt them, too?"

She seems more worried about them than the fact she's our prisoner.

"I didn't think to check on them. But why would he do anything to them?" I ask.

"Rob hates them… for some strange reason."

Probably because he knows they are magical creatures. But I keep that one to myself. This has been enough of a revelation tonight.

"If you plan on keeping me prisoner, please take them to a shelter so they don't die of neglect?" Her sad green eyes undo me.

Apparently, Maxum is affected too. He sighs as if this is sending him over the edge. "I'll check on them." He gets up and goes into the backyard to portal out. I find it telling that he's so kind in easing her into this world.

I'm also happy that she seems to accept most of this without solid proof.

Although, I won't be surprised if she relapses. I've seen it before. Then we will have to show her our true forms to make her understand.

After a moment of her sitting quietly dazed, Maxum calls out that the animals are safe.

"Thank you," she whispers. Her eyelids droop. She sways in her seat and falls sideways over my lap.

"I'm putting her in my room," I announce and carry her into my small space, setting her down on my bed. I brush her long hair from her face and pray she will forgive me when I confess my sins.

## 27

### HERE WE GO

JADE

"*A*m I losing my fucking mind?" I ask the darkness that surrounds me.

I'm back in the shadowscape, as Osen calls it.

"No," Osen says as the room we're in lightens up enough for me to see his shadowform standing in front of me.

I'm in my bedroom, not passed out on Arran's couch.

"You are a witch… as I've been telling you since we first spoke," he reminds me.

"Your kind hates my kind." Feeling utterly depressed about being their enemy, I sit anxiously on the edge of my bed.

My mind registers that I'm naked, and I cross my arms in a futile attempt to cover up.

"No need for that here," Osen says gently, his shadowbody moving closer. "If you are uncomfortable with your nakedness, even after all we experienced together, I can conjure clothes for you."

Osen's right. He's seen all the goods. He's been inside this version of my body—which is very much like my actual body.

"You control all of this?" When he nods, I ask, "Then why do you have me look like this? Is it to make it feel more real because it appears to be my own body?"

I watch for his reaction. I find it's easier to do because he is more solid now. I can see hints of confusion on his face. "I like the way you are made."

"You *like* the way I look?" I try not to be insecure, but after Rob, it has been harder to accept that men want all my curves and imperfections.

His shadowhand strokes my hip and trails up my side. "I enjoy all your softness, your plump ass, and full tits."

"But usually, you're attracted to males, aren't you?" I ask, because that's what it appears to be from his memories.

"I'm attracted to the individual. I believe the closest thing I am is what humans call pansexual or omnisexual nowadays. Yes, typically, I enjoy my males big and brawny, but not necessarily. And I often delight in my females being curvy and soft. Which isn't a common trait for supernatural women."

"Most supe women are thin?" I wonder aloud.

"It's what got me in trouble. Witches are human-born, so they are often thicker. When I was just awakening to my powers, I was attracted to such a witch. She tortured me for a month until I was on death's door. Fortunately, Maxum saved me from that fate. Then years later, I let my guard down and trusted another witch. She tried to end me too."

"Oh, my god, I'm so sorry." I almost reach for him, then realize he might not want my touch.

"Oh, my *Goddess*," he corrects and places his hand in mine. "Those witches are why I hate your kind, but they aren't the only ones who have committed horrible deeds."

"So you believe all witches are your enemy?"

"Maybe not. Being inside you, here in the shadowscape, I merged with your spirit… I see not all witches are cruel."

YVE VALE

"*I* changed your mind?" I'm a bit surprised since he's been clearly anti-witch.

"You offered yourself willingly, while also knowing I could possibly do you great harm when I fed."

"I was nervous, but didn't believe you were a bad person."

"Jade," his use of my name is disarming. "I'm afraid you're too trusting."

"And you aren't trusting enough," I add.

"Perhaps." He nods. "But I'm older than you, and I've had more experience with deceit. I've had a dozen people close to me attempt to end me. Rob was just the last of them."

"What did Rob do?" I ask. "I don't remember a thing."

"He knows you're a medium," Osen explains. "He attempted to trigger a mind-control spell that he has in place. He chanted a phrase and then asked what you knew about me and the ASO investigation."

I curse, anger rising up in me. Rob's violated my trust more than I could have ever imagined. "Rob hypnotized me to do his bidding? Like a sleeper agent?"

"Yes. Technically, you were working for my enemy."

I sit in shock, but as I process this, I find it fits with my strange 'dream' experiences, his interest in my dreams, and why he was with me when he didn't seem to like me all that much. "Go on."

"Well, since I had taken over your body, his spell didn't work on me. He realized right away that it wasn't you he was speaking to. He attacked with a spell I've never seen before."

"He tried to... kill me?"

"It was a very close thing. I don't know if he was only trying to exorcise me, kill you, or both." Osen's shadow wraps around me like a hug. "But I was able to keep you bound to your mortal coil. I shared my energy with you...."

"Why?"

"Because I recognized you were a victim, just as I was."

I want to believe him, but part of me is now souring to look for the best in others. Perhaps everyone is only out for themselves. They have played me for a chump.

Arran and Maxum only dated me to get information about Osen.

At least Maxum didn't lead me on and play with my emotions. We had brunch together and nothing more.

When I think about what Arran did with me sexually under the guise of liking me... hurt stirs in my soul.

"You didn't save me for my sake but for your own," I say, and it feels like venom dripping from my mouth.

"Yes. I benefitted, because I'm trapped in your body. But I didn't want you to die. Not when I could help."

"Sure," I say, not wholly believing him. "What about your buddies?" I demand.

"You mean Arran?" Osen sighs. "I'm afraid he really likes you. He would have let me die to save you."

"You're just saying that." I stand up and want to get away from him, but I'm not in control here. Osen is.

He moves in front of me, the shape of his face clear. He slips one arm around my waist, and another moves up to cup my cheek. "I'm not lying, not about my motives, and definitely not about Arran. I sort of wish I were."

"Because you love him?" My heart slightly softens to his plight.

"Yes."

"But he can't want me."

"I'm afraid we both want you. I suspect the others do, too." His lips brush over mine. "*I* want more of you, little witch."

He kisses me. I realize this is the first time. He did almost everything else but this. As if this simple act was sacred to him. It makes sense. This is more than sex. This is intimacy.

A warming wave rushes through me. I sense him, his soul. Osen's telling me the truth. He wants me. He cares, even if he doesn't want to.

"We have this time together," I say, snaking my arms around his waist.

"Yes, but you're about to wake, and it will have to wait." He holds me tightly to his shadowy but firm chest. "Until next time, my sweet, fuckable little witch."

The light of day streams in and makes me curse as if I'm a sun-shy vampire.

"Do vampires exist?" I wonder aloud as I throw my hands up to cover my eyes as the nuclear-level amount of sunlight shouts at me.

"That's a weird waking thought, and yes they do," Arran sounds amused. "Except they aren't what humans have made them up to be. Although they have fangs, love drinking magical blood, and are fast."

I try to sit up and look around, but honestly, my body isn't having it. I'm exhausted.

"Water?" Arran asks, coming to sit on the edge of the bed to inspect me.

"My throat feels like a dehydrated bitch, so yeah," I practically croak, my voice sounding as rough as I feel.

Arran slides his muscular arm behind my upper back and lifts me enough as he places a glass of water to my lips.

My hand automatically clasps over the glass, and I touch his warm fingers. Another lightning bolt of energy hits me with our touch. My heart pounds in response to his proximity. I don't know if his interest in me is real, but my feelings for him definitely are.

I pull back to let him know I've had enough water.

He gently rests my head on the pillow and sets the half-empty glass down.

I study the fairly stark room instead of looking at my sexy-as-fuck-maybe-boyfriend. Things just feel awkward now. I don't know what last night's news means for my future.

Our future.

Do I have a future? Or will one of his buddies kill me because I was born a witch and because Rob used me?

"Where am I?"

"My room, in our safe house." He tucks me in, tapping the blanket edges around my hips. He's nervous too.

I finally look directly at him. "What are you going to do?"

"What do you mean?"

"Are you going to kill me?"

"No. I'm going to keep you safe." He strokes my cheek.

"But why?" I turn my face away. I need to stay focused. "You think I'm your enemy—a witch."

"*You* aren't my enemy. You were being used, from what we can figure out."

"That's what Osen said." I sigh and rub my eyes with both hands. "He told me what happened with Rob. Not that you or your friends will believe me."

"What did Osen say?" Maxum is suddenly in the doorway. Damn, he takes up the entire space.

"He said that Rob was using my ability to talk with spirits without my knowledge and tried to trigger some kind of hypnosis spell. When Rob realized that I had been compromised by having Osen in charge of my body, he attacked and left me to die."

Arran looks at Maxum. "It makes sense—why Rob was so possessive and why we sensed her innocence."

Maxum grunts in agreement. "How are you doing?" he asks me. "Why aren't you running down the street screaming like a maniac about the existence of a magical world?"

"Because I don't like running?" I shrug. "I'm sure my panic attacks will come in waves." I try to sit up, and Arran helps me, placing pillows behind my back to prop me up. "Maybe I'm okay with it because I suspected magic was real with my abuela saying she was a witch and the weird dreams I've had my whole life. I just didn't know it was *this* scary."

Maxum grunts. "You're telling the truth about that."

"Are you a walking lie detector?" I ask.

"I can be." He nods. "But usually, it scrambles the person's brain, so I only do it if I'm desperate or desperately bored."

My eyes widen. I believe him, even with my limited powers of reading people.

Giving Maxum the side-eye, Arran asks, "How much do you remember from last night's conversation?"

"That you're supes. I'm a witch. You hate me."

"We don't hate *you*," Maxum corrects with a sigh, and I'm surprised it's him who does.

"Then why were you mean during brunch?" I ask.

"I thought you might have had something to do with Osen's death." Maxum narrows his eyes and reminds me, "You did spy on us at the bar."

"I said I'm sorry about that." My eyes widen when I think about how he said I wasn't wrong about how I had guessed their personalities. "Wait a damned minute. Was I right? About all your supernatural abilities?" I almost feel giddy that I might have nailed the magical spy thing without having known it.

"Yes. I'm a demon," Maxum confirms.

Arran squirms away uncomfortably.

"What about you?" I ask.

"Let's come back around to that later," he says in an ominous tone.

I pout but then recognize there is a lot to his situation if Osen's dream is to be taken as fact. They mentioned Arran had a terrifying beast that his friends might have to kill if it took control.

Oh…

Arran's beast might kill me after all and not even mean to.

I scoot back from him.

"You need to tell her everything," Maxum says with a firm

tone. It's not quite a command, but it doesn't leave room for argument. "You have no excuse now."

I glance back and forth between them. "Tell me what?"

"You're tired." Arran tries to stand up, but Maxum takes his shoulder and presses him back down to sit on the edge of the bed again.

"I'm a shifter." Arran doesn't even look me in the eye.

"That was my guess." I gain a bit more energy with my confirmed projection.

Then it hits me.

"Hold up... are you a *wolf* shifter?" My voice has hit a high pitch. My heart drops to my gut and swirls in confusion.

I loved Beast. But I thought he was just a dog.

"Are you the fucking *dog*?" I cover my mouth and try to remember all the interactions with Beast.

Arran has been eerily still during my enlightenment, which confirms it without his words. "I am."

"You slept in my bed. You ate off my floor. You shit in my yard." I shake my head in disbelief. "I trusted you as both a dog and a human. And you weren't either."

"I'm sorry. Initially, I didn't intend to spy on you inside your home, but you invited me in. I thought at first you knew what I was. Then, I realized you didn't. But I was entrenched at that point and had to know if you were involved in Osen's death."

"You went through my things, didn't you?"

"Yes, but—"

"You pretended to want to date me and protect me from Rob, but that was all a ploy to know all the details about my life."

"It wasn't a ploy." Arran tries to catch my hand, but I pull away. "I didn't want to see you hurt. I fell for you."

"You accuse me of spying, but wow. You guys take it to another level." My eyes burn. "So licking my pussy was just a day at work? A spy's job is never done, huh?"

"Goddess, it's not like that." Arran falls to his knees at the side of the bed and clasps his hands as if praying. "Please believe me. I wanted you the first moment I saw you, but thought you were the enemy. When I sensed you weren't, I was relieved and set out to prove your innocence. I want to protect you."

"I'm supposed to believe all that?" I huff, "What about Osen? Did you use my body to fuck him?"

"What? No!" Arran draws back in horror.

"I remember kissing you. Maybe you did more?"

"You kissed me," he defends himself. "But all I did was talk to Osen."

"So you've known all along that Osen was possessing me?" I hold my forehead. I was barely holding on to my sanity before this conversation. Now I want to crawl away and sleep for a million years.

"I wouldn't have had sex with your body," Arran says.

My first instinct is to be offended, but there's more to his loaded statement.

"What do you mean?" I ask, staring into his golden-amber eyes that radiate pain.

"I wouldn't do it, because I can't." Arran frowns as if this is the hardest thing he's had to say in his life. "I've been cursed by a witch. When my emotions are riding high, I turn into a true beast—not just a wolf. I would hurt you. And I don't want to hurt you."

He's telling the truth because I can see it on his face, and I recall Osen's memory.

"You led me on." I glower at him. "We can't have something between us, anyway,"

"I could only be with Osen after it happened because he can immobilize my entire body. But with you, I was hoping…"

"What?" I demand. "What could you possibly be expecting from me after all this?"

Maxum answers when Arran doesn't, jarring me with the

reminder that he's still here watching this whole love life fiasco. "He was hoping you could keep his beast under control."

"It's true," Arran agrees. "Your presence seems to keep him quiet. Calmer."

I don't know if it's his answer or my fatigue from apparently dying, but the room fuzzes out a bit. My head feels light and heavy at the same time.

"She needs to rest." Maxum waves his hand at Arran, encouraging the shifter to leave me the fuck alone.

I'll have to say the demon is winning some points here.

## 28

# HEALING

JADE

*I*'ve been in and out of consciousness. I wouldn't be so presumptuous to call it sleep. This "rest" has been elusive and in no way restorative.

I haven't even seen my new incubus friend when I've been passed out.

Arran has been here a few times when I open my eyes, looking sorrowful and repentant. I believe he murmurs his apologies even when my eyes are closed.

Twice, I discover Maxum keeping vigil in Arran's room, watching over me. I read the concern in his eyes. And maybe something more, or perhaps I only wish to see that he's as attracted to me as I am to him.

Even Flint shows up, staring at me like I'm a great mystery of the ages.

His gaze is distant as I peek through my lashes at him, studying him. He fascinates me. I want to know more about this quiet, brooding presence. His fingers fiddle with some worn scrap of fabric. I have the sense that it's precious to him.

"Hi," I say, opening my eyes.

"Hello." His unease is visible. "You need something?"

"To talk. Is that okay?" I wince, expecting him to tell me to stuff it. I don't know how this guy feels about me. I am a wicked witch, after all.

"On what topic would you like to converse?" he asks.

"Anything." I want to ask him about his fabric treasure, but I don't want to shut him down. "But I suppose I'd like to talk about Arran, what he did. What do your friends want from me? Are all supernatural beings real? What's it like being a gargoyle? Do you protect places or people from evil? Do you turn to stone? Do you have other kinds of magic?"

"You have a lot of questions," Flint states, a slight upturn of his lips makes me think he's amused by aggressive curiosity. "In which order should I answer them?"

"I don't know." I pick at the blanket, feeling vulnerable. "I suppose I mostly want to know if I should believe Arran's apology and forgive him. But I also want to know more about the supernatural world... the real one, not the crap I make up."

"It sounds as if the stories you invent aren't excrement, but hold value and truth. At least, that's what Maxum and Arran have told me. I haven't read them yet. I don't read fiction." He glances at his fabric and sighs. "Yes, I can turn to stone, but only when I need to safeguard myself from injury. And I have a protective nature. I can't say if I know what it is to be a gargoyle. I just *am* me... and don't know what it's like to be anything else."

"That's what fiction does. It can give you a glimpse into how someone else feels," I say when he pauses.

"Perhaps I should try reading one."

"It doesn't have to be mine. I won't be offended," I add.

He nods and continues, "Maybe you can suggest something

for me to begin my literary journey. Maybe not something heavy in a romantic theme?"

"Okay. I can do that." My mind races, compiling a list of books he might enjoy.

"As for Arran, he didn't mean to destroy your trust. He thought you were a threat. But his instinct to be near you made it impossible for him to pull away. He couldn't confess his true nature because you didn't know about your own. It was foolish of him to pursue a relationship with you."

"Because I'm a witch?" I ask, tears welling in my eyes. I believe I stupidly fell in love with Arran, and my heart hurts with the idea he can't be with me because of what I am.

"No, because he is a monster," Flint corrects, his voice soft. "We all are."

"Oh. You think he will hurt me? That you will all hurt me?"

"The odds are not in your favor."

"Are all supes monsters?"

"No. Most are much like humans. Perhaps they are more arrogant, which seems impossible. Supernaturals are often devastatingly beautiful. Obviously, I'm not like most supes."

His face and body are wide, and he epitomizes masculinity to the point of being absurd. "You are extremely handsome."

"This isn't my true form. You wouldn't find it appealing."

"My tastes are broader than most." I offer him a smile, hoping he will show me.

He grumbles, but changes the subject. "Arran cares about you. He didn't mean to damage the relationship you were developing."

"But his beast might accidentally hurt me?"

Flint nods. "None of us want to see you hurt. I don't even think Calder wants that, no matter how he blusters."

"Do you believe me when I say that I didn't hurt Osen? I didn't even know I was a witch. If I helped the witches and warlocks kill your friend, it wasn't my choice."

"I know. You were being used." He frowns.

My fatigue hits me again, and my eyes flutter shut.

"Sleep, sweet witch," he whispers, perhaps not intending for me to hear.

Waking up, I feel like crap, and that's putting it mildly. It seems as though each time I wake up, I feel worse.

My dry throat makes me cough, and it's enough to rouse me to move and seek water. Of course, this is the one time when I open my eyes that no one is here to help me.

With great effort, I get the covers off me and sit on the edge of the bed, summoning the energy to get up.

It takes another few minutes to remember how standing works.

I shuffle to the open doorway, zeroing in on the doorframe as my next life goal.

My hand settles on the frame, and I gasp in a breath, basking in my victory.

My grip slips, and I tumble forward.

At the same moment, someone turns from the hall into Arran's room.

A male voice is cut off mid-word, "Wha—"

My body crashes against what feels like a wall.

Massive arms wrap around my torso, and they freeze.

I look at the literal rock-hard body my face is pressed against —tan-colored marble. I didn't know a gargoyle's flesh was so unyielding.

*Flint… the gargoyle version.*

"Okay, buddy, you can let go." My arm wanly pats his biceps.

He doesn't move or respond to me.

"Flint?" I call.

Nothing.

I'm worried he's debating the merits of crushing me with his humongous arms. Heck, I think his pinky fingers could crush me all by themselves.

I tilt my head back to look at his face, but it takes some effort with my debilitating exhaustion.

Flint is solid stone.

His eyes are locked onto me but appear to be unseeing. They are no longer filled with their usual quiet inquisitiveness. His face looks as though he is frozen with fright.

Do witches scare this huge guy enough to defend himself like this?

He might scare me more if I didn't get the feeling that he has a gentle soul under all his group's talk of war and revenge.

I try to slip down and out of his hold, but his arms are locked tight enough around my waist that I can't move.

"Fuck," I mutter, my face still pressed against Flint's smooth marble chest.

Is this his true gargoyle form? He appears to be in his human form, but only now, made of carved marble. I was hoping he would have tusks and wings.

Oh, well, another fantasy bubble burst. Unless he has a shifted form since he said I would be turned off by his true form. But I see no other change than his solidity.

Back to the matter at hand... I wonder what could be wrong with him to make him turn. Has someone spelled him?

Can a witch's mere touch do that? Did I hurt him? Accidentally cursed him?

The guys are going to think the worst of me... especially Calder. I hope he doesn't discover us first.

I wiggle to break free, but it's no use. I'm pinned to him. As it is, I can barely take a full breath.

"Arran?" I call to the empty house. I don't know how I know it's empty, but I feel it. "Maxum? Calder?"

I don't know what they could do about this, but maybe they have some anti-statue spell.

Fatigue washes over me again. I tuck my arms into my body,

lean my head against the gargoyle's massive chest, and pass out.

"Jade!" I hear Arran shout from a distance.

I open my eyes and see him peering over Flint's broad shoulder. He's stuck on the other side of the bedroom door that Flint's giant body is blocking entirely.

"Arran?"

"Oh, thank fuck," he sighs. "I thought you might be…"

"Dead?" I finish for him. "No. But this might be my new life now, caught in Flint's hold."

Maxum asks, "What happened?"

"I was going to ask you that," I say. "All I did was get out of bed to get some water, and Flint quickly came through the door. Since I could barely stand, I accidentally fell into him. He grabbed me and froze. I swear I didn't mean to hurt him."

"He's not hurt," Maxum assures me.

"Thank goodness," I breathe out.

"Did he hurt you?" Arran asks.

"No." I look up again at his strange frozen expression. "What's going on? Why did he turn to stone? Did my witchiness do this?"

"Witchiness?" Maxum chuckles, then mutters, "*Womanness* is more like."

"What do we do?" Arran asks Maxum. "We can't get around him even to see how tight of a hold he has on her."

"It's pretty tight," I inform him. "I can't budge."

"Shit." Arran's frustration worries me.

"Is there a spell or something to wake him up?"

"He's not asleep," Maxum grumbles. "He's petrified."

"Forever?" I screech. That's not a great sound.

"Hopefully not," Maxum says with a sigh. "We need to calm him."

"Isn't he a battle-tested warrior? Why would colliding with me in the hallway upset him?"

"He doesn't like to be touched," Arran answers.

"Shit!" I lift my arms away from where they were resting on his. "Can he hear me?"

"Yeah," Maxum says. "He's aware of what's going on in his stone form."

"Flint?" I begin, my voice soft. "I'm sorry I touched you. Please don't be upset with me. I like you, and I didn't mean for this to happen. I will be more careful around you, I swear it. I need you to just soften your stone, and I can stop touching you."

Tears fall from my eyes, because I don't like that my budding friendship with him is on the line. I wanted to get to know him, and now he won't ever want to be around me again.

"I'm so sorry. I keep messing up, making mistakes." I sniff, feeling like a failure. I don't know why, but all my problems tumble out of me. Maybe it's because I'm certain I will die soon. I can feel my life force slowly slipping from my body. Or maybe because I'm so damned exhausted, I can't think straight.

"I didn't even know I was a witch. My abusive, warlock ex-boyfriend only dated me to brainwash me and use me to channel dead people. I caught the attention of the wrong hot guys. I invited a wolf shifter who wanted to kill me into my house. I went on a brunch date with a demon who wants to scramble my brains. I'm possessed by a sex ghost who tolerates me only so he can power up. And I'm pretty sure I'm still dying from Rob's spell. And now? I'm stuck in the arms of a sexy gargoyle who can't stand my touch."

Yeah, I'm leaning into my self-pity.

I'm 'whining'… *whatever*.

People can be sad once in a fucking while. I'm sick of always having to keep my shit together.

Why is it that the only accepted form of emotional expression is snarky anger?

Be tough. Be strong. And be an asshole.

No. Sometimes we just need to grieve. Say how we feel.

Sometimes, we need to call out how fucked life can be.

If we don't acknowledge what's wrong, what makes us depressed, then we rarely make the changes we need to get out of it.

Besides, it's justified for me to have a fucking breakdown after all that's happened. Even the emotionally resilient need a vacation from being strong.

Apparently, my sadness shakes something loose in Flint as I hear a moan that sounds like gravel grinding on itself.

Flint's grip on me loosens until I can slip downward. He still hasn't let up entirely, though. Of course, as I move down, my face drags over his... not six, not eight, but ten-pack abs. I feel a generous package under his pants. I try my best to not be a perv and ignore that, making this as nonsexual as possible.

But the gargoyle does something to my heart. If I thought he'd be into it and had any strength left, I'd enjoy this trip along his body more.

Finally free from his hold, I collapse onto the floor. I don't have the energy to get up.

Flint returns to his flesh form and staggers backward until he slams his body into the hallway wall behind him. His eyes are wide with panic and shame. "I'm sorry, Jade. It's my fault, not yours." He runs off before I can tell him it's okay.

I feel something wet under my hand and see a glass of spilt water that Flint must have been bringing me when I crashed into him.

He was trying to take care of me.

Arran rushes inside and lifts me into his arms. "I got you, sweetness."

This little misadventure took more out of me than I realized. "I don't feel well," I say as I pass out.

My eyes are still closed when I hear the guys talking.

"Jade needs healing," Arran says to Maxum. "The killing hex is still hurting her."

"She won't want it from me," Maxum argues.

I slowly open my eyes. "Why not?" My words come out slurred.

"You would see my true form, and the healing is... sexual in nature," the demon sounds contrite.

"My beast won't like you touching until he's claimed her," Arran whispers to Maxum.

I start to giggle until I'm in full chuckling mode.

"Why is that funny?"

"Because, of course, it's *sexual!*" I believe I've lost my mind. "Why can't anything be simple?" My humor drops like a stone. "Besides, you want me dead. So you wouldn't want to sex magic me up anyway, right?"

"I didn't say that," Maxum says quietly.

My mind spins as I turn to look at him. "What part?"

He squares his broad shoulders. "I don't want you to die. And I would share my magic to heal you."

"But you seem hesitant." Nervousness crawls over me. I wonder what his version of sex magic is. "So I'm guessing you don't want to fuck me."

"It's not that. My true form will scare you." Maxum nods to Arran. "And it will trigger his berserker beast if I have sexual relations with you."

I snicker at the use of 'sexual relations.' I turn to Arran, "Will your beast hurt us if Maxum does his sex magic thing on me?"

"Hold on." Maxum's usually calm exterior cracks. "Are you saying you want to fuck a demon?"

"It's on my bucket list," I joke. Well, I sort of joke... It's totally on my imaginary bucket list. Or it was, when I thought it was fictional.

"Arran?" Maxum looks at his friend. I know he's not asking

permission per se, but he doesn't want his beast to hurt us… probably me.

"I… I want to say that I'll be okay." Arran turns to me. "But my beast is riding me right now, since I've messed things up with you."

I take a moment to consider what's really happening. On the one hand, this all feels like I'm caught in some strange fantasy-nightmare. On another, I look at it as if I'm writing one of my paranormal novels. Rules don't apply the same way in a supernatural world. I'm familiar with this concept.

And sure, Arran made mistake after mistake, but I still don't get that icky feeling like Rob gave me.

I believe I've already forgiven Arran after I've thought about all of it and what Flint said.

"Why didn't you tell me before?" I ask, knowing why, but needing it confirmed.

"You didn't know about supes. I thought you'd turn me away. I knew I was over the line with my behavior."

"If I were to forgive you, what would you want from me moving forward? Really want… not just the answer you *think* I want to hear."

Arran gulps. He knows this is his test. It comes down to this. "I want to make you my mate. Love you. Protect you."

Geeze. These supes don't play around. It's let me 'lick your pussy, and then I'm mating you for eternity' in the next breath.

Do I mind? Not really. I write this shit because it turns me on. I've desired to have someone consumed by my existence.

"How can we soothe Arran's berserker *and* have you do what you need to do to heal me?" I ask Maxum.

"I think he's going to need to be inside you when I am."

My body heats with that image. Do I take one in the mouth? One in the ass? I wonder which I would prefer where. And I love all the ideas. I can't choose.

"Oh, wait, what about STDs?" I hold my hands out like they

are about to rip my blanket away and fuck me stupid... well, *more* stupid.

"Supes don't carry diseases," Maxum assures me. "You aren't worried about me breeding you?"

Oh, shit. I'm dying inside with his use of the word *breeding*.

I wonder if he has a kink. But I wait as the impulse to giggle passes, and I shake my head. "I'm on birth control."

Maxum looks at his crotch, and then at Arran's growing bulge. "I'm going to get something stronger. Our magic might negate your prevention."

Even though I feel weak as a fragile wilted flower, I apparently died and don't exactly feel double penetrated fresh. "Maybe I can clean up while you get that?"

"You can't even sit up." Arran fidgets, his hands poised to snatch me up.

"Can you help me?" I ask, feeling vulnerable. I've been so independent and isolated. It's a foreign sensation asking for help.

Arran exhales, and his tension falls away. "It would be my honor."

"I'll be back soon, little witch." Maxum nods and heads out of the house.

My shifter smiles sadly. "I'm so sorry. I wish I wasn't cursed. Then I could let you be with Maxum alone."

I hold my arms out to him so he can help me up. When his strong arms lift me and carry me to the bathroom, I confess, "It's okay. I want both of you."

## 29

## BUCKET LISTED

ARRAN

When Jade confesses to wanting us both, I almost stumble with her in my arms. Which is not great since we are now on the slip-sliding away bathroom tiles.

I steady myself and try to remain calm. But my beast is waking the fuck up.

What's worse, I don't know how long Maxum will be away.

I need him to keep her safe... just in case my beast loses control. And losing control is on-brand for that part of myself.

"Arran?" Jade calls me softly.

I realize I'm gripping her so tightly that she probably can't breathe. "Sorry."

I loosen my hold and pull the throw blanket away from her naked body—well, almost naked body.

My arm is bracing her against me. Her full breasts are begging to be released from the thin bra she's wearing, and I wonder why she even bothers with wearing the flimsy thing. I want her naked all the time, ready for me to fondle her beautiful tits.

She's strong enough to pull the thin sports bra over her head. I have to resist the urge to lean down and nibble her mounds and suck on her hardening nipples.

Using my free hand, I slide her underwear down her thick thighs.

My eye catches on the only thing she has left on—her golden pendant. She seems to wear it all the time. "What's this?"

"My abuela gave it to me—my grandmother. She said it was a protection pendant." She fiddles with it nervously. "I guess it doesn't really work that great."

"Well, you are still alive, so maybe it does?" I offer.

Jade nods sadly, then glances at my clothed state. "What about you?"

I was ready to go in the shower with my sweatpants on because if I'm naked with her, it will be much harder to resist plunging into her slick heat.

"You are too tempting, and we can't start messing around without Maxum," I warn.

"Because of your beast?"

"I could hurt you."

She nods and assures me, "I'll be a good girl. Promise."

Jade can barely move, so I didn't expect her to be the problem. But the thought sobers me. She's completely at my mercy. Her life is in my hands. I'm alone with the woman I want to make my mate, and I could kill her.

I'm also as hard as Flint in his gargoyle form. And I don't want her to freak out with my eager cock.

I turn on the water to warm it and try to command my dick to deflate.

Slowly pushing my sweats down, I say, "Don't freak out."

"That's not an alarming phrase while revealing a dick for the first time. No, not at all," she says sarcastically.

My cock pops over the waistband.

Jade gasps.

Ugh. I knew she would hate it. I close my eyes and wish I'd been born a warlock instead.

"Holy magic eight-balls." She sucks in a breath. "Do you actually lock inside a woman?" Instead of sounding disgusted, she sounds intrigued about my knot—excited.

"I can. But that's usually done with other wolf shifters."

"Does it stay that size or get bigger?"

"It would swell a bit when I lock in." I blink with surprise. "Do you want that?"

"Uh, I've written about all this fancy peen, but to have the chance to try it out, with a real, live supernatural being? Sign me up."

I frown. "Why do I feel like a glorified boy toy right now?"

"Does that mean you don't want to fuck me with it?" she asks. "Shame."

I smack her ass lightly. "You are a brat."

"If I admit I am, do I get to play with my new toy?"

I smack her ass again, and she moans.

Somehow, my dick hardens even more.

Remembering that I can't fuck her yet, I lift us into the shower, and she squeaks when the water hits her backside.

I lather up my hands with soap and use them to clean her body—slowly and methodically.

When I massage her breasts and slide my fingers over her cunt and asshole, she murmurs how much she loves it.

I can scent her arousal even through the water pouring over her. She's driving me mad with desire and doesn't even realize it. I'm afraid I'm going to be a two-pump chump once I sink into her.

Once she's clean, I lift her out of the shower, set her on the vanity, and dry her off. Her hazel-green eyes watch me with a sly smile. Her gaze wanders over my entire body as I also take in her tantalizing, exposed flesh.

I wrap a dry towel around her and carry her back to my

room. I set her down on my bed, sitting up, so she hopefully feels less fragile.

"You're sure you want me?" I ask. It seems like a dream. I pray to the Goddess this fantasy doesn't turn into a nightmare if my beast loses control. Maybe I should have Maxum take me far away and chain me up while he heals her.

"I want you." She gently strokes my cheek. "Are you sure you want me? I don't know if you know, but I'm a criminally ignorant witch." She gives me a sassy grin.

"That's a whole step down from evil witch, so yeah, definitely on my bucket list."

Maxum returns a moment later. He clears his throat and hands Jade a small vial. "It's safe. Safer than human birth control. Effects are immediate."

Thanking him, she swallows the entire bottle with a wince.

"Give us a second?" Maxum asks me.

I don't like it, but his needs come into play here too.

I don't go far, just outside the door. It's as far as my beast will allow. It gives them the illusion of privacy, at least.

# 30

# HORNS AND ALL

## MAXUM

"You don't have to do this," the witch tells me.

It's true. I don't.

But I want to.

"If I don't do this or find another safe way to help you, you will likely die," I explain. "So I have to."

Do I sound desperate to slide my cock inside her? Because that's all I've been able to think about since I left to get the potion. Fuck, that isn't entirely true. I've wanted her since she told me to fuck off during brunch. I love a feisty woman. So few are that way with me. Either they are begging me to fuck them, or they're scared of the power they feel radiating off me and run far, far away.

Let's just say it's been a while since I found a female I wanted and one who wanted me, too. I don't want to admit it to either Jade or Arran, but I want her around more than for one fuck.

"Is there another way?" she asks.

"Not a guaranteed method, which I am. As for healers? I don't know who to trust. I'm fairly certain someone betrayed Osen within our outer circle. I won't expose you to that risk. Besides, the fewer people who know you are alive, the better. Rob believes you're dead, and I intend to keep it that way."

"I don't want you to do anything you're uncomfortable with." She tugs her towel higher as if that half-inch of skin offends me.

"All I do is shit I'm uncomfortable with," I chuckle darkly. "But I would assume you'd be the one who wouldn't want me since I was an asshole before."

"You thought I was the enemy. I understand that."

With my psychic senses, I pick up that she indeed understands.

"I must be in my true form for this to work." My words come out soft and a bit shy.

"Will you show me who you really are?" Jade adjusts as she leans against the wall, as if to brace herself.

I remove my shirt so she'll see my markings first—ease her into this.

The red lines cover my entire torso and arms.

Her eyes widen as she stares.

I nervously wait for her to respond to my markings. They are sacred to my people, and I don't want her to hate it.

*Fuck. Am I falling for her?*

"Do they have meaning?" Her hand lifts as if she wants to touch them.

"Sacred markings of my spirit. They appear magically when I have a significant experience. It's written in my flesh."

"That's amazing," she says with awe.

I sit down on the bed and offer my hand. When Jade slips her hand in mine, I place it on my forearm so she knows she can touch me.

She smiles. "You are so warm." Her eyes catch on the

broken, jagged lines in the center of my chest. "This shows how you've lost ones you loved."

She gets it—*me*.

I take her finger and run it over one particularly fresh-looking line. "This is Osen's death."

Tears well up in her eyes. "I'm so sorry. I know you meant a lot to each other."

"You've seen some of it?"

"I didn't mean to invade. I didn't see much. However, I saw this isn't your true form. I saw horns in one of the memories, but it was dark."

"Don't be afraid," I say and shift, showing off my deep red skin and curled horns.

This crazy woman, who just discovered the magical world, doesn't look the least bit afraid. She looks entranced by me.

Is it horrible that I'm disappointed that I didn't startle her a little?

Her hungry gaze makes up for it though. She licks her lips as she eyes my horns.

I unfurl my bat-like wings, and she squeals with joy.

*She squeals… what the actual fuck?*

"Wings!" she claps happily.

Might as well see if she can deal with the rest of it. She's going to see it in a few minutes, anyway.

I yank down my pants and reveal my tail wrapped around my waist and my already throbbing, hard dick.

"A tail!" She bites her lips in anticipation, the crazy witch. "And your cock is…"

Arran bursts back into the room, his skin rippling with a barely contained shift.

"Oh, Arran, come here." She holds her hand out to him, inviting him to be part of this. "How do we help you handle what's going on?"

"If you touch him, I need to be touching you at the same time."

"But you're okay with him touching me?" she asks, because it is an interesting distinction.

"I know I have to share you, but until... *if* I claim you, my beast will be on edge about sharing your affection." Arran looks me in the eye. "If I look like I will hurt her, do what you have to do to stop me. Even if it means ending me."

"Arran!" she cries. "I don't want you to be hurt."

"I'll never forgive myself if I injured you." He presses his forehead to hers. "I believe my beast wants to pleasure you too, so I think we will be okay."

I nod at both of them, and Jade ogles my jutting member again. "You wanted to touch my cock?" I ask.

She nods and looks at both our dicks. "I want to feel both of you."

Her eyes linger on my unusual cock. It's similar to a dragon cock, but with spiky-looking ridges around the head and along the top and bottom of its length.

"Textured for pleasure," I say, stroking myself to show her they aren't sharp.

We each take one of her hands and place it on our cocks at the same moment.

Wisely, she strokes Arran first and lightly squeezes his knot.

He jerks in her hand. "Fuck. You keep playing like that, and I'm going to knot you this fucking second."

She gives Arran a kiss, and he deepens it, claiming her with his intensity. His hand cradles her jaw as he slowly rocks himself into her hand.

Jade turns to me and slowly slides her hand down my length and back again. "Oh. That's different."

Arran growls.

"Be a good boy and suck on my tit," she orders him.

Both our dicks twitch in her hold.

Arran snaps to it. Cupping her breast, he guides her plump nipple into his mouth.

Her hand squeezes me as she's overcome with pleasure.

Tentatively, she strokes me. I have to bite back my moan. I don't want either of them to know how much she affects me. Not yet.

With Arran distracted by his feast, my tail slides up, tickles her thighs, and brushes over the V where her mound disappears between her closed legs.

I need her on her back and open to me.

Besides, she's pushing her limits, and I can feel her energy failing her. I don't want to be fucking her while she's unconscious.

"Open your legs," I order.

She obeys quickly. Both Arran and I slide our hands up her inner thighs, brushing over her apex. Arran presses her backward as he sucks on her other tit.

"I'm going to taste your pussy now," I inform them. I need to make her ready for me.

Arran's barely handling this, but he's keeping the beast on lockdown for the moment. He grunts to acknowledge my announcement.

I kneel between her legs as they hang off the edge of the bed.

Slowly, I spread her thighs farther apart.

My fingers trace over her folds and I familiarize myself with her cunt, finding the bundle of nerves they now call a clit. She bucks when I do.

I lean forward to lick and suck on her nub.

"Oh, damn. Is your tongue forked?" she cries out the question as I use it to stimulate her clit.

"Does that turn you on, little witch?" I say with a smirk. I know it does with how wet she's getting. I flick my tongue in the air at her, and her eyes dilate.

"Fuck, yes." She grabs my horns to pull me in, and I bury my face in her pussy.

I swear I almost spill my seed right then, but that won't help her condition. So I maintain my control and slide two fingers into her, then I add another.

She grinds into my hand.

Goddess, I want her again when she's at full strength. I want her bouncing herself on my cock, my tail in her ass, gripping my horns, and screaming my name.

Pumping my hand into her, I tell them my idea. "I want Arran under you, taking your ass. I will take your pussy as I work my healing."

"My ass?" she pants. "But..."

"We can see if both of us can take your pussy at the same time," I suggest. "Or you can suck him down while I fuck you?"

My hand is instantly drenched in her juices with my dirty talk. My little witch is so responsive.

I wonder if we can share her all the time. Would Calder ever want her, too? Maybe Flint will finally get over his celibacy stint if he sees how she enjoys my true form. And that she can survive a monster fucking.

"What do you want, little witch?" I ask.

"I... uh." Arran pinches her nipple, and she shouts, "I want him to fuck my ass."

"I need your pussy first," Arran snarls, and I move out of the way.

I look for her consent, and she nods as Arran lines himself up. Then he realizes his frenzy. "Jade?"

"Yes, fuck me," she pants.

Arran shoves forward, and she moans with his thick shaft, where his knot pounds against her labia.

"Don't let her come yet, and you'll have to come in her ass," I warn.

"Goddess," she says, picking up on our lingo.

Her eyes glaze over. She's losing her ever-loving mind.

"Arran, on the bed, now," I order.

He glares at me, wanting to finish in her pussy. But he pulls out, lies on his back, and brings her on top of him.

I grab some lube and work it into her ass and over Arran's

dick. It's been a while since I've touched him like this, but he moans with pleasure.

"Ready?" I ask.

They both nod. Arran has both hands on her tits, cupping both entire mounds and pinching the large nipples. I'll need a suck on them too.

As soon as I get Arran distracted, I will make it my mission.

I line him up to her back entrance, and he presses inside. Slowly, he slides to his knot, her body welcoming him inside.

I watch the show for a moment, enjoying how she gasps and moans with his steady thrusts. I'm not sure how he's maintaining his composure, but when I look at his hands gripping her breast and one now over her low belly, I see his hands have shifted into fur and claws. The points are dangerously pressing into and dimpling her soft skin.

"Arran?" I question his control.

He looks at me, his eyes glowing amber and his teeth elongated. His mouth and nose have become a snout.

"Arran?" Jade calls him, caressing his monstrous hands. "It's okay. Just be careful with me."

He seems soothed by her words—that she accepts him even as his monster.

My hand rubs over her clit, and I slide my fingers inside again. "You ready, little witch?"

"Yes?" She hears her own nervousness and says with more certainty, "Yes."

I notch my enormous cock at her pussy and slowly press inside.

Arran groans and snarls, equally irritated and turned on by my invasion. I'm not even fully sheathed in her glorious body.

Jade pants as if she's giving birth. Her forehead is beading with sweat. "It feels... so... good. So full." She can do nothing but take what we are giving her. "Keep going," she insists, grabbing onto my waist to encourage me to move deeper.

Her legs drape over Arran's beastly thighs, and his knot teases her back entrance.

I lean forward and suck her unattended nipple into my mouth.

"Hurry, get all the way inside me. I think I'm dying," Jade whines. She isn't taking a bad turn, but I love that she's begging for my cock.

"Whatever you need." I work myself deeper until I'm finally seated. I'm surprised she's taken all I have to give. If she were to become ours, she would be perfect.

I love how her pussy squeezes my dick.

"Look at you, taking our cocks so well," I praise, sliding in and out of her.

Arran begins to work her ass, matching my rhythm.

She smiles, glancing up at me and looking blissed out of her mind.

I use this moment of her attention to give her a show… one I believe she will appreciate, as her monster fucking kink is loud and proud right now.

I pull back, slam into her, and flare my wings out, casting her in shadow, sheltering all three of us from the world.

"Fuck!" she screams and climaxes with the sight. Her pussy clenches my dick so hard I think I might pass out. Her face is lost in the pleasure we're giving her and I've never seen a more beautiful sight.

I begin the chant to heal her, my ancient language droning as I pump into her, extending her pleasure, grinding into her hips, my tail flicking over her clit.

I warn Jade, "Arran's about to come."

I pull the magic he releases with his orgasm into my magic to heal our witch. Her body starts to glow. A pattern of light shines over her.

I'm not sure what this is… a witch's protection warding?

However, it doesn't feel like that. I'll have to investigate later, when I'm not balls-deep inside her cunt.

Fortunately, whatever the glow is, it doesn't stop my healing magic from pouring into her body. I feel her gaining strength. I sense the damage from Rob's hex being repaired.

As I unload my cum deep into her cunt, I finish my sex magic spell and pull my wings tightly around us. I want to be with her again. Without Arran. For hours.

I want to learn everything I can about her body.

I want to teach her things she's only imagined in books.

Her body pulses with the unusual glow, and finally, it fades.

When I catch my breath, I acknowledge there's something *other* about Jade.

She isn't a mere witch.

That might explain her ability to channel and hold Osen's spirit.

And it might mean she is meant for us after all.

## 31

## AFTERCARE

JADE

*I*'m spread-eagle over the top of Arran's monster form with Maxum curling his massive body over mine. They are both buried deep inside me.

"That was..." I can't finish my sentence as I'm dizzy with euphoria, fatigue, and with the healing magic Maxum just used on me.

Arran's fur tickles my back, and he's huffing, recovering from his orgasm. He's stuffing me full, and I can feel his hot release leaking out of my ass.

Maxum's wings are still wrapped around us, and I don't want to break the moment by moving or saying anything more. While I do feel better health-wise, I'm still exhausted.

I'm also blissed out of my mind. I've never had an experience like that. I'm fairly certain my soul left my body... in a good way this time.

It feels like this is the place I've been seeking my entire life, in the arms of Maxum and Arran. I don't want this moment to end. I want to pretend for a while longer that we aren't enemies and this can somehow work out. To pretend as if I'm one of my own characters, and I can finally have a happy ending too.

The demon dick inside me twitches, and I suck in a breath. Those bumps and ridges do things to me, and I need to experience them again when I'm not at death's door.

I want to take him again, but slowly and with no distractions. I want to use my tongue to explore his cock and everything else. I need Maxum—all of him.

My hand skims his wing's hard ridge, and he bucks into me.

Oh, they're sensitive. Nice. But I should ask before I assume to touch. "Sorry."

Maxum pushes up and off me just enough to look into my eyes. His obsidian orbs have a warm glow to them—magic radiating from him. "You can touch me. I'm just hypersensitive during sexual activities."

His tail flicks over my clit and my pussy clenches. Since Maxum and Arran are still deep inside me, the three of us groan with the sensation.

"Like that," he chuckles.

"Arran? Are you okay?" I ask, turning my head to see him. I have no idea what his berserker beast looks like, but I'm curious.

"Don't look at me." His clawed hand moves to prevent me from seeing him, and he turns his face away. "I'm not fully shifted back yet." His voice doesn't sound quite human.

"I have your huge cock and your cum in my ass, and you won't let me see you?" Realizing this might not be the time for being sassy, I soften my voice. "Arran... I want to know you, all of you." I gently run my finger over the claw on his index finger.

I must have convinced him since Arran warns, "Maxum, get ready to take her away if she screams."

Now, I'm a bit nervous.

When he moves his hand, I see his beast, but he's actually

more attractive than I was expecting. His face is mostly wolf-like but with a humanized look to it.

His shoulders are bulkier than his human form and have a thin coat of fur. He still won't look directly at me.

Since my back is on his chest, I can't see more than that. To reassure Arran of how I feel about him, I give his snout a kiss.

His eyes fly wide with shock. "You kissed my beast!"

"Is it mad?" I ask.

Instead of answering, his body shifts back to his human form. Wow. That was weird, but cool. I sink a few inches lower since he's smaller in his normal body.

Arran gives me a searing kiss that conveys all his appreciation that I've accepted his monstrous side.

Maxum hums with interest at this exchange. I turn back to study him.

His demon form is so sexy that I could believe this was a dream. His face is almost the same, with his brow slightly more pronounced. I dare to drag my fingertip over the base of his horn. I peer into his eyes to see if this is okay, but they are closed, and he's smiling in bliss.

"That feels good?" I ask.

"Very much so." He opens his eyes and strokes my cheek. "I sense you're much stronger. But I need to stay inside you for a few more minutes. Is that all right, my little witch?"

He's being so sweet that I want to cry.

I have not one but two males caring for me, and sending me into emotional territory.

I nod so I don't have to risk my voice cracking.

However, Maxum sees beyond my walls which are pretty much windows at this point—and not even double-pane.

He presses his forehead to mine in a gesture of compassion that undoes me.

Tears drip over the sides of my face and land on Arran.

"Sweetheart?" my shifter coos from beneath me. "What's wrong?"

"Nothing. Everything." I inhale and exhale slowly. "You both think of me as the enemy but are still here healing and caring for me. Yet my ex, who told me he loved me, tried to murder me."

"You aren't our enemy," Maxum assures me.

"*You are pack*," Arran says, his voice deep and authoritative.

Even I recognize the magic in his statement. Goosebumps erupt over my skin as I feel the power wash over me.

I'm one of their people... as far as Arran is concerned. At least, he feels like that at the moment, with the pleasure of release running his brain.

But I've been betrayed and abandoned too many times to trust even a magically imbued claim. My own mother disowned me.

One of my arms goes over my shoulder to cup Arran's strong jawline with my palm. At the same time, I caress Maxum's face with my other hand. "Thank you for saving me."

The demon presses his lips to mine in a tentative kiss, but when I respond to him, his kiss becomes more urgent and consuming.

His hips rock into mine, and the squelching sound from his release makes my pussy throb with need again.

Maxum quickly lifts me off of Arran and cups my ass. When Arran gets up to follow, Maxum warns, "Your beast has been quelled. Let me satisfy mine. *Alone*."

His textured dick is still inside me, and as he walks, I'm rubbed in all the right ways. I finally let out my groan once we are in another room.

While still holding me to him, he grabs a clean towel and wipes the mess from my backside.

"I'm impressed with your staying power," I say about his cock that hasn't softened one bit.

"You turn me on, little witch." He nuzzles my jaw, and I lean back so he can kiss and lick my neck. His forked tongue feels amazing.

"What's happening now?" I ask, since I'm a virgin to this whole sex magic ritual.

"My own beast needed to have you to himself." Maxum kneads my ass. "I want to fuck you again."

"Oh." I check in with my body, and it feels absolutely on board with this suggestion. It also demands to know why this isn't happening already. If I don't agree quickly, my body is putting in a complaint with the manager.

"Would you like that?" Maxum cants his hips to make me take him deeper again.

"Fuck. Yes, I would." I'm completely supported by his cock and powerful arms around my ass, so I'm able to move my arms freely, exploring him. I stroke over his broad shoulders and then dip behind to see if I can reach where his wings attach to his back.

He curls inward to make it easier to reach around his enormous body.

When I feel and caress the tendons and bones where the wings connect to his back, Maxum bucks hard into me. Apparently, I've found the demon's G-spot.

His tail slides over the back of my thigh, teasing my asshole.

"Are you…"

"Yes, I am." He growls. "I'm going to fuck you with my tail and my cock."

As he slides inside me, where I've been made slick with Arran's cum, I about lose the few marbles I have left. "Are you sure you aren't trying to kill me through pleasure? I'm not objecting, by the way."

"I don't kill what's mine." He licks my nipple, playing with it with his forked tongue.

"Yours?" I ask, breathy from how he's working my body and a bit shocked he would want me.

"Mine." Maxum's voice is rough and possessive. "I can't let you go after this." He thrusts into me. "You're perfect."

I never expected my grumpy, snarky demon to say that. "No. You are."

He claims me with a kiss so passionate that it feels like our souls intertwine.

My hands are at the base of his horns, stroking them.

When he pulls back, he grins wickedly. "Such a good little monster fucker." His fingers lace into my thick hair at the base of my skull, and he fists a handful, tilting my head back until my neck is vulnerably arched and fully exposed. His sharp teeth graze my soft flesh.

I wonder if he'll bite me.

Do I want him to?

"Now that you're mine, all those fantasies you write about? I'm about to make them all come true, little witch." Maxum chuckles, then lifts me up and slams me down onto his cock while he's standing.

I grind against his pubic bone with every downward motion. I'm so fucking impressed with his strength that an orgasm quickly approaches. His tail pumps into me, stirring me higher. When I climax, I cry out at the sensation of his double penetration.

"Maxum!" I take hold of his horns again and ride my bucking bronco.

"Say it again!"

"Maxum!" I shout as I milk his cum from his textured cock.

His wings once again circle around me.

I feel unimaginably protected and cherished, cocooned within his embrace.

My head falls forward against his chest. All the energy I had from the first round has dissipated.

"I got you, little witch," Maxum murmurs, carrying me into the shower.

I fell asleep in the shower and I'm not sure how I ended up back in Arran's bed. I vaguely remember a bit of arguing about where I would sleep when we came out of the bathroom.

Apparently, Arran won. Maybe they are taking turns. Sometimes when I'm half-wake, I feel one or both of them in the bed with me, snuggled up closely.

I sleep and sleep.

It's dark out when I open my eyes, and there's a legit furnace at my back... named Arran.

"You awake?" His hands stroke up and down my side as if they have been itching to do that for hours, but he didn't want to wake me.

"I'm waking up." I rub the gravel from my eyes and turn to face him. I'm not sure if I hoped for the beast. Am I crazy that I find him just as hot? "How long have I been out?"

"A full day." His brows pull down in concern. "Are you hungry?"

"I think so." Then I panic. "Are my fur babies okay?"

"They're fine." He grins like he knows something I don't. "Better than fine."

"Can I see them?"

Arran helps me stand and get dressed in his sweatshirt and shorts. I'm glad for the assistance since I'm still wobbly on my feet.

He holds me to his side as we walk down the hallway.

He pushes a door open to reveal another bedroom and flips on the light so I can see.

Calder curses and covers his eyes.

He's been caught. All my animals are snuggled up with him on his bed. It has to be the most adorable scene I've ever seen.

I squeal with joy and take a couple of steps to pet my guinea pig.

"Thank you, Calder." I smile as he cracks his eyes open, looking chagrined. "You found their food and stuff okay? I'm sorry I didn't think to give you instructions about their care."

"I told him what to do," Trouble, my guinea pig, says proudly.

"What the actual fuck?" I fall back into Arran. "Am I dreaming? Did you hear that too? Did you break my brain through my vagina?"

Arran chuckles.

"You heard me? Well, *finally!*" Trouble shakes his head like I'm dense.

My shifter holds me as I sway with shock. He consoles me. "Calder and I can hear them since we are shifters with the gift to communicate with magical creatures."

"Magical creatures?"

"Well, obviously, not *all* animals can talk," Trouble sasses.

I blink at him. "Obviously?"

Now, even Calder has a smirk. But I think it's because I'm the butt of the joke. "He's been wondering if you were broken," Calder tells me.

"I think I am now," I admit. "You've always been able to talk?"

"You weren't listening. I think your witch hole was blocked."

"My... *what?*"

Calder grumbles, "Well, Maxum and Arran have fully inspected her witch holes now."

Arran smirks. "You're just jealous."

Calder's eyes flare with some sort of emotion, triggering his magic.

I believe he might be jealous, but not about me. Maybe he wants the guys.

"I know you don't like me, so it probably won't mean much to you, but I appreciate you taking care of my friends," I say to Calder as I give my fur babies each a touch.

He grimaces and says nothing. I'll take that as a win. Maybe he will realize I'm not his enemy.

"But seriously, why can I hear them now?" I ask.

"Perhaps it is as simple as accepting that this world exists?" Arran suggests.

"Maybe. I used to have paranormal experiences when I was a kid." I sway on my feet.

"You need to eat, sweetheart." Arran wraps his muscular arms around my waist and practically carries me out of the room and into the kitchen.

"Where is Maxum?" I ask, sitting down at their kitchen nook table.

"Miss his tail already?" Arran teases, fussing in the fridge.

"And his forked tongue," I add.

He grins. "*Fuck*, right?"

"So are you and Maxum…" I make a poking gesture with my two fingers. "Fuck buddies?"

"We used to be—to blow off steam, mostly. We don't mess around anymore, not since I was cursed. As far as our relationship? I don't know if we ever defined it. We're all best friends, care deeply about one another, and since we have trust issues, we've all had our moments together."

"Except for Flint?"

"Yeah, not him." Arran doesn't elaborate, and I don't want to invade the gargoyle's privacy about what happened to make him hate my touch so much. My shifter adds, "Flint doesn't fool around, but he's solid."

"*Solid?*" I roll my eyes and suppress a chuckle. "I see what you did there."

"You'll come to understand just how clever I am," Arran boasts, then he places a beautiful charcuterie board in front of me.

"Will you or the guys mind if I ask questions about being supes? It's just blowing my mind that you are real. But I don't want to get too personal and upset any of you."

"I had my cock in your ass. You can ask me anything now."

"Fair point."

## 32

# DUNGEONS

JADE

*I* feel much better since Maxum used his girthy, textured healing 'wand' to cure me.

I don't remember Osen visiting me in my dreams after I passed out from what I'll refer to as *Double D-day*.

I worry Osen used too much of his magic to keep me from dying. Can a soul be injured from something like that? Will the guys want me around when I don't have an incubus stowaway?

Is Osen the actual source of my new appeal?

It sort of makes sense they would sense their former lover inside me and become attracted to me by his presence.

Shit. That is far more believable than them wanting me for me—a middle-aged witch.

Oh, well.

I'll just have to enjoy the ride, hoping they don't come to their senses and kill me when Osen leaves my body.

I'm restless. I don't have my computer or phone because the guy's magic in the house would blow up my devices. I can't check my book sales, promotions, or emails. I can't work on my edits for my next release.

Maxum gives me a pen and paper to help take the edge off, but I prefer typing since I can't read my writing when I write too fast.

"You seem agitated, sweetness," Arran says from his spot, snuggling up to me on the couch. It's borderline puppy behavior. And I love it.

"I feel a bit lost and like my life is over." I doodle on the paper instead of writing. They are sketches of shadowy figures with claws.

Maxum comes back through the front door and frowns. "What can we do to make you feel better? Would bouncing on my cock help?"

Arran glares at him. "Not everything is cured with a cock."

"It is with *my* cock." Maxum gives me a wink. "How about a mission then?" he asks. He leans over, captures my chin in his huge hands, and inspects my face. "But I don't know if you have it in you to learn the details and to make the journey."

Last night, Arran told me a bit about the supernatural world. There are three primary realms—Fae, Mortal (where I live), and the Underworld.

I perk up. "I can go on a trip? I want to see the other realms. Can you portal us someplace?"

Maxum shakes his head. "Rob might have spies everywhere."

Giving him a disappointed glare, I huff, "Then where did you intend to go for this *mission*?"

"Calder!" he shouts. "I'm calling for an adventure!"

The grumpasaurus storms out of his room, where he's been hanging out with my magical creatures, aka fur babies. I still haven't asked what kind of supernatural he is, and the guys haven't volunteered. I don't know how touchy the supes are about their other forms, but it seems that Calder wouldn't want me to know since my name is written in an indelible marker on his shit list.

Calder looks at me, then Maxum. "With *her*?" He curls his lip in disgust.

"Yes. You owe me a favor."

The jerk's eyes bulge. "You're calling in your favor—for her —for *this*?"

I don't know what the hell is going on, but it sounds like a big flipping deal. "Don't call in favors for me. Calder doesn't want to be around me."

"He's going to get over it… starting now." Maxum steps up inches away from Calder and glares down at him. Wow, he makes a six-foot-tall man look petite.

What do I look like next to him? A hobbit?

"I don't think she can handle it," Calder snarls.

"My money is on the witch." Arran laughs.

Okay, not sure why he's laughing. This appears like a harrowing task, one in which Calder doesn't think I can keep up.

"Five minutes, and it's go time." Calder surrenders, throws his hands in the air, and retreats to his room.

"What about Flint?" Arran asks Maxum as he hurries to prepare for our misadventure.

"He's due back from his scouting any second." Maxum then informs me. "Flint's never late unless there's trouble."

"Is he okay to be around me?" I ask, feeling confused if I should be changing out of my makeshift pajamas or not. "I haven't seen him since the incident."

"I'm fine," Flint says as he enters the house.

I swear these guys can hear through several walls. I blush, thinking of all the obscene noises I made with Maxum and Arran.

The gargoyle walks up to me and wisely gives himself six feet of personal space so I can't accidentally fling myself at him again.

He lowers his eyes and says, "I apologize for putting my hands on you. I could have hurt you."

"Flint, I know you were only trying to bring me some water. Your touch did not hurt or upset me. I'm only worried that you'll feel awkward around me. I enjoyed talking with you, and I would like to be friends."

"You enjoyed talking to me?" he sounds surprised.

"Of course." I smile. I itch to reach out and hug the massive male, but I stop myself. Why is he so endearing? All I want to do now is cuddle him.

He gives me a shy grin and nods. "Friendship sounds nice."

Gah. He's killing me. Maybe one day I could get him to hug me without freezing up.

"Go get your gear. It's adventure time," Maxum orders.

Arran and Flint rush off to get ready.

"Do I get gear?" I ask.

"Let's see what you are made of first," Calder grumbles as he stomps back into the great room.

He glares at me as he sets a wooden box on their dining table. The table and the box look old and beat up, as if it were from an actual medieval tavern. Maybe they are. With these guys, anything is possible.

"Does she know what she's getting herself into?" Calder asks Maxum.

"Not a clue," Maxum smirks wickedly.

*Ruh-roh…* I think I'm biting off more than I can chew. "If this is going to be too rough for a recovering witch, I'll manage being bored."

Maxum snatches me by the waist and draws me to his hard body. "One, you shouldn't be *bored* living with four monsters. Especially when two of them are frenemies with benefits." Maxum cocks his brow at me. "Two, I wouldn't push you beyond what I know you can handle. You can do this." He cups his large hand over my cheek in a show of comfort.

Calder announces, "We are going to the village of Caranth to capture the rogue mage."

"Shit, I thought you said I can't be seen?" I ask Maxum.

"We aren't leaving." Arran struts into the room dressed as if he were going to a Renaissance Faire as a knight.

Flint is also dressed in period clothing but with a light cloak, simple leather armor, and a lute.

*What is this fuckery?*

I look to Calder, and he pulls out a leather-bound book.

"We need you to pick from these races." He hands me a sheet. "Dragonborn, dwarf, elf, gnome, halfling...," he drones on, listing them all. "Then we will discover your strengths and attributes." He explains, "You will roll the dice. You have some items, such as armor and weapons, as a default, but others you can buy if you have money."

Internally, I grin and look at him like a deer caught in a monster's gaze.

"Are you following what I'm saying?" Calder snaps.

"Yeah, I think so... If you're done Monstersplaining me... I have a level 17 Tiefling Bard with a plus-five initiative, leather armor, a light crossbow, and a pair of daggers. Is that good enough for us to start off with?"

"Excuse me?" Calder's eyes widen in disbelief.

Loving the shocked reaction I'm getting from all of them, I continue dramatically, "Orianna believes that freedom and compassion matter more than rules. And she'll never explain her scars."

Calder looks like steam might blow out of his ears. "*You...* play DnD?"

Arran howls with laughter as Maxum chuckles at his shock.

"It's been a decade or so, but yeah." I eye the guys' outfits and their weapons. "And it looks like you guys are *really* into it."

Maxum waves his hand dismissively. "It rarely comes to bloodshed."

"Rarely!" I step back. "I think this game is too rich for my blood. Literally."

"We won't attack you," Maxum coos in my ear and sets his hand on my lower back. "Well, I might with my cock. I'm so hard for you right now. You are too perfect."

I chuckle. "How long have you been playing? And I'm assuming Calder's the dungeon master?"

"He used to be in more ways than one." Maxum swats me on the ass, pushing me toward the table. As I sit down, he pulls me onto his lap. His flesh sword presses against my ass crack. "Fuck," he hisses. "I think this is a bad idea. I'm going to have you riding me right here in a few seconds."

"Let Jade have her own seat. *Please, and thank you*," Calder growls as he sets up his Dungeon Master supplies.

"What's your character?" I ask Flint.

"Elmell Smoketail, a halfling ranger with a love of music." He points to his legit lute strapped to him.

I think I might die of cuteness. "I love it."

"And you two?" I ask.

Maxum grins playfully. "Neluthel, an Elven rogue, who loves to steal the hearts of his lovers. After he's done with them, of course."

I'll unpack that later…

"I'm a Dragonborn Beastmaster named Gorkilwyrm the Awesome," Arran says shyly.

We play for a few hours, and the guys act out the skirmishes. I see how this helps them let off some steam. However, I find it odd since this is practically their lives. But to each their own.

They gouge some new marks into the table with their swords. And yes, an actual mace gets lodged in the wall at some point.

Calder stretches and pats his belly. "Pizzas?"

We all heartily agree.

The brat asks me, "What does the bard want on her pizza?"

"I don't think I should eat a whole pizza by myself."

"Not up to the challenge?" He shakes his head. "How disappointing."

"I didn't say I couldn't," I laugh. "Challenge accepted. Thin crust though!"

He orders us pizzas from their rotary landline. When they show up at our door, Maxum pays with cash and hands them out to us.

"Is it rude to ask about what supernatural species a person is?" I ask and shove a pizza slice in my pie hole.

"Why do you ask?" Calder watches me.

"I was just curious if you were a dragon."

"Why would you think I was a dragon?" He looks more confused than irritated with me, which is a step up in our dynamic.

"I felt like you were fiery when I first saw you. I imagine dragons can be… standoffish."

"Don't blow dragon-smoke up my ass." He rolls his eyes. "Most dragons are complete dicks."

"There really are dragons?" I bounce with excitement.

"Don't be too happy. I just told you they were jerks." He huffs.

"I can handle jerks—obviously." I give him a pointed look. "So, was I way off base with my guess?"

"Phoenix." His tone is flat.

"Holy crap! A Phoenix! That's so awesome!"

Maxum grumbles. "I'm feeling a touch jealous. Just me?" He looks to Arran.

"Yeah, but he is super rare." The wolf-shifter shrugs.

"You're rare?" I bite my lip so a million questions don't pour out of my face. "I mean, it makes sense. Most legends are probably close to truths, yeah?"

"In my case, yes. I come back to life, and I have a bird form." He doesn't sound like he wants to talk about it, so I let it drop. "Thank you for sharing. I won't pester you any more about how cool you are."

A strange expression passes over his face. Disappointment, perhaps?

## 33

### REMEMBERED

JADE

*T*he day has been lovely, spending time with all four of them.

Then they inform me they need to catch up on their normal routine of patrols for ASO activity.

By the evening, I'm feeling healthier, emotionally and physically, but also tired.

Currently, I'm curled up on the couch with my head on Maxum's lap as he reads and idly strokes my hair. I love that the demon is so well-read. That alone could make me fall for him, never mind all the sexy he has going on otherwise.

As much as I love his affection, I need a proper sleep. "I'm heading to Arran's bed to sleep for the night," I say.

At the same moment, Calder rushes inside the safe house, looking about ready to burst into flames. "There's been another ASO attack. An explosion."

"Where?" Maxum shoots up from his seat.

"The supes' community center," Calder reports.

"Was anyone hurt? The younglings there?" Maxum's red fists are clenched so hard they are almost white.

"It's chaos. People were inside. They need help. Arran and Flint are already there."

Maxum looks at me, and I can see it written on his face clearly. He wants to go help, but he doesn't want to leave me alone either.

"Go," I urge him. "I'll be okay. I'm just going to bed. No one knows about this place, right?"

"She's right," Calder says, but he still looks like I'm about to betray them. Damn, I was hoping we'd made progress today. "Let's go."

Maxum rushes over to me and gives me a passionate kiss. "Stay safe, sweet witch."

He rushes out the door, unfurling his enormous wings as soon as he's outside the front door.

Damn, that's hot.

Calder doesn't immediately follow. Instead, he uses this rare moment alone to threaten me. "If you betray us or hurt one of them through your callous, witchy ways, I *will* end you."

"I don't have *witchy* ways." I glower at him, refusing to let him intimidate me, although he should terrify me. "If anyone gets hurt, it's going to be me. By the way, I'm not an asshole. And I don't betray or hurt people intentionally."

"Watch your step." In a blink of an eye, Calder is out the door and soaring after Maxum.

I slam the door shut and lock it.

It's eerie being left alone in the guys' house. After checking on my pets, and the doors and windows, I curl up in Arran's bed and fall asleep.

I don't know how quickly, but it seems almost immediately that

Osen, in his shadowy form, is standing near Arran's dreamscape bed.

Is it wrong that I sort of enjoy his dark shadows? Yet, curiosity pecks at me, wanting him to reveal that part of who he is… or *was*.

But I believe he was drained while constructing imagery in the shadowscape. I note we are in Arran's room now, and I think that's the reason for it. He doesn't have enough power to create anything different than where we actually are in the astral plane.

"So you are claiming my men?" he asks, and I detect a bit of jealousy. Maybe only because he can't touch them anymore.

"I thought you were okay with me having sex with them." I sit up and notice I'm undressed under the covers.

"Sex, yes. But you're stealing them away."

"Are you asking me to stop?"

I don't know what I would do if he said yes. Part of me doesn't expect this whole fling with them to continue. The other part realizes I might not have a choice against an incubus who can take control over my body and mind. I may have to do as he says or find a way to exorcise him.

Regardless, I should probably eject him. I doubt this is healthy.

*Being possessed is a generally frowned upon condition.*

But at least the sex has been phenomenal.

Osen studies me. Maybe he can read every thought I just had. This is not good.

"I don't think you can stop being with them now," Osen finally answers. "They have claimed you."

"I doubt that, but why would you be upset?" I don't think they've claimed anything but my holes, which I'm perfectly okay with since I've not orgasmed that intensely in my entire life—especially not with a partner. I suspect the sex will only get better since I was half-dead when we fucked.

The guys have kept it casual in their little fuck circle. So I will keep my heart out of the sex—to 'blow off steam' and 'fool around'—as Arran put it.

Osen shrugs. "Does it matter if I am upset? I'm dead."

"Well, I'm sure I'll be moving on as soon as we get you sorted. It's not like Calder appreciates my presence. Flint barely tolerates me." I shake my head and try to not let the uncomfortable burning sensation in my chest take hold. I need to let go of any attachment or feelings of connection I believe I have for them. I stare up at Osen, seeing the outline of the male he used to be. "I'll leave soon enough because I don't want to drive a wedge between the guys. I understand they are family, and I'm the enemy."

"Unfortunately," Osen agrees, and I don't know why that's what tears me up.

Pull it together, Jade.

He continues, ignoring my wave of emotion. He feels me crumbling, of that there's no doubt. "I need you to help me access my last moments."

"How?"

I want to solve this case just as much as he does. One, I'm a fucking curious person. Two, that means he can leave, and I can move on with my life. I'll sell my house and go where no one knows who I am—far away from Rob and the rest of this mess.

"I need to study my death spot." He moves closer, crowding me. "Now."

"Why now?" I try to scoot back, but he presses against my body.

"The guys won't let you go."

"Why not?"

"Rob thinks you are dead. And they intend to keep it that way. Until Rob and his organization are neutralized, I doubt you'll be allowed to leave. But that day might never happen."

"I can't leave... ever?" This sucks.

"I'm certain I learned the ASO's secret right before they

killed me. If I can remember what happened before my death, then Maxum and the guys can take them down."

"Okay, let's go solve this."

Fortunately, Maxum and Arran had grabbed a few things from my house earlier today, including my sneakers and some clothes. So at least I won't only be dressed in a guy's flannel shirt and socks for my adventure with Osen.

They also left the Rambler here, so I snatch up the keys from the entry table and steal their car. *Borrow* their car.

I memorized the address and location of Osen's death spot when he gave it to me in the shadowscape. I feel him vaguely in the back of my mind, thrumming with energy.

It's a weird sensation to feel him like this when I'm awake. But he told me that me having sex with the guys has empowered him. He's so much stronger now.

At least he agreed to let me be in control of my own body for this trip. Although he plans to take control briefly when we arrive at our location.

I don't like the idea of that.

But what's a medium supposed to do when there's a murder to solve?

The roads are empty as we get closer to our destination, which isn't completely unusual for this part of town. It's mostly abandoned warehouses. There's not much reason for the city's residents to be here.

Now that I know there's an entire world I never knew existed, I imagine these buildings aren't as abandoned as I had previously assumed.

I feel Osen agrees with my thoughts.

Great. That means he probably has access to all my wandering thoughts.

Again, I get a sense of agreement. Ugh.

YVE VALE

When I turn down a dark street, Osen insists I pull over and park. I do. With nervousness pumping adrenaline through my veins, I step out of the car.

I almost stumble because Osen takes that moment to shove my soul aside and take over without warning.

*What the fuckity fuck?*

However, this time, I'm still conscious of what's happening, but I have no ability to move or speak through my own body. I'm not sure if that's worse. I hate the feeling of being out of control. I'm just his puppet now.

*"Remain calm, or I'll put you to sleep,"* Osen threatens in my mind.

*"Some warning would have been nice, asshole."*

*"Keep quiet. I need to stay alert for danger,"* he reprimands.

We step forward slowly. He casts our eyes up at the rooftops and down the road. This is the strangest experience I've ever had. And that's saying something since I've just been double-teamed by a werewolf and demon.

Oh, yeah, and I died. There's that.

*"Shush,"* Osen snarls in my mind.

*"So I'm not even allowed to think?"*

He doesn't answer, and I'm immediately distracted when he pushes his psychic awareness outward. Or maybe it's my power?

*"Yours,"* he answers. *"You need to learn how to use your powers."*

I won't argue about that. This is cool. I can sense the emptiness of the street and the strange echo of magic ahead of me. I realize I've felt magic and power before, but I've always brushed it off as my imagination.

As a child, I perceived so much, and it was all lost because of my controlling mother, who repeatedly told me I sensed nothing.

But she was wrong, and now, I'm weak. I wish my abuela

was still alive to teach me. Although she was a bit... intense, too.

*"You could try calling on her spirit,"* Osen suggests. *"But not now."*

"Is this close to where Rob and the witch person went after he attacked me?" I ask.

*"Close, only a few blocks."* Osen walks down an alleyway and circles a spot, studying the ground.

*"There's a dead zone here. Forgive the pun."* We don't sense any magic in this spot.

The sound of cars in the distance reminds me we are still on Earth, but for some reason, it feels otherworldly here.

*"I agree."* Osen rubs our chin, thinking.

*He allows his thoughts to drift to the night he died...*

I see a moon above and a man in silhouette walking toward us.

"You shouldn't have pushed," the male says. The voice... it sounds so much like Rob, but this is only a memory, and can't be trusted completely. Perhaps it's only my fears in play. "I warned you to walk away."

"You expect me to heed your message from the lips of my dying ally? You truly didn't expect I'd seek justice for what you've done to my kind?" Osen remembers himself asking the mystery man.

"I was hoping you might be smarter than the rest since you have gotten closer than the others to discovering what's truly going on."

"I know the witches are behind the ASO. And it's the Witch Council members."

The man laughs—genuinely amused.

I sense Osen's doubt.

*Could he be wrong?*

Suddenly, Osen is hit with a blast of energy—magic—from behind. Someone has used the man's distraction to sneak up on him. This energy doesn't feel like anything Osen has experienced before. It's a new magic filled with dark intent.

Osen wonders how there can be new magic.

But he realizes that magic has been dwindling in the realms… and if that's so, then maybe, like most things in the Universe, when one thing dies off, something else slightly different replaces it, filling a void.

Osen's body trembles. Someone is stealing his magic, and his soul feels as if it has detached from his body.

*Is this his death?*

Osen's spirit floats above the scene.

"I told you he'd come, my liege."

And a woman, who looks very much like me, appears from the shadows. A wicked grin spreads over her face.

*What in the Freaky Friday?*

"*Why are you in my memories, Jade?*" Osen snarls.

"*I don't know. But that can't be me.*" I feel the pressure of Osen's anger, as if he's attempting to crush my actual soul. "*Wait! Didn't you say Rob hypnotized me?*"

"*You don't look brainwashed to me now,*" Osen argues.

He's not wrong. This woman appears to be in *complete* control.

"*Why would I come here if I was behind your death?*"

"*Maybe you didn't think I'd remember?*"

I feel my spirit fading. He's draining my life force. "*I didn't do this!*"

"*That woman looks just like you,*" Osen points out.

"*She does, but actually put together—polished. I'm a warmed-over mess most of the time, not even a full hot mess.*"

"*Jade, the game is over. Just tell me why.*"

"*Yeah! If I'm some witch mafia boss, why would Rob kill me yesterday?*"

"*Because you were compromised by me.*"

"*Maybe it's a glamour like Maxum or Flint wears?*"

"*Unlikely.*"

"*And I live in a tiny house with magical creatures? And write romance books?*"

"*That's just some stupid cover story,*" he says, but sounds less certain.

"This was you!" he growls in my voice out loud.

"*Hell, this woman looks more like my crazy grandmother than me!*"

Osen stops his stranglehold on my soul. "*What did you say?*"

Now that I take a moment to put a pin in my terror, I realize it's true. "*She looks like my abuela. I swear the women in my family don't age.*"

"*Witches* don't *age like humans.*" He shouts, "Fuck!"

# 34

# BETRAYED

## CALDER

*I* don't have much magic outside of my phoenix gift of regeneration and shifting, but I have premonitions, especially concerning death.

It's one reason I was so close to the community center's attack when it happened. My psychic senses were pinging.

In the middle of the cleanup and pulling survivors from the rubble, I have another ping.

Osen's death spot.

I glance over to see Maxum, Arran, and Flint removing debris to get to another victim. They are needed here. All of them are stronger than I am. And I don't want them to get involved if it's nothing.

My mind flashes to an image of the witch.

I'm unhappy that I seem to be mistaken about her innocence. It's getting under my skin.

Her magical creatures adore her as if she were their pet and not the other way around. Magical creatures are usually not wrong about a person's character and are rarely corrupted.

I've been trying to catch them in a lie, but they appear as innocent as they look.

It shouldn't bother me that I might have messed up my chances to spread her thighs and plunder her depths.

I don't want to lust after women—especially witches.

I'm pissed that I want to hear her make those wicked sounds while she chokes on my cock.

Maxum and Arran made her scream so loud with ecstasy that I still hear it ringing in my ears and in my balls.

Maybe she could be the woman to make me forget what happened during my last death.

Sneaking out the door, I take to the sky and soar over the buildings. Osen's death spot is only a mile or so away. So if my instincts are nothing, I'll be back before the guys know I'm missing.

Thankfully, I have enhanced supernatural eyesight, since there aren't many working streetlights in this industrial area anymore, and the moon hasn't risen. The supernaturals who inhabit the supposedly abandoned area like to move in the dark since they don't easily pass as humans, even with glamour. They are far too big or some other inhuman shape. Most have lost the magical power to maintain a glamour at all, even with charms or spells.

As I approach, I see my Rambler parked on the street close to where Osen was killed.

The witch.

Why would she steal our car when no one was home? Why come here? Was I right all along?

I land on the building to observe her as she stands in the dark alley.

She seems strained, her body twitching and bowed as if fighting an invisible force.

*Osen?*

Has he found some evidence in her mind and come here to confront her?

"This was you!" she shouts, sounding very much like Osen.

Then a second later, Osen screams, "Fuck!"

A man appears at the end of the alley. "Ah, there you are." I'm not sure if he means Jade or if he's speaking to Osen.

The man looks like Rob. I sense he is indeed a warlock.

I want to fly down there and protect Osen, but I also want to see how Jade-Osen reacts to Rob.

"He's still inside you, hm?" Rob throws his hands out.

I expect to see the glow of a warlock's spell, but a shadowy tendril shoots out instead. It looks and feels like Osen's magic.

Osen gasps, realizing the same thing.

Jade's arms fly up in a stop motion, but whatever magic Osen has left is too weak to prevent Rob's assault.

The shadowtendril wraps around her middle and yanks her forward until she's only a few feet from the warlock.

"Don't worry, we'll take care of it," he tells Jade and plunges a shadow into her forehead.

Fuck. Rob's attacking Osen.

I dive off the building's edge to rip Jade away from Rob just as a black sedan pulls up.

I grab the witch around the waist to break her free from his shadows. Then I swing my Katana with my free arm, slicing Rob's chest.

He releases Jade.

His shadow hits me so hard that I fly back into the brick wall.

Somehow, I manage to hold on to the witch.

However, her head cracks against the brick.

I clutch her unconscious body to my chest. I thought I was only saving Osen, but I find I don't want to lose Jade either.

With my last bit of strength, I charge at Rob, my blade poised to end him.

He's smart enough to run.

My head spins as Rob jumps in the car and drives away.
Blood pools around me... my own and hers.
My vision fades to black.

TO BE CONTINUED...

Grab your copy of **<u>Charming Her Monsters</u>** right now
and discover what happens next!

And...
If you enjoyed this book, please
consider leaving a review on Amazon.
It means the world to me!

# THANK YOU FOR READING!

Check out some of my other books and series below:

If you love Maxum, he has an appearance in
**Shadowcraft Academy Completed Series**
*I didn't want magic. I was supposed to escape.*
I'm forced to attend a magic academy with five males
who won't leave me alone—my fated mate dragon,
a dangerous vampire, a protective druid, a seductive incubus,
and a hot professor wolf shifter.
https://books2read.com/ShadowcraftAcademy1

**Fae Hearted Series**
A human servant with a secret.
A tempting deal with an Elven prince.
Three elves willing to break all the rules for her…
https://books2read.com/faehearted1

**Chained Fates**: Shadow Myths Book 1:
*Four Demon Warriors. The last Serafim. One dark cell.*

I find myself imprisoned with four gorgeous males
from a violent warrior species.
With their massive size, horns, and tails, I worry they will seek
revenge for my reluctant part in their torment.
When my healing hands wander, their growls turn to purrs.
Will they take me with them if we can escape?
Will they give me what I crave—their touch?
https://books2read.com/chained-fates

**Rebel Fates:** Shadow Myths Book 2
*The Egyptian gods were aliens, and their people still exist...*

I'm done with Earth. The moon base has to be better.
Famous last words…
However, my plan didn't go as I had hoped.
I end up on a ship with three intense warrior aliens who look
like gorgeous Egyptian gods—all who I begin to crave. They
have heads of animals and bodies of men. They look like
Anubis, lion man, and a minotaur.
And they're furious I'm a stowaway.
*I'm not out of trouble yet...*
https://books2read.com/rebel-fates

Need bonus content? News on new releases?
Visit ValeRomances.com to sign up!

# ALSO BY YVE VALE

## SHADOWCRAFT ACADEMY:

(Dark Paranormal Academy Trilogy + Bonus Novella)

**Hexed ~ Jinxed ~ Cursed ~ Blessed**

## BEWITCHING MONSTERS:

(Grown-Ass Woman & Monsters Trilogy)

**Bewitching Her Monsters**

**Charming Her Monsters**

**Enchanting Her Monsters**

**Possessing Her Monsters**

## SHADOW MYTHS:

(Science Fantasy Standalones)

**Chained Fates ~ Rebel Fates**

## FAE HEARTED:

(Fantasy / Shadowcraft Universe Origins Prequel)

**Between Realms**

**Tangled Secrets**

**Chaos Tempted**

**Bonds Eternal**

## GODS ARE HIRING:

**My Karmic Destiny**

A Why Choose / RH continuation of

**My Instant Karma** by Raven Vale

# ALSO WRITING AS

## WRITING AS RAVEN VALE

### *GODS ARE HIRING:*

M/F PNR Standalones

**My Instant Karma**

**Cupid's Last Arrow**

## WRITING AS JADE VALE

### *CAGE BROTHERS:*

M/F Dark Billionaire Contemporary Interconnected Standalones

**For more book details, visit:**

**ValeRomances.com**

# ACKNOWLEDGEMENTS

A special thank you goes out to my husband, Mr. Vale, for supporting me. Thank you for being my editor and catching any rogue plot points or typos. He actually constructs a detailed timeline for my books to keep track of the story's dates!

Thank you to all my author and reader friends for their great advice, support, and friendship.

Also, I appreciate all of my wonderful fans! I love reading the beautiful reviews you leave or when you reach out to talk about my books. They are gifts to my heart and soul.

And my deepest gratitude goes out to all of you who have encouraged me in my life.

# ABOUT THE AUTHOR

Yve Vale loves spicy romance, fated mates, and redeemable supernatural bad boys who end up as cinnamon roll alphas for their woman.

She writes about strong females and their magical males, all set in paranormal worlds.

She is a lover and a fighter. This is why her books feature a fair amount of action, both in romantic endeavors and in battle.

For more information: ValeRomances.com